I knew undercover work could be dangerous, but I hadn't expected that this assignment could get me killed...

I started up and drove about two blocks when I noticed the headlights turn the corner and hold back about two hundred yards again. One thing was certain. The tail car made no attempt to hide itself. It seemed that the driver didn't care if I knew of his presence. Though I didn't know where Chester Avenue was, I did know this neighborhood since it had been in my patrol area for over two years. I pushed the gas pedal to the floorboard and the tires squealed around the corner. When I got to Whitmore Avenue, I slid around another corner and was a few hundred feet from Riverside drive where I turned right again and gunned the gas. This time I was sure I had lost my tail. Driving straight down Riverside, I mixed in with the few cars on the road. For the following nine minutes, there were no headlights behind me.

In all the sudden twists and turns, Stan's body flopped back and forth like a rag doll and his wig had fallen between the seat and the center console. He was now half-awake. With his false eyelashes, heavy make-up, and his short hair askew, he looked like a music-hall clown. A block away from his apartment building, I stopped and waited. One car approached and passed, as did a second one. Assuming I had lost my tail, I pulled up in front of his building in a loading zone. After I fished out his keys, the two of us made our way into the courtyard. When I unlocked the door to Apartment number 7 and we walked in, the lights suddenly turned on. There in the living room sat a man in his sixties, holding a pistol pointed directly at me.

Victor Espinoza, a short, youthful LAPD patrol officer, is sent undercover as a cross-dresser to catch a serial killer. His ambition to become a detective gets snarled when, ignoring his captain's orders, he goes it alone and establishes himself at the Velvet Glove, a Hollywood bar that caters to transvestites and drag queens. The secret nature of his assignment not only strains his long-term relationship with his girlfriend, Jannine—who wants to marry and start a family—but hot on the trail of the killer, Victor gets a little too close—and now, he's targeted as the next victim.

KUDOS for *Dressed to Kill*

In *Dressed to Kill* by Charles Alvarez, Victor Espinonza is a patrol cop who desperately wants to be a detective. He gets his chance when his captain asks him to go undercover as a cross dresser to catch a serial killer. But he's not supposed to tell anyone, so his partner wonders if he's dirty, his long-time girlfriend thinks he's having an affair, and his main suspect thinks he's gay. Just a few of the complications that can arise when a straight man starts trying to dress like a woman. Alvarez did an excellent job of portraying the problems of an over-achiever, under-sized Latino cop who will do almost anything to get promoted to detective—well, anything but kiss "ass or any other body parts." The plot is well thought out, with plenty of twist and turns to surprise and intrigue you. ~ *Taylor Jones, Reviewer*

Dressed to Kill by Charles Alvarez is a mystery/detective novel that has an interesting twist. Instead of the hunky super cop that we so often see in novels today, the main character, Victor, is only five-foot-two, slender, and insecure. Because he is also Latino and fairly new to the force, he suffers some discrimination and has to work twice as hard to get promoted. But when he finally gets a chance to go undercover, it's not the cloak and dagger assignment he longs to get due to his skills and graduating from the academy in the top five of his class. No, this is one he got because he's short and slight of build. He has to go undercover as a cross dresser. *Dressed to Kill* is well written, well researched, and thought provoking. It gives us a glimpse, not only into what a short man suffers in today's society, but also into the world of transvestites, gays, and cross dressers. All in all, a worthy endeavor for this first time author. ~ *Regan Murphy, Reviewer*

ACKNOWLEDGEMENTS

Though my name stands alone as the writer of this book, there is an army of helpers that brought the story to life. WGA writer David Alexander my mentor and my guide gave me focus. My fiction writers' group, LAwriters, who were critics with love: Jennifer Moss, Rick Rice, Richard Stouvenel, Michael Christensen, Kevin Badt, and Dennis Johnston. Thank you to my teacher, Tricia Bevan, for inspiration and encouragement.

Thank you to my wife, Patricia, and my children for their input and suggestions about the story line and the characters.

Finally, Lauri Wellington and all the editors at Black Opal books, who have been instrumental in helping, shape my raw material into a finished novel.

I owe a special thank you to Captain Will Gartland of the Los Angeles Police Department for his measured guidance and suggestions concerning technical accuracy.

Charles Alvarez

Dressed

to

KILL

charles alvarez

A Black Opal Books Publication

GENRE: MYSTERY-DETECTIVE/SUSPENSE

DRESSED TO KILL
Copyright © 2014 by Charles Alvarez
Cover Design by Jennifer Moss
All cover art copyright © 2014
All Rights Reserved
Print ISBN: 978-1-626941-67-0

First Publication: AUGUST 2014

Published by Black Opal Books **http://www.blackopalbooks.com**

DEDICATION

For Patricia, my reason for life.

Chapter 1

The Address of Murder

I was in that zone between a sleep-dream state and the real world. Fantastic events unfolded in my mind's eye and the cold details of daily life overlapped each other. In the dream, I was soaring on imaginary wings, sweeping up a mountainside that guarded a verdant valley below. In the real world, the telephone next to my bed was tearing me away from the magic of flight. I just lay there, not moving, hoping it would stop.

It did.

I turned toward Jannine who was asleep in her own dream world and she responded by moving closer so that various parts of our bodies touched. That nudged me farther back into the real world. Suddenly, touching was better than soaring. As I put my arm around her cool and inviting body, my iPhone, somewhere in the room, rang. I lifted my head just far enough to see the digital clock. Its red-orange letters glowing. 3:32 a.m. Jannine stirred, turned to face me, and whispered, "Ignore it."

After the fourth ring, she lifted herself onto her elbows and said, "Oh my God, no. Maybe someone in the family has died." So she too had been awake when our bodies touched and faked sleep. Why would she do that? The phone was on its sixth ringtone. Soon the message machine would go on.

I not only felt naked, I was naked as I climbed out of bed and searched for my pants and my iPhone. When I saw the caller ID, I stood bolt upright at attention. "It's Captain Wilson," I told Jannine.

"Oh God, someone is dead. Why are they calling you? Let it ring and come back to bed," she said as she reached out and playfully patted my naked butt.

That was unfair of her to put me in such a momentary crisis: the captain or Jannine. My eyes shifted from her dreamy swoon to my police uniform draped over a chair. Her warm hand on my cheek produced a paralysis of mind and body akin to the deer in the headlights syndrome. I took a short step away.

"Hello," I said.

Jannine sat up and pulled the sheet up over the most beautiful breasts in the San Fernando Valley, maybe even all of LA. "Victor, no. Tell him no," she pleaded.

I put my finger over the tiny holes on the mouthpiece. "I can't."

Jannine slumped down and shook her head back and forth. Saying no to my captain would not fly when I was a routine patrol cop. Saying no to Jannine's naked body would not be a violation of the Fair Employment Practices Act. I tapped the screen.

"Why didn't you just let it ring?" she whispered.

"Did I get you out of bed?" Captain Wilson's feeble attempt at humor went right over my head. Nothing is funny at 3:30 in the morning.

"Yes sir. I mean no. I had to get up to answer the phone, sir." That was stupid.

"That's good." He rattled on about duty, honor, public safety, and other forms of official LAPD bullshit, all of which was drilled into me at the Police Academy. He wondered if I could report to a murder scene. When he said it was an unusual case and perhaps I could help, I didn't have to think twice. Besides, he didn't have to ask, he could have ordered me.

"Of course, sir. I will. Where, sir?"

"I'll call you right back," he said.

I turned off the phone and pumped a fist into the air. I looked weird, butt-naked, prancing around the room shouting, "Yeah!" at the top of my lungs. "This could be the break I've been waiting for. This is great, Jannine."

She covered her head with the sheet.

"I gotta go. It's probably nothing and I'll be right back." I was manic. "On the other hand, I don't know what he wants me to do." I suddenly remembered the last gig I did for the Narcotics Division. It came to nothing. They were baiting me with promises of promotion and future benefits, but it depended, of course, on budgets and priorities. Money never materialized nor did any promotion.

Jannine stood, pulled the sheet around her, and started to pace about the room. Not a good sign. She was pissed but I tried not to notice while I dressed and avoided eye contact. When she stopped at the foot of the bed, I suspected it was the beginning of a battle we had fought in the past. The sheet twisted around her ankles so many times she almost tripped.

"I arranged to take off today—if you remember—we're going to the Dodger game." Her voice changed from reasonable to full-battle-dress, code blue and not Dodger blue. "I paid ninety dollars apiece for the tickets. Did you forget how much you hate the Giants?"

I thought not answering was the best plan.

"You do this to me all the time," she said.

Actually, her *all the time* meant it had happened twice before. I wasn't going to argue because I had no choice. I had to meet the captain at a crime scene. Unofficially, I was ordered to. I wanted to be able to count on adding a murder investigation to my background.

"Not all the time," I said, "maybe twice."

I hoped she wouldn't pick up the pathetic pleading in my voice.

"What? What about the time you had to go undercover at that crazy high school. We hardly ever saw each other for more than three months. Damn it, Victor, What kind of a relationship do we have?"

Here it comes.

"Why is it we never seem to have the time to start making plans for ourselves? It's been five years, Victor, five. What the hell are we waiting for?"

I buckled my boots. "Let's not start this again. I have to go."

"Why?" she demanded. "It's your day off. Take it. The victim's dead already, so what's the big hurry?"

"Because it's my job." There was a tone of indifference in my voice, which annoyed her even more. I checked my weapon, snapped it into its holster, and then spoke in a low soothing tone. "We've been over this before." Now it was my turn to get pissed. "I don't want to be a patrol cop all my life. I want to be a detective. I've passed the exam. I would *like* to be a detective; I *need* to be a detective. And in order to get it, I have to take whatever duty they give me. I want them to consider me when an opening occurs. Be reasonable, Jannine." I hated to plead. It diluted my testosterone.

She plopped down on the bed. "And I suppose our dream to get married and start a family doesn't count? Or am I being unreasonable after five years?" It blossomed into a full-fledged argument. "It's always what you want and never mind me and what I want." Her brown eyes darted back and forth as though searching for an escape route.

"And I want that, too, but we can't talk about it. Not now. If I can make detective, it will mean more money and then we'll be able to afford for you to have—"

I stopped myself before I said the wrong thing, which would escalate to an even bigger argument. She tipped her head forward and her long, blonde hair cascaded over those magnificent breasts. I thought she began to cry. I hated that part, especially the crying. I felt so helpless. Women always seemed to pick the worst time to take a stand with tears, logic, and emotion. However, she wasn't crying. Instead, she was seething with anger.

My iPhone rang again. It was Captain Wilson. He was just leaving for the crime scene. "This is a case I want you to be involved in. I want you in every phase of the investigation. Are you up for it?"

"Yes, sir."

"Now when you get there try not to ruffle the feathers of Detectives Fryman and Murray. It's their case and they may not like you poking around. Murray's the lead on this. I'll explain the whole thing to you and to them when I get there."

"Understood." I sounded like a buck private taking orders.

"And another thing. Don't discuss this with anyone. Got that?"

"Yes, sir."

"By the way, how the hell old are you, anyway?"

"I'm twenty-seven, sir. Does it matter?"

"How tall are you?"

"Under the new rules, I qualified and passed my basic, sir. Does it matter?"

There was a long pause. Captain Wilson answered, "Probably."

"How, sir?"

"Never mind that now. Just get yourself down there as soon as you can. Here is the address."

I jotted down the numbers and estimated that I could be there in about fifteen minutes considering the early hour and no traffic. After I hung up, Jannine stopped raging and began to dress herself.

"Why don't you go back to bed? Get some more sleep. I'll probably be back in a couple hours."

"No. I'm going home."

She sounded definite. I marveled at how stunningly beautiful she looked. Even though Jannine was two years older than I was, and three inches taller, she was blessed with the freshness and vigor of a teenager. Whenever she smiled at me, my knees felt like I'd just swung at a low curve ball.

"This is probably going to amount to nothing so I might be back in time for us to go to the game." I inched my way toward the door as I checked my belt for all the fourteen pounds of equipment strapped to it.

"I'll put the tickets on the dresser," she said. "If you finish early, you can take one of your buddies."

She looked up and gave me a glare that would penetrate a Kevlar vest.

"I can't believe that I'm still going on with the same old routine of yours," she said. "On your priority scale, just where do I fit?"

At that moment I didn't need conversation; I had to go. "Jannine, please."

When I walked over to give her a good-bye kiss, she remained motionless like the statue of Aphrodite—cold and indifferent—and I, at that moment, lacked the courage, the words, and the time to change her mind.

"You have as much chance of becoming a detective as I do," she whispered.

I stopped at the bedroom door and looked back.

"Can't you see they just use you to get what they want?" she shouted. "And me, I get nothing I want. Five years. Oh, Jesus, why am I wasting my time?"

"Let's talk tonight, okay?" I said as she turned her back to me.

I left and grabbed an apple on the way out, happy to get away from the turmoil. I was certain all this would smooth over as it always did. The East Valley air was crisp and refreshing with the predawn stillness that heightened my excitement at the prospect of real police work. The night-blooming Jasmine that lined the drive-way of my house was at the end of its blossom time but still hinted of sweetness.

When I backed the car out of the garage, I stopped at the curb and looked at the windows of my house just as she pulled back the curtain to watch me leave. In that in-stant, I remembered her cool body and our naked touch-ing, but mostly her anger. I jumped out and ran back into the house. Without saying a word, I took her in my arms and kissed her, not from passion but from love. I truly did love her. She didn't really kiss me back. It was more like a neutral response. Her eyes remained open and unfo-cused. Her arms dangled at her side. We just stood and looked into each other's faces. She bent down, gave me a quick peck on the cheek, and said, "Go. Your captain awaits," then gave me a mocking salute.

"I just couldn't start our day this way," I said and I meant it. "You know I love you and I want us to get mar-ried."

She smiled, walked to the bedroom, and pulled back the tangled bedcovers. I hoped she wouldn't jump back in and force me into making another choice. After picking up the note I had written the address on, she handed it to me like it was contaminated contraband. Her forefinger and her thumb barely touched the paper.

"Oh! Officer Espinoza, I think you're going to need this," she said, sarcasm dripping from every word.

"Oh wow. You're right." It was way too late to try to explain that I really did come back for her and not the address of the murder. I wondered if she knew that I wanted and needed both. It felt like her anger had cooled from rage to indifference. As I left, I noticed the Dodger tickets on the dresser and remembered that Keller was pitching that day.

Chapter 2

Cloak and Dagger Secrets

As I raced along on empty Chandler Boulevard, I tried to reconstruct where I had gone wrong again and what had made Jannine so bitter. How could she not see how important it was for me to accept assignments that could lead to a promotion? Of course, we were going to get married, when the time was right. When I almost went through a red light, I realized that I had to clear my mind and be sharp when I met the two detectives on the case. In the protocols of LAPD it was unusual for an ordinary patrol officer to work with seasoned detectives on a murder case.

I felt lucky, racing through the empty streets of the East Valley. I wondered if Jannine and I had passed the magic point that was total commitment. Perhaps I had reached a level of convenient comfort in the status quo. Marriage would only have us finishing each other's sentences. It would become, *we always*, and *we love*. There would be no more *I*. However, I couldn't imagine life without her.

Captain Wilson's message directed me to the murder scene behind the Quick Stop Convenience Store, in the 6600 block on Lankershim Boulevard in North Hollywood. I pulled up to a group of uniformed LAPD officers standing guard at the location; orange DO-NOT-CROSS tape stretched across the entire front parking lot. I flashed my ID card and got signaled in. The entire minimart parking lot was yellow taped with four black-and-whites and an unmarked car inside the perimeter. After I parked, one of the uniforms questioned me about who assigned me and what division I was from. I felt a pleasant rush of power to name drop, Captain Wilson. The uniform regarded me suspiciously, even though I assumed a false mantle of authority.

"Is Captain Wilson here yet?" I asked, using the deepest voice I could muster.

"Don't think so. The detectives are out back with the body."

As I made my way to the rear of the convenience store, I let my five-foot-five frame swagger the way I thought a real detective might.

"Hey," he called after me. "You gotta log in."

I wanted to say, "I knew that," but instead, I snapped back, "Where is the log?"

He looked disgusted as he held up a clipboard. When I signed in with my serial number at 4:15 a.m., I was number 11 on the list. I noticed eight officers and two detectives, Murray, number five, and Fryman, number six. The few cars on Lankershim slowed, causing a minor traffic jam of rubber-neckers. Nothing was visible from the front of the Quick Stop as one uniform was directing the cars to keep moving.

I made my way to the back of the store and stopped cold when, from a distance, I saw the body of a woman spread out on the pavement at the rear entrance to the

Quick Stop. The two plain-clothes detectives were bent over her, but not touching anything, just looking over the body. The small flood light at the roof of the building cast long shadows over the scene. LAPD flood lights had not arrived yet. It took two hard swallows and a clenched fist for me to muster the courage to move forward. My stomach did a couple back flips because I had never seen a real dead body before, let alone a murdered one. I was anxious and nervous. Two other officers with trademark LAPD haircuts searched the perimeter of the parking lot with high beam flashlights. With the shadows and the poorly lit back parking area, it looked like the cover of a cheap detective novel. I felt tightness in my throat as I moved forward very slowly.

Murray pointed at me and yelled, "Stop. Dammit."

I froze.

"Who the hell are you?" he asked.

"I'm Victor Espinoza—sir."

"Get the hell out of here. This is a crime scene," he hollered.

I was sure he had seen my uniform.

"Captain Wilson sent me here and wants me to kinda observe what's going on."

Fryman and Murray exchanged a look that said "What the hell?"

I was certain they thought I was a spy for the Captain or the Chief of Police. "Wilson eh," Fryman grunted.

"Yes, sir...I mean...yeah." I took three cautious steps forward like someone playing hop scotch in a school yard even though there didn't seem to be anything to step on.

"What the hell are you supposed to observe?" Murray almost spit out the word *observe*.

"I'm not sure...er, sir...er, detective."

"Just so you know, Espinoza, and for your record,

Wilson may have sent you but I'm the lead on this case. We make all the calls. Get it?" Murray said. "There's nothing here for you to observe."

"Yes. Of course. Captain Wilson already told me."

Fryman leaned over the body and said to Murray, "Same as the one five weeks ago."

Murray nodded as he reached his forefinger toward the victim's open left eye. He touched it lightly and then waited. He tapped the eyeball again. I inched a few steps closer and leaned down to get a better look. The open eyes felt like death looking back at us, the living, but in particular at me. It caused my stomach to flutter again.

"Don't touch anything and watch where you step," Murray added.

"Why?" I asked since I was at least eight feet away.

"I don't need a cop's bloody foot prints recorded as physical evidence."

"Why did you do that?" I asked.

"Do what?"

"Touch her eyeball."

He stood up and folded his arms in an exasperated pose. "I told you to get the hell out of here. Go wait out front."

"Well, I can't—sir. But what about the eyeball?"

He shook his head in disbelief. "We gotta make sure he's dead before he gets a thermometer plunged into his liver. Now get out of my way."

Some detective, I thought. Doesn't he see the four-foot diameter of blood surrounding the body? And what does he mean *he*?

I stepped in closer to get a better look and then I realized the dead woman was not a woman at all. It was a man dressed in a blue evening gown. The front of his dress was ripped open, and a huge gash just below his breastbone looked like he'd been filleted. His internal organs were on complete display. I assumed the large blackish mass was his liver but I wasn't sure.

The odor, which almost made me retch, came from a mixture of blood, urine, and excrement. In the victim's violent death, all three spilled from his body. I took out a handkerchief and pressed it to my nose. When Murray stood up, he almost knocked me over and both of us wobbled. Then we steadied ourselves as though our shoes were glued to the ground, like the red-light, green-light game that kids played in a schoolyard.

"Shouldn't we check his wallet for an ID?" I asked.

"Is that what you're supposed to observe?"

I got more of Murray's disgust.

"Look, kid, nobody can touch anything until the M.E. gets here. *Capish*—er I mean *comprende*?"

It took me a minute to remember that detail from my studies for the detective exam. And what the hell was he speaking Spanish for?

"Where are your gloves?" Fryman asked me.

Oh shit, I forgot the gloves. It was then that I saw everyone else wearing white latex gloves so I headed back out front to ask the log-in cop about a pair. A large group of bystanders had gathered outside the tape. One man leaned in and asked what happened. A police helicopter was scanning the neighborhood in case the killer was still at large. Captain Wilson arrived with a grand flourish that none of the spectators behind the yellow tape could mistake. Not only was his aura big but his physical stature was as well.

He caught up to me and stopped me. "You must be Espinoza."

I wondered how he knew me since we had never officially met. "Yes, sir, I am." I glanced at my last name sewn over the lapel of my breast pocket.

Wilson stopped and turned just as the coroner's

wagon arrived. The medical examiner signed in at 4:58 a.m. Behind him, the police photographer drove up. He signed in at 5:05 a.m. Across Lankershim Boulevard the Channel 5 News van parked in Bobby's Hamburgers parking lot and a crew of three emerged, running up to the tape asking for a spokesperson. Captain Wilson ignored them and, instead, ordered the perimeter search expanded to two miles since the killer or killers might still be in the area.

Two more police helicopters arrived and the thumping noise turned on lights in the nearby houses. Their bright beams scanned backyards, side streets, and anything that moved.

One chopper made a pass over the crime scene, giving the whole area a surreal atmosphere. For a few seconds, we were looking at reverse negatives.

I joined Wilson, the M.E., the photographer, and two additional uniforms as we all headed back to the dead body. The captain grabbed my arm and wanted me to stay close to him, but not close to the body while the pictures were being taken.

"I don't want you in any of the photos," he said.

"Understood," I said, but I wondered why he excluded me from official police pictures. It certainly wouldn't hurt my status to be in a few official photos. I could use copies of them in my applications.

The M.E. plunged a long probe into what he said was the liver and the dead man's whole body twitched. The victim's right arm jerked outward through the pool of blood, setting off small ripples. The skin on the back of my neck crawled. For a moment, I thought the man was still alive.

As the M.E. waited for the temperature reading, he joked with Fryman. "What are you going to be for Halloween?" he asked.

"I don't know. I was thinking of being a ballerina in a red tutu."

"You've got the legs for it."

I wondered how they could be talking about costumes at a time like this. My heart rate must have been over a hundred but the vision of this big M.E.in Halloween dress made me relax a bit. For these hardened cops, black comedy trumped the ugly reality of murder and violence.

After the M.E. finished his examination, it seemed as if they took a hundred pictures. Several angles of the corpse, close-ups of his face, each piece of evidence before it was placed in plastic Ziploc bags or paper bags, and finally a long shot of the large bloodstain completed the photo shoot. Two tiny yellow flags posted several feet away marked bloody footprints. They, too, were photographed.

"What about the store clerk?" Wilson asked.

"The store is closed now and we have a statement from the night clerk," Murray said. "He said there wasn't much business after midnight and he didn't hear anything unusual. He had some music playing kinda loud." He paused. "I tried to convince him we were not interested in his legal residency status. We were the police not ICE, but he still seemed guarded."

"Where is he now?" I asked.

Murray scowled at me. "Why don't you run out front and check if he's still behind the counter."

He probably wanted me out of the way.

The Captain broke in. "No. Stay right here, Espinoza."

Murray seemed annoyed to be over-ruled by the captain, but he just shrugged his shoulders.

Later I noticed Wilson and the two detectives off to one side. They appeared to be arguing. I felt uncomfortable when Wilson pointed to me twice. Murray shook his head back and forth and waved his hands in circles. It appeared that my short career as a junior detective was over even before it started. The way my stomach was reacting at that moment, it sounded like a good idea. There had to be a better way to become a detective.

After the M.E. gave the all clear, Wilson waved me over and Fryman and Murray returned to the corpse. They pulled out his wallet from a purse that matched the color of his shoes.

"Stay with them," Wilson said. "They will complain and bitch and moan, but that's okay. Don't worry about it."

Murray brought over the wallet with me practically hanging on his arm. He looked over his shoulder and gave me a disgusted glance. I knew then that he'd gotten the message from Wilson that I was to be included in all aspects of the investigation.

"What have you got?" Wilson asked.

"His name is Fredrick Carlyle, thirty years old, 4107 Ridge Road, Tarzana. Here's a picture of him, a woman, and two little boys who look to be about five and seven maybe, but this could be an old picture. Probably his wife and kids."

"Does he have a wedding ring on?"

"Yes," Murray said.

Fryman flipped through the rest of the wallet. "Here's a work ID card from Rocketdyne in Canoga Park. No cash was taken because there's eighty-three bucks still here and three credit cards. The AAA membership card is current. A couple a receipts, one with a note scribbled on the back and that's it."

"What about a cell phone?"

"We've got his iPhone bagged. Oh and here's something interesting. He has red lipstick on but the tube in the purse is a shade I'd call light blue. We've got that bagged, too."

"Maybe he was color blind," I said and all three looked at me as if I was from another planet.

Wilson shrugged and Murray raised his arms in the air like a referee signaling a touchdown. "Captain?" he said in a begging whine that said, "Are we going to have to put up with this guy?"

"Okay, after the wagon leaves, you, Murray, take a uniform with you, not Victor, and go to the address on his driver's license, break the news to the family and, if that's his wife, ask her to come down to ID the body."

"Do you think she knows about his being dressed as a woman?" I asked.

"We'll find out soon enough," Murray said.

Wilson signaled Fryman to come over. "I want you to talk to the Channel 5 News people and answer their questions. That is, don't give them any information because I want you to stall and distract them. We've got damn little to work with here, but I don't want them to know that."

"What should I say?"

"Give them the standard *on-going-investigation* routine. Tell them we need the help of the public and ask anyone who may have been a witness to call the East Valley Division." He looked up and down to make sure no one was within earshot. "Here is the plan. I want the camera crew occupied while you, Victor, make your way to your car without anyone noticing. Leave as quickly as you can without drawing attention to yourself. The place is already crawling with cops, so you should be okay."

"Now?" I asked.

"No, not now, you—I'll let you know when."

I was sure he wanted to say "you idiot" but stopped short for my benefit.

"Am I off this assignment?" I asked.

"Well, we'll talk later today. I want you in my office at 10 a.m. sharp tomorrow." He started to leave then stopped. "And another thing, I want total secrecy. No one, nether your wife nor your girlfriend or your parents, your friends or your fellow police officers are to know about your involvement in this investigation. It must remain a total secret. Got that?"

"But—"

"No buts. My office tomorrow."

"Do I report to my home squad first?"

"No. I'll take care of that. I've already talked with Captain Bledsoe in Van Nuys."

When I looked back at the dead body sprawled on the pavement, I wondered what this poor man was doing in women's clothes. I also wondered why I, a patrol officer, was being asked to be involved in every aspect of the case. The whole "secrets" idea puzzled me, even though my undercover work at the high school had to be kept on the down low.

The coroner's wagon had arrived and a short, balding man about forty was trailed by two plain-clothes police women. Captain Wilson huddled in conference with them for several minutes.

He then made his way to the side of the Quick Stop where he signaled Fryman to come forward and talk to the TV and press representatives.

They were occupied, pinning a microphone to his coat, as their camera scanned the corner's wagon.

A few minutes later, he waved me on. I walked directly to my car, keeping my head low. The shock of seeing a corpse for the first time wore off and I started to enjoy the cloak-and-dagger aspect of my assignment.

This could be exciting, I thought, if it wasn't for the dead woman or dead man or, I suppose, dead person.

As I drove away, I began fantasizing about detective work, even though I was still considered a newbie.

It was exactly what I wanted to do as a member of the Los Angeles Police Department, however, I wondered if I could ever tap a dead man's eyeball.

Chapter 3

Undercover

I felt very nervous and a little scared sitting in Captain Wilson's office like a high school student waiting for detention from the assistant principal. It reminded me of the day I got caught smoking in the boy's toilet at Notre Dame High School and had to sweat it out in Father Damian's office.

Occasionally Wilson looked up but said nothing. Not talking was a chore for me because I was compulsive about filling empty air time. The longer the silence, the more uncomfortable I became. The windows of his office looked out on a large room with the various people in the East Valley Division moving about, answering phones, and working at two white boards that had information scribbled on them for the Carlyle murder case. Wilson closed the manila folder, got up, walked to the front of the desk, and looked directly at me.

"Stand up," he said. "How tall are you?"

"About five-foot-six." I always rounded up from my five foot five and a quarter.

"And how much do you weigh?"

"Well the last time I checked I was—"

He never let me finish. "How in hell did you pass the physical at the academy?"

This line of questioning began to annoy me because other cops and administrators always asked the same questions. I wanted to read them the new regulations, which had changed when there was pressure for more women in the force.

"I graduated third in my class, *sir*."

My pointed emphasis on "sir" didn't escape Wilson because he glared at me from deep set eyes above puffy red cheeks. The interrogation stopped when there was an announcing knock on the door and Fryman and Murray entered. I sat back down since both men looked through me as though I didn't exist.

"What have you got?" Wilson asked.

"You were right, captain," Murray said. "The MO is the same as the James Burgess murder and the Nicholas Jordan one last year, both of which are still open. Even down to the detail of how the murder was done; a twisted knife into the midsection. Canvasing the locals resulted in zilch. Burgess was murdered in the back of the Vons store at about 4 a.m., and he too was married but no children."

He paused and tossed the murder book onto Wilson's desk then added, "And, of course, the blue lipstick and the elegant women's clothes. The dress he had on was from Dillard's, which means he bought it somewhere back east. And here's the kicker, he visited the Velvet Glove in North Hollywood."

He opened the murder book and flipped to another section. "The note scribbled on the back of the receipt we found in Carlyle's wallet was the address of the Velvet Glove."

"Carlyle sounds like a repeat performance," Fryman said.

"And so does the Jordan victim," Murray added.

"Any responses from this morning's news broadcasts?"

"Nada. Nor did anybody come forth from the two-mile perimeter scan around the Quick Stop."

Wilson shifted in his chair. "I got a call from the chief this morning. He wants a daily report on the progress. He asked about a connection between the four cases."

"What four cases?" Fryman asked.

"Vickers, Jordan, Burgess, and now Carlyle," Wilson said.

"I doubt it because Vickers was shot and Burgess and Carlyle were stabbed or should I say eviscerated," Murray said.

Wilson heaved a sigh and I wished I knew more about the two previous cases.

"What was the Vickers's murder?" I asked as Fryman and Murray gave me a look that felt like "Mind your own business." I also wished I knew exactly what eviscerated meant but decided not to ask. Certainly, these men were not pork chops.

"This past February a man was murdered on Van Owen Street near Coldwater Canyon. There were no witnesses and robbery wasn't the motive," Wilson said. When he turned to me, I sat up straight. He opened another manila folder and studied it for a moment, then spoke directly to me, his gravel voice dropping into the low notes for authority.

"Narcotics sent over the file from your Metro High School assignment. It says 'excellent work.'" Wilson kept on reading the report and I could feel my heart starting to pound. "Your commander says here you were directly responsible for getting information about the drug ring operating there. Can you tell us something more about how you were involved?"

I always liked an opportunity to brag about myself but this time it made me uncomfortable with two veteran detectives staring at me. "Well, sir, I went undercover and posed as a high school student. The administrators at Metro knew about the assignment but the teachers didn't. They thought I was a transfer student because I entered mid-semester. The classes were a snap. In fact I had to act a little stupid at times so as not to raise any suspicions."

"That must have been fairly easy for you," Fryman injected as his lips hinted at a smile.

Wilson glared at him.

"It didn't take me long to learn who was doing lines and who the supplier was for crystal, weed, and ecstasy," I said "It turned out there was an empty house for sale near the back entrance of the school and that became our hang out."

"And nobody suspected you were in your twenties?" Murray asked.

"No, sir."

"They took you into their circle, no questions asked? You musta been damn good," Wilson said.

I began to wonder why they buttered me up, even though I was "damn good."

"Yes, sir. I was. I did have to take a few hits from a communal pipe, once, just to prove myself and I figured it was in the line of duty. There was no way to wiggle out of it. My cred was at stake."

"You do know that's a felony whether done in the line of duty or not?" Murray said.

"Do you have a history of drug use?" Wilson asked.

"No, sir. I wanted to make sure they accepted me as

one of the players. Most of the guys were part of a gang they called RCs which was part of the Crips."

"Go on."

"Well, there's not much more. The information I got helped set up a sting with Narcotics and they busted eleven people. Two of them were high school students. That's about it," I said and sat back, feeling very smug.

"What kinda grades did you get?" Fryman asked with a note of sarcasm.

"You're lucky the defense didn't nail us for illegal entrapment," Wilson said. "So what else?"

"I was hoping that after the trial I would get a promotion, but I didn't."

"Yes. Yes. That's a different matter," Wilson said. "You have to take the tests and get on the various lists."

"I have and I am, sir."

"Right now, I want to know if you are interested in doing some undercover work on the Carlyle case. It certainly won't hurt your future applications and requests for advancement." Wilson paused and looked directly at me. "The department is always looking for officers with special talents that help the team."

"Like what kind of undercover?" I asked, making sure that I didn't sound too positive or negative.

I purposely didn't tell the Captain that I enjoyed the high school assignment but there were parts I hated. Once when we were on the back patio of the house, I couldn't get out of taking a hit of a joint that was being passed around.

Since I didn't smoke cigarettes, I worried that I would start to cough and look like a first time user. Afterward, I didn't like the feeling of not being in control of myself or the mental confusion between the past and the present that weed produced.

"Fryman, give him a little briefing of our morning

meeting while I check on something." Wilson returned to his desk.

Fryman began to outline the strategy they planned to use in the effort to capture Carlyle's killer. "We don't have a lot of leads but we do have one positive one. There was a case about a month ago that was very similar to this one—a James Burgess.

The victim's mid-section was splayed open, cosmetics were found near the body, and an anonymous witness said he saw the dead man's picture in the paper and remembered seeing him in a notorious bar a few nights earlier."

Fryman took several police pictures from Wilson's desk while the captain was dialing a phone number. He showed them to me and I was, again, shaken by them. I had seen similar ones when I was training at the police academy, but now a direct connection to the violent deaths of two victims made my skin tingle.

"The Burgess case was handled out of the Devonshire Division and at the moment it remains an active case," he added. "The lead detectives are Raymond Carlucci and Jeff Reed."

"In the Carlyle case we found a store receipt in his wallet with just an address written on the back of it," Fryman offered. "It was the address of a bar in North Hollywood called the Velvet Glove. That same bar turned up in the investigation of the earlier Burgess case."

"Why not just go there and check it out?" I asked, as if I was some official of the logistics department, giving advice to rookie detectives.

Both men stared at me as though I had just landed a Manny Paquiano round-house punch. Their jaws dropped open in unison.

Wilson finished his conversation and hung up the phone. "They approved the budget."

Fryman and Murray frowned at the news and I wondered why.

"It's not that easy," Murray said. "The patrons there don't like cops. As soon as they see a badge they clam up."

"The place has a history of fights and complaints from the neighborhood people." Wilson walked to the front of the desk and perched himself on it. "Here's where you come in, Espinoza. We need someone to go in there, become a regular, and keep his eyes and ears open for leads that we can follow up, sort of what you did in the high school activity."

"In a bar?"

"Yes."

"I get carded every time I order a drink anywhere and even when I buy beer at the liquor store," I said, sounding very tentative.

Fryman and Wilson nodded almost in unison and Fryman said, "You actually drink beer?"

"What do you say," Wilson asked. "Son, are you interested?"

Of course, I was interested because it sounded like real police work. I wasn't interested in being called "son." I wondered how Jannine would take the news since she wasn't very happy during the high school assignment. "I have a lot of questions about the hours, the costs, and...the danger. I guess I would have to think about it."

I actually didn't have to think about it because it fit into my plan of advancement. I would do anything to get out of street patrol duties.

Captain Wilson stood up, walked over to me, put his meaty claw on my shoulder, and said, "Of course there would be no cost to you. I just got the approval to requisition funds...well in this case we would have to ask for extra funds because of the added expenses. The hours might be a problem because you would have to work late most nights and probably the week-ends as well. As far as your safety is concerned, LAPD takes care of its own. We would have your back at all times. We would never put you in a situation where we can't move in and protect you."

"Protect me? From what?"

Murray chimed in with, "In police work there is always some degree of danger. No more than a little courage and determination can't overcome." He sounded like my high school history teacher giving us homework.

"That's why we make the big bucks," Fryman said.

"There is no danger, son," Wilson said. "You're just going to be observing. No direct confrontation. We work together as a team with one goal; catch a murderer, but we need as many leads as possible. Sometimes the most inconspicuous thing like a word or a cigarette butt, or even a hair, can lead to an arrest."

"Sounds to me more like we're after a serial killer, sir," I said.

"Serial killer or killers, a copycat killer, or an avenging lover. Who knows?" Murray said.

"So," Wilson injected. "What do you say? Is it something you're interested in? Naturally you can say no, and there would be no hard feelings and even if you say yes, you can back out anytime you want. I don't want you to feel any pressure from me or anyone else. Of course, I would have to put the request and your answer in your personnel jacket."

I wondered what else would go into that file, now that he knew about my pot smoking on the job.

"Okay, I guess. I'll do it." I smiled and boasted, "I can nurse a drink like any other man."

I stressed the word *man* for Fryman's sake. His one eyebrow arched and the other pressed into a frown.

"There are a couple of hitches," Wilson said. "You'll have to shave that mustache you're starting to grow. When it's full grown it will be too big for your face anyway."

"I've had this mustache for two years. It's fully grown—sir."

He ignored me and returned to his desk to make another phone call.

"It looks it," Fryman interjected.

"And those scruffy side burns will have to go," Murray said. "No Pancho Villa look, either."

"Because you have to look clean and clear with no facial hair," Fryman chimed in.

"And what's the second thing?" I asked.

Murray stood directly in front of me, sizing me up and down. "You'll have to dress as a woman. You know, wig, high heels, makeup, the whole nine yards."

"Well, in your case maybe about five yards," Fryman added.

"What?" I yelled. "Why?"

"Well, the Velvet Glove is a bar where cross-dressers hang out," Fryman said. "A sort of drag bar like the one on Lexington Avenue in Hollywood."

"You mean a gay bar?" I blurted out.

"Yes, some of them are gay men, but more than half of all cross-dressers are straight men who like to dress up as women. Some of them are secretive about it and wear women's undergarments under their regular street clothes."

Wilson finished his phone call and began reading from a report he had on his desk. I was dumb struck which, for me, was unusual.

He put down the report. "Your size and weight are good but your narrow hips might be a problem."

"Maybe we can get him one of those butt enhancers that Victoria's Secret sells," Fryman said.

"How do you know about Victoria's Secret?" Murray asked.

"I bought my girlfriend a gift there once and they've been sending me catalogs ever since," I told him. "You should check it out."

I didn't think it was funny and I was starting to not like the assignment. Captain Wilson must have picked up on my body language because he reassured me that dressing in women's clothes was, like Halloween, no big deal. Didn't he realize that for a Latin man, any hint of femininity was a serious ego issue? He then continued the conditions with, "Speaking of secrets, remember this has to be completely confidential. Nobody may know about your undercover activities or your dress-up."

No problem with that, I thought.

"Sort of like Victor's Secret," Fryman said as he clasped his hands over his mouth.

"Can I think about it?" I wanted to talk to Jannine and try to convince her that this was a wonderful opportunity for me—something that would look positive on an application for advancement.

Wilson picked up all the paperwork on his desk and put it in a side drawer.

"Sure you can," he said. "You've got about 60 seconds. If it's not you, we'll have to get someone else on the force to do the job. This is not some game, son, this is serious business. We are looking for a man who slaughtered innocent citizens on our streets right here in the San Fernando Valley and, God knows, there may be more. We will do all we can to find this killer."

The manner in which he stood up, confident and self-assured, with body language that spoke louder than his words, convinced me he was serious.

He waited for my answer.

Jannine was right. This was another kiss-ass job. Saying no would mean I would be a patrol cop until I quit or retired. Saying yes would keep the door open for me when an opening occurred. Saying yes meant the embarrassment of trying on and buying women's clothes, wearing falsies, and, heaven forbid, a padded ass. Saying yes meant more time away from Jannine. It was a foolish mental argument on my part. Of course, I wanted to do it.

"Okay, I suppose, when do I start?"

"We'll have to do some planning for a couple days. In the meantime, resume your regular patrol duties while we get some outfits for you and check on your necessary female movements and gestures. I'll have my wife get some clothes at Goodwill just to get an idea of sizes and stuff."

Then Wilson added, "Remember this is a highly secretive assignment. I don't want anyone here in the department to know what's going down. These things often start with some jokes and then it becomes common knowledge." He turned to Fryman, "And that includes you too, Robert."

"I'd start by shaving," Murray said. "Maybe even twice a day."

Fryman stood, then smiled. "Maybe you should rent the movie *Bosom Buddies*, Victoria Espinoza, or should I say Vickie?

"Okay, cut it out!" Wilson said.

"Oh, sorry. I meant *Tootsie*," Fryman added as he walked out the door.

He stood outside the glass window, mocking me by licking his finger and rubbing it across his eyebrows.

He didn't seem concerned that others in the station

were staring at him and mimicking his gestures. Halloween was only two weeks away, but lipstick, falsies, and a padded ass still made me feel uncomfortable and a little worried. I was more worried about how Jannine would take the news.

Chapter 4

The Brown Bag

Although Aaron Weiskoff was known as Bubba in our Van Nuys division, I called him Aaron. We had been partners for the past two years and Jannine and I had become close with him and his wife, Carrie. In fact, the four of us took vacations together and shared intimate knowledge of our respective lives. A year ago, Aaron and Carrie asked us to be God Parents for their newborn son, Alexander.

Aaron was more than a working colleague, he was a loyal friend. When it came to their two children, both Carrie and Aaron were like lions—you didn't criticize or the wrath of hell would befall you. I knew I fell into the same category.

We sat in our patrol car parked in front of a large truck on busy Burbank Boulevard. He was the driver and I was the book man, riding shotgun. I kept the records, did the reports, worked the radio, turned on the videocam, and the computer. Even though I was the better driver, he outranked me. Our assignment for the morning was to nail motorist violations: no seat belts, cell phone talking, texting, expired tags, and speeding.

"What the fuck happened to your mustache?" he asked.

"Oh, I got tired of it."

Truth was I felt naked without it and even found myself touching my upper lip repeatedly like someone who had lost a limb.

"I'll bet Jannine is happy about that."

"Happy? This morning she almost broke my neck hugging me so hard and kept kissing me. It was the kissing that made me think of calling in sick."

The light had turned red on Hazeltine Avenue and there before us was a blue Honda with last year's expired orange tag on the rear license plate. We eased in behind the car and I logged into the computer. Once we were past the intersection, I turned on our flashing lights but no siren. The Honda continued for another block then pulled over to the curb. The routine was preplanned and *boring*. I moved to the right rear of the car with my holster unbuttoned and my hand on my weapon. Aaron did the same as he approached the driver's side window and stood behind the center post so that the driver had to turn around to face him—handbook safety, regulation number 1710.

"May I see your driver's license, ma'am? No, don't get out of the car. Just your driver's license and the vehicle registration."

Our dialogue was right out of the handbook. Generally, we wrote the ticket and returned to our roost in front of the truck, but not this time. The expiration was longer than six months so the car had to be impounded. She would cry. We would remain stoic. The tow truck would arrive. She would stand on the sidewalk. We would leave. It was beyond *boring*. It was mind numbing. This was not the police work I envisioned when I graduated from the

Police Science program at LA City College four years
ago. The thought of doing this for twenty-five more years
sent a shudder through me, but for Aaron it was his life's
blood.

"I think you're bullshitting me about the mustache,"
Aaron said, after we'd finished with the lady and gone
back to our patrol car.

"What the hell are you making a big deal about it?
What? I have to ask permission to improve my appearance?" My voice was just testy enough to make him back
off so we sat in silence like an old married couple.

"Jesus," he yelled. "Did you see that? That poor kid
walking his bicycle had to jump back."

A black Corvette had barreled through the crosswalk
then accelerated, narrowly missing the boy about ten
years old. It took lights, siren, and five blocks to bring the
driver to a stop. Aaron was pissed. He rattled off numbers
like 23103 (reckless driving), 23582 (speeding), and
maybe even evading arrest. Despite two years on patrol, I
still had to look up the violations in the codebook.

The driver was impatient. "Look," he said. "I gotta
be downtown in thirty minutes. I plead guilty, so skip the
lecture and give me the ticket."

He had lowered his window about six inches then
pushed his driver's license and registration out like the
thrust of a fencing stab. That was all Aaron needed to put
him in slow mode. I wondered why he had to make so
many trips back to our cruiser to "check on something."
It was his way of stringing out the action.

"Step out of the car, sir," Aaron said. "Please stand at
the rear of your vehicle."

Watching Aaron was the highlight of the day. The
driver's body language and grumbling sent Aaron into
super-thorough mode where he not only dotted every "I"
he circled the dot as well.

I watched my partner peer into each window of the car. For me the routine was a welcome change from the boredom of traffic detail. It was past our lunchtime and I hoped the driver—shifting his weight from foot to foot—wouldn't hear my stomach growling.

"Sign here," Aaron said as he looked at his watch.

The driver scowled and didn't read the entries on the citation. He scribbled a few lines. Behind the stoic face, I knew my partner was smiling. The Corvette's tires squealed as the driver pulled away without signaling.

"So, where are we going for lunch? Or is that brown bag on the floor your lunch?"

"No, it's not," I said as I nudged it away from the driver's side. We headed for the *4 and 20* pies on Laurel and Riverside. After we parked, he glanced down at the bag then at me.

"Come on. Be straight with me. Why did you shave it?"

"No reason."

Here was another lie I had to keep track of. Once you started lying, it became a Ponzi scheme where one new lie must pay off a preceding one.

"Bullshit. I remember how you couldn't wait for it to grow in so you could look older. Remember that?" Aaron said.

"Well, now I am older and I don't need it."

"Look in the mirror, Victor. You just took off about ten years and when you smile you're like someone expecting to get a hard on any minute."

Before I took the first bite of my sandwich, my cell rang. I looked down at the screen and it showed LAPD so I cupped my hand over the mouthpiece.

"Hello."

Captain Wilson shouted so loud I was certain Aaron could hear so I pressed the phone hard against my ear.

"Channel 2 is going to do some extended time on the Carlyle story and that means the rest of the TV stations will probably follow with their own versions," he bellowed. "I want you to come in tomorrow morning at eleven. Do you have a shift?"

"I do, sir."

"I'll get it cancelled because we have to move up the schedule of your involvement. I'll see you in the morning."

"Anything else, sir?"

"Yes. After our meeting, I want you and Robert to follow-up on a phone call we got through Crime Stoppers. Murray said it came in just a little while ago and looks like something solid. By the way, did you shave that mustache of yours?"

"I did, sir."

As soon as I said it, I wondered if Aaron heard the Captain's bellow because he looked up with wide eyes and a smile.

"So, you just felt like it, eh? Who were you just siring, a captain or a commander?"

"Look, I can't tell you. Okay? Can we just leave it at that?" I was getting nervous about how much he already knew.

"You don't have to tell me. I'll find out. Secret shit in the squad room travels faster than the speed of light." He looked about for the waitress. "You gonna have pie?"

"It's not that I don't trust you. I do. I'd trust my life in your hands, you know that, but I've got orders."

Aaron waived at the waitress. "See. There's another little piece of the puzzle: who gave you the orders? A couple more and I'll know everything. Besides, you're not supposed to keep secrets from your partner. Even though you're an asshole, I tell you everything."

We made quite a pair. With his Bubba-built six-foot-two frame and my five-foot-five one, we looked like Laurel and Hardy in police uniforms. Like the famous comedians, we rarely expressed our feelings for and about each other. We were both better off by demonstrating through action that covered each other's back. Like the time a year ago when a drunk at a bar on Laurel Canyon Boulevard lunged for Aaron's gun. They both fell to the floor with the drunk on top of Aaron.

"You son-of-a-bitch," I'd yelled and immediately pulled him off. Aaron rolled him over and, with my baton, I pummeled him repeatedly.

"Stop," Aaron yelled, but blind with rage, I reared up to hit him again.

There were at least ten witnesses. Aaron grabbed my fist and stopped me. Once I was back in control, I stood the dazed man up. Had I continued, it would have meant an internal affairs investigation and needless paperwork in my personnel file. A certain hurdle for any promotion.

I remember Aaron being honest with me after the fight. "I don't get it. You short guys always have short fuses."

Now he just sat there staring at me then finally said, "What are you goin' to have?"

"Yeah. I'm thinking banana with whipped cream," I said.

"If you want to look older and tougher, you better make it apple ala-mode. That's the macho Jack Armstrong all American pie. And if you really want to look tough, skip the fork and eat it with your hands."

The waitress came, flirted with Aaron, then asked him, "The usual boysenberry?"

"Yeah," he said.

And I wondered how she knew. Did they have a history? If they did, when could it have been, since I spent almost every day with him?

"And you?"

I hoped my voice wouldn't come out squeaky and weak. "Apple pie, ala-mode."

We were about half way through our desert when the squawk box crackled, confirming our location. We were instructed to stand-by, as we might be needed at a domestic scene at 6615 Lankershim Boulevard.

"Damn," I blurted out. "That's the same block where the Carlyle victim was murdered."

Aaron cocked one eyebrow and stared at me. "Carlyle?"

He was expecting an answer, but I just kept eating the all-American pie which probably should have been crow pie.

"Isn't that a case over in East Valley Division?" he asked.

I cringed at the thought of word getting back to Captain Wilson that Aaron knew of the plan.

After another big bite and mouthful of ice cream, I mumbled, "I guess so."

"Come on, Vic, level with me. What's the story?"

"I can't discuss it. I will tell you that you'll probably have a different partner for a while because I'll be on a special assignment. But that's all I can tell you."

"Oh great, now I gotta break in a new asshole."

Aaron continued to stare at me as he ate his pie, sometimes stabbing his upper lip with a fork full of boysenberry filling that planted a purple mustache. He set down his fork and assumed the pose of a cross-examining attorney.

"Let's see, we have a shaved mustache, a captain or a commander giving orders, a special assignment outside our division, knowledge of a murder scene, and a secret kept from your favorite partner." He set his elbow on the table and leaned his jaw into his hand in a mock analysis.

"It all adds up to another undercover assignment similar to your high school gig. Am I right?"

"Aaron, I can't"

"Okay, I'll wait. By the way, what's in the brown bag?"

"Nothing."

"Pretty big nothing." He knew I was avoiding his question because he didn't push for an answer.

"Okay, but listen," I said. "If you find out, promise me you won't say a word to anyone, including Carrie. My involvement can't get out."

Aaron sat back, puffed out his chest, made the sign of the cross over his heart, and gave the "scout's honor" sign.

I leaned in closer to him and spoke in a whisper. "The murderer has killed two men dressed as women. So, they want me to dress up like a woman, go to a bar where cross-dressers hang out, and keep my eyes and ears open for info about the case."

"Holy shit. You as a woman? Why?"

I regretted my lack of control and not keeping the orders given to me by Captain Wilson.

Aaron shook his head in disbelief.

"Because they suspect the killer goes after men dressed as women," I said.

He looked at me with a silly grin. "Sooo…you'll be a drag queen?"

"I will report back to the two lead detectives. They want me to be like the third detective on the Carlyle case."

"I doubt that. It sounds to me like you'll just be bait. And at the looks of you without a mustache, jail bait."

"No, I'll be talking to people at this bar and getting whatever information that might be useful as leads in the case."

"Just bait, baby."

"I don't think so because Captain Wilson said they would have my back at all times."

"You're on the hook, so start to wiggle. Or do the shimmy or whatever you drag queens do."

The squawk box crackled again, "Twenty-seven Charlie, proceed immediately to 6615 Lankershim for a domestic violence dispute in apartment 3B."

"Let's go. At least there might be some danger there that should spark up our day," I said.

Unfortunately by the time we got there, the fighting couple was all kissy-kiss and I'm sorry and I love you.

Boring!

The watch ended with Aaron and me completing our paperwork at the station while I clutched the brown paper bag. We said our good-byes in the locker room. When I was certain I was alone, I slipped off my shoes and socks and tried on the black high heeled shoes I'd bought at the Goodwill store, eyeballing the size. They looked right for me. It was a painful, impossible squeeze to get them on and, with that, came a slight rush of feeling taller. I stood straight up and weaved back and forth, before I tried a few steps while leaning against the lockers. Twice my left ankle twisted to the side, but I retained my balance. I tried a few steps without holding on. This was going to be a snap. After I braved a few steps to the end of the row of lockers, I picked up my speed. I was almost prancing when I noticed my feet starting to hurt. I made a quick turn and fell flat on my belly, just missing my head on a bench, then crashed into the lockers, producing a series of loud bangs. The handle of one locker dug into the top of my right wrist. Fortunately, I had unstrapped my belt—else there would be police gear all over the room. I sat down on the bench and then could not get the shoes off.

The soft leather and my sweat had bonded the black pumps to my feet.

The noise of my fall attracted the attention in the outer office because several cops came running into the locker room. I had just enough time to throw a towel over my feet.

"What happened?" the duty cop yelled.

"I tripped. No problem," I said. "I'm fine." I rubbed at the pain in my wrist.

"Are you sure?" he said. "You look sweaty."

I pulled my feet under the bench, waved away the two cops and a trainee then said, "I'm fine. Thanks for your concern, guys."

The duty cop kept staring at my wrist and said, "Something's not right here. You're bleeding." With that, he pulled the towel off my feet. The open toes of my pumps stuck out like headlights, and three grown men's eyes widened as their jaws dropped open.

This was sure to get back to Aaron and God knew who else.

Chapter 5

Very Cold Cream

At 6 a.m. Jannine and I moved around her tiny kitchen like a couple of silent ballet dancers. She had to leave for work before eight and usually I had a 7a.m. roll call at the Van Nuys Division. Toast, cereal, juice, and coffee, accompanied by the morning news hour on channel 2, all had to be orchestrated on schedule. Neither of us spoke much before work. We were well-matched night owls, needing about twenty minutes of morning coffee to flood our blood streams. She stopped and watched during the freeway traffic report.

"What did you do to your wrist?" she asked. The black and blue mark looked like a tattoo gone wrong. "Or did you get into one of your fights again?"

No, Mother, I didn't and I'm not going to tell you.

As the smallest kid in every grade at school I attended, I'd learned to fight anyone that crossed me. Unfortunately, it left me with the short-guy-chip-on-his-shoulder affliction. In any fight, my lightning fast moves were always a problem for the big guys.

My ears piqued when the announcer said, "New developments in the murder of a cross-dresser after this short break."

Four commercials later, the reporter segued to last night's interview from city hall in downtown Los Angeles.

I ate my cereal, watching the screen where city councilman Alan Kemper was being interviewed by reporters from various TV stations. He decried the mayor and the chief of police in front of a bank of microphones pushed toward his mouth, almost obscuring the lower half of his face. Kemper was a short, intense man in his middle-fifties with a full head of graying hair and frown lines between his eyes. Behind him, towering over the councilman stood Captain Wilson. Kemper waited for the jostling reporters to settle down and then began his rant.

"Another innocent family man has been slaughtered on our city streets. The second such murder in less than two months and the police don't have a clue. This is a disgrace. Someone is not doing their job."

A reporter from ABC shouted out, "Captain Wilson, why was the victim wearing women's clothes?"

Kemper did not give Wilson a chance to answer.

"The man was probably in a Halloween costume. But that makes no difference. It's still a gruesome and senseless murder. As chairman of the Police oversight committee…"

Jannine stood behind me listening. As she cleared the table she asked, "Isn't that case in your division?"

"No. It's out of East Valley."

"What do you know about it? Was the guy really wearing women's clothes?"

"How should I know? I'm not in homicide."

I couldn't lie to Jannine because she had a tuning mechanism that nailed me every time. Remembering

Captain Wilson's edict about secrecy concerning my involvement in the case, I tried to act indifferent. I knew that letting Aaron in on the program was safe since I swore him to secrecy. I turned off the TV. Even though I wanted to hear every detail of city hall's take, I wanted Jannine to see my disinterest.

It didn't work.

"Is that the same Captain Wilson that called you in the middle of the night last week?" she asked.

"Hmm? Yeah, it probably is. Why do you ask?"

She turned the TV back on just as the cameras switched to a nearby gathering of planted shills holding placards and chanting, "*Vote Alan Kemper. Vote Alan Kemper.*"

When the councilman came back on the screen he was holding a prepared statement. "This afternoon," he began, "the council voted unanimously to offer a reward of $25,000 for the arrest and conviction of the killer or killers of Fredrick Carlyle. Even in these difficult financial times, the city must explore every possible avenue to apprehend a vicious killer."

The reporters all started shouting questions at the same time. I clicked off the TV again.

"So why does Wilson want you involved in the case?" she asked.

"It's more BS about the coming election," I said to divert attention from the murder news.

She was annoyed and rightly so. I hated not being able to tell her about my involvement.

She dropped dishes into the sink and put milk back into the refrigerator, slamming the door closed. "Shouldn't you be getting dressed? You're going to be late for roll call."

"No. I'm on a late shift today."

"What? Then you had better call Aaron because we

were supposed to meet him and Carrie tonight for drinks at their house. Or did you forget again?"

"Forget what?"

"What's going on with you?" Her voice had gone up at least two octaves. "Or is this like the Dodger game we missed?"

There was a strong edge to her question, which I tried to ignore. "Stop nudging at me," I shouted.

"Me? It's you that's being evasive."

"I'll call him," I said.

We never left each other without at least a peck or a quick squeeze. Instead of another argument starting, she sent me a clear message by leaving without a kiss or a word good-bye. I washed up the dishes and hurried to the bedroom where I turned on the small dresser TV set in hopes of getting more information on the case, but all I got were more commercials and a story about a dog that could bark words.

Jannine and I kept toothbrushes, some clothes, and other essentials at our respective places. Life would be easier and less expensive if we both lived in one unit— preferably my house. She was steadfast in refusing to do so because she wanted to set an example for her younger brother and sister. I couldn't understand how fornication practiced in two households had a higher moral value than fornication practiced in one. Jannine got angry every time I reminded her that fornication was a dying sin. Naturally, I didn't dare compare it to missing Mass on Sunday or going to purgatory.

Jannine was taking the fall for both of us by insisting that we maintain separate households. My parents— staunch Mexican Catholics—would blow a bible gasket if Jannine moved into my house. They would remind me how hard they worked to send my brother and me to an all-boys Catholic high school. A lot of good it did.

After a vigorous brushing and flossing, I began to in-
spect the myriad of bottles, jars, and tubes in her cabinet
and on the counter. I read and smelled each item: one for
base, another for vanishing, still another for cleansing,
and finally one for softening. They had weird names like
Lucidity, White Linen, and Estee Lauder. I rubbed a little
of each on my cheeks, but the stubble of my unshaven
chin caused caking. It looked and felt strange as if I just
passed through a snowstorm.

I opened her closet door and marveled at the number
of dresses, skirts, and blouses she kept in neat rows. At
first, it looked like hundreds of shoes on the floor and in a
rack, but actually it was more like a few dozen. After I
pulled one of her dresses off the hanger, I held it up to me
in front of the mirror on the door. It hung below my
knees. The thought of going out in public in a dress and
make-up produced a twinge of fear in my stomach. This
was not going to be like the undercover assignment at the
high school where all I had to do was act and sound im-
mature and use words like cool, hey bro, and like.

I dropped the dress on a chair and took a blue blouse
with ruffles along the collar, held it up and it seemed like
it might fit.

I whipped off my T-shirt, threw it on the bed, slid my
arms through the sleeves, then tried to button the row of
hooks behind me. The hooks ended up in the wrong eye-
lets. When I stood in front of the mirror, I looked like a
circus clown with the black hairs of my chest curling out
along the ruffles of the blouse. Maybe turtleneck dresses
would work for me. Otherwise, I would have to shave my
chest.

Suddenly, I wondered if her shoe size would fit me. I
pulled out several pairs and held one against the bottom
of my bare foot which, because of the high heel, gave no
indication that it would fit. After my experience in the

locker room at the station, I did not try on any. The good news for me, even though Jannine was taller, my feet were bigger.

I panicked when I heard a car door slam. From the front window of her bedroom, I saw her climbing up the stairs. I ripped the seam of her blouse as I tore it off, throwing it and the dress into the closet. I scooped up her shoes and tossed them in, too. The front door opened.

"Vic, where are you?" she said jingling her keys.

"In here," I yelled.

Jannine appeared in the bedroom just after I slid the closet door closed. She looked puzzled, first at me, then at my T-shirt on the bed and then to the TV that was re-playing the interview with Alan Kemper. Though she didn't say anything, I felt I needed to make a comment which was probably a wrong-headed idea, considering her ability to detect deceit.

"Wow, it's warm in here. I was just going to make the bed." I tugged at the sheets and punched up the pil-lows. Then I walked to the window and pulled it open.

Her eyes widened since I had never made her bed or mine in the five years we had been together.

"What's come over you?"

"What? Can't I do something nice for you?"

"No, you can't. And what's that white stuff on your chin?"

I was amazed at how one lie necessarily led to an-other and then still another until you forgot about the first lie. I pushed the palms of my hands across my face sever-al times. "I was going to shave but then changed my mind. What did you forget?"

She put her hands on her hips then smiled. She walked slowly, almost gliding, toward me.

"I couldn't just leave and start our day on that angry note."

48   Charles Alvarez

She came up to me, put her arms around my neck, and we kissed. Her cool hands on my bare back and chest almost made me forget that I didn't want her touching my face. What if she could see or smell the various test applications? I moved my head up, kissed her neck, and rubbed the small of her back. Her fingers dug into my scalp as I moved from one side of her neck to the other. She arched her head back as an invitation not to stop.

"Whoa," she said. "Don't get me started. I have to go."

Then she wiggled closer to me. Talk about getting started, for me it was too late. All systems were on full throttle.

I pulled her closer and we kissed. "What about *me* getting started?" I said. "Can't you be a little late this morning?"

"Maybe," she said and kicked off her shoes toward the closet.

I was amazed that I could undo the buttons on the back of her dress but not the buttons on her blouse when it was on me. At the rate we were going, she wasn't going to be that late for work. I pulled her closer to me so that my chin rested on her shoulder. We finished undressing like we were on steroids: fumbling, clutching, and panting.

In the large dresser mirror across the room, I watched the small of her back move rhythmically. There was something erotic in seeing my hand coursing along her picture-perfect tush. The double sensation, of watching what I felt, registered in my brain, heightening my pleasure to a new intensity. I completely forgot about the cosmetic, the torn blouse, and the shoes.

We fell onto the bed as I lost nearly all sense of hearing and seeing. The intense passion blotted out all awareness of time and place. We were interlocking puzzle pieces that pressed and hooked into each other. Rapt in pleasure, we lay there, overcome from spending ourselves within each other. Time was no longer measured in its passing. There was no future, no past, only the intense present that demanded helpless submission.

Neither she nor I realized she was kissing the very spot on my chin where I tested her potions. She rolled over on top of me and pinned my back to the bed like a wrestler, but I was down for much more than a count of three. I was a modern day Sampson, losing his hair and his strength. Our senses were askew because sound did not register for me. The end came with a shudder and soon our bodies slackened. While I was still in a semi-trance, she disappeared into the bathroom. In the glow of the moment, I never noticed she had dressed. The world had stopped for a short twenty minutes. All our cares had vanished. Now we were back to the reality of the phone call to Aaron, the sigalert on the freeways, the captain's meeting, and my worry about the torn blouse. Perhaps the vanishing cream did it.

The TV announcer gave the traffic report as very heavy. "Be careful, folks," he said. "It's a jungle out there."

I somehow found the strength to get up and change the channel in search of one covering the murder. I had two hours to languish in bed and daydream about Jannine and the chaos of the East Valley Division.

Jannine, fully dressed with not a hair out of place, stood next to the bed, smiled, leaned down, and kissed me. "Since when did you start shaving with cold cream?" she asked, then she turned on her heel and left.

Chapter 6

Cross-dress Lessons

Nothing Wilson or Fryman could say would upset me that day. Even the usual wait in Captain Wilson's office didn't bother me. He was now a half hour late but when you were a captain, tardiness was a luxury and a privilege of rank. At eleven-thirty, he entered, holding an armful of files and folders, which he dropped on his desk. Several papers spilled like an avalanche.

He turned to me. "You're early. I like that in a team player."

After he sat down, he shuffled through the various files and selected two which were set down in front of me.

"What do you know about cross dressing?" he asked.

"Nothing, sir."

"Have you ever dressed up in women's clothes?

I hesitated to admit it. "Only once."

"Great, that's a start. Was it for Halloween?"

"No, sir. I went to an all-boys high school and Miss

Mackey, the drama teacher, drafted me to play a girl in the senior musical, *Annie Get Your Gun.* I got more applause than anyone else in the cast. My dad was really angry that I accepted the part."

"Hmm. Well, for this assignment you won't have to sing or dance but you will have to dress, look like, and act like a woman."

"I could pitch my voice a little higher like this." I cleared my throat and said, "'The rain in Spain stays mainly in the plain.' How was that?"

"What did you play, Eliza Doolittle in a Western? For this assignment it's more than just pitching your voice and putting on a dress."

"What do you want me to do?"

"The Velvet Glove caters to all types of cross dressers. You have to know about all of them. You have to know who you're dealing with when you engage them in conversation. You have to understand their reason for cross-dressing."

I liked the thoroughness of how LAPD approached a problem, even though I wasn't that interested in cross-dressing.

However, this was now beginning to sound like the police work I wanted to do. The part that troubled me was his comment to "engage them in conversation." What did you say to a man dressed in women's clothes? I remembered Joey on *Friends* would open a conversation with 'How are *you* doin'?'

Wilson went on to give me a complete lesson. "There are a group of men who are amateur crossdressers. They only dress up occasionally with no particular motive."

"I got the amateur part down already," I said.

"That's not what I have in mind," he said.

The second group he called Drag Queens. "These men dress up in wild fashions and extreme get-ups. Watch a couple shows of *Ru Paul's Drag Race* on television. These cross dressers spend all their money on custom gowns, hair, and head pieces. I can't even imagine what the shoes cost them," he said.

I remembered my shoes from Goodwill had already cost me a lot in reputation at the station. Most of the guys bought my lies about putting together a costume for Halloween. I was beginning to zone out as the captain droned on.

"Then there are the secret cross-dressers," he continued. "They wear women's undergarments in place of their jockey shorts and under their regular clothes. For them the silky touch satisfies their needs. For them it's an erotic fetish. They become aroused at the feel of silk on their skin. You can't tell when you see them because they look like normal men." He stopped and caught me gazing out the window.

"What do you think of Spanx?" he asked.

"I don't know. It sounds a little kinky to me. But if I have to do, it I will."

He dropped his head down and rubbed his forehead. "I hope I'm not making a mistake here." Walking to his desk, he pulled open the bottom drawer, took out a pint bottle of Jim Beam, and took a long swig. "They're trying to hide their manhood."

"If they're hiding it, why do they go into the Velvet Glove?" I asked, realizing that I was asking why again.

"Psychologists tell us they want to be with their own. For them it's a time to totally relax and relieve built-up stress and tension caused by the fetish and the pressures of living a secret. It's like opening up a relief valve on a steam engine."

As he shuffled through a file on his desk and produced several pictures of men who looked normal but were classed as secret dressers, Murray entered, said nothing, and sat down next to me.

"Eventually they lose it and do something outrageous and get arrested," the captain said. "A different kind of cry for help. Then there's the hookers," he continued. "These men are primarily gay who give head to johns looking for that kind of action. Not long ago, an African American comedian named Murphy was arrested for his involvement with a male cross-dressed hooker. These guys get very aggressive and annoy straight men right on the street. Vice hauls them in on a regular basis."

"How do they dress?"

"Provocative and sexy in a caricature sort of way. The johns know exactly what they're looking for. You'll probably not run into very many of this group at the Velvet Glove bar."

"Would they be aggressive enough to kill?" I asked, trying to sound like a real detective who was part of the team.

"No. But often they themselves are the victims of violence. Then there are the professionals that cross-dress for a living. These are entertainers. Dame Edna from England has toured all over the States. There is Jim Bailey who does impersonations of Judy Garland and Carol Channing. You won't see any of those at the Glove, though I understand the bar puts on shows of their own on Friday and Saturday nights."

"So how do you want me to dress?"

"None of those," he said and appeared to be enjoying his listing of cross-dressers. I thought maybe he was trying to impress me with his knowledge of the cross-dress culture. I couldn't care less about what rang his bell because I wanted to get to my involvement.

"There is another group of cross-dressers called gender fuckers. Sometimes they're called Half Drags or Spit
Drags. These guys purposely mix masculine and feminine
appearances as an in-your-face statement." He paused
then added, "It's their way of saying to social standards,
fuck you. They get into fights and generally cause may-
hem."

"The penal code has no category for them," Murray
added in a tone of disparagement. "They bother everybody and anybody that bothers them."

Wilson smiled, not out of humor but of tolerance.
"These guys come into the bars wearing a dress, make-
up, and panty hose with army boots and sporting a beard,
tattoos, and long side burns."

"I could be one of those," I said.

I had visions of myself more as a female pirate than a
cross-dresser. Even so, growing the beard could be a
problem.

"A major group of cross-dressers are men who want
to pass. That is, they want to dress and look like normal
women and move through the everyday world without
being suspected. If you rent the movie *Some Like it Hot*
you'll get the idea. Those two men needed to pass as
women when they joined an all-girl band. That's where
you come in."

"Then why me? Why not just get a professional actor?"

He opened another file and spread out pictures of
Burgess and Carlyle, along with a few composite drawings of the two men. Attached to each picture were details of their physical characteristics before and after the
killings.

"Would a professional actor agree to do this?"

I nodded but still didn't get it because I didn't have a
clue why the litany of types.

"Notice they look alike. Each man was very youthful looking and no taller than five-foot-five. Each had similar bone structure. They were both olive skinned Caucasians. From all accounts Burgess was virile, outgoing, and very athletic, but very convincing as a woman."

He sat back and just stared at me. I was slow to catch on but eventually I saw myself in those pictures and drawings. The resemblance was uncanny even down to the hairstyle, the narrow muscular shoulders, and full lips.

"I guess I fit the type," I said, more out of resignation than acceptance.

"Burgess and Carlyle wore expensive clothes. Not the kind you'd buy on Rodeo Drive but close. Theirs came from Nordstrom's and Bloomingdales'. Both were hard driving, successful men: Burgess was an account executive at Price Waterhouse and Carlyle was a space project engineer at Rocketdyne."

"And I'm just a vanilla flavored patrol cop."

"More than that, son. They were ambitious men with deep desire to be successful and get ahead. I see some of those qualities in you, especially your desire to become a detective. You have the drive."

I knew I was getting an "Atta-boy" work-over but, oddly enough, I liked it. I hated being called son. Coming from Captain Wilson, it seemed to have sincerity behind it, a vein of honesty not usually found in police administrators.

"I guess I still want to know what I'm supposed to do."

"I want you to dress and act in such a way as to pass. If you get on a bus, heads shouldn't turn to look at you. When you're at the Glove, I want you to act like a lady. I want you to mingle, get to know people, and then report back to Murray any info you get: names, phone numbers, where parties are held, what kind of cars they drive, anything."

"Do you want me to go to the parties?"

"Absolutely," Wilson boomed. "That's where you're apt to get the best information."

"I guess the hardest part will be acting like a woman."

"No. The hardest part will be not raising any suspicion. If they get wind that you're a cop, the show's over for us. And another thing, don't do or go anywhere without clearing it with either Fryman or Murray."

"I can do this. I know I can," I said and Wilson looked pleased.

I felt a rush of excitement from my brain to my stomach—as if I was batting in the bottom of the ninth with two outs, two men on, and the game on the line.

"Get up," Wilson said. "Walk from the door to my desk and back again."

I stood up, confused, as I looked at Murray and Wilson who had expectation written across their faces. I took a few hesitant steps and then walked back and forth a couple times.

"You're going to have to learn how to walk, sit, and gesture with your body. Have you ever seen John Wayne walk?" Wilson asked.

"You mean the cowboy?"

Wilson nodded. "Go over to the Sherman Oaks Galleria, sit down on a bench, and watch how women move, sit, and stand. When you walk, don't swing your arms close to your body like the Incredible Hulk. When women walk, they swing their arms six to eight inches away from their body, palms out. Watch and learn," he said. "And when they walk they put one foot in front of the other so it makes their hips undulate."

Reality was sinking in. I wondered if I could act well

enough to convince and not make people laugh. "Tomorrow, I'll go to the mall," I said.

"There's another hitch. We gotta get you in that bar ASAP. The chief and the city council are on my ass, especially that damn Kemper. Go to the mall this afternoon and tonight you can start doing some research on the internet. Just Google cross-dressers and you'll get tons of sites to study."

Fryman knocked on the door then entered just as Wilson was wrapping up. All he heard was Wilson saying, "Tomorrow, we buy clothes." He paused. "I just wish you had a bigger ass and weaker shoulders."

"Wow! Am I interrupting something?" Fryman asked.

"Yes," Wilson said. "We were just talking about you trying to figure out what category of cross-dresser you could be to help you get in touch with the woman within."

"No way," Fryman snapped back. "My feminine side is all in my tongue."

"Yeah. We'll be testing that tomorrow. I want you and Murray to go with Victor tomorrow and advise him on buying a wardrobe. We're not going to use the usual drag queen shops in town. It's important that we move up the calendar on the Velvet Glove part of our investigation."

"Go with him where?" Fryman asked.

"The women's department at Macy's."

Chapter 7

Shopping

I waited for Fryman and Murray at the women's dressing rooms at Macy's on the boulevard. I walked
through the entire area of women's garments, avoiding the lingerie section, and any areas where there were
shoppers. I probably looked silly, pretending to shop. By
eight o'clock most of the shoppers were gone so I started
to make some choices. It seemed like everything was on
sale at forty and fifty percent off. The regular priced
items, I thought, even a woman wouldn't wear.

The selection of dresses, skirts, and blouses I made
were piled on the checkout counter. Besides the sales
clerk, there was one woman shopper who seemed to be
browsing and circling around the area more like a store
detective than someone wanting to make a selection. Perhaps word didn't get to her about my appointment.

Captain Wilson's wife instructed me that the store
did not allow men to try on dresses during regular store
hours. She had made us an appointment for near closing
hours on Thursday. For me it was a relief to know that

nobody would see me prancing around before two men whose goal would probably be to make obscene comments. When they arrived, just at closing, Fryman started right in.

"I hope you picked out something in black because white will make you look fat," he said, loud enough for the sales clerk to hear. She maintained custody of the eyes as she choked back a laugh. For me, Fryman's taunts still hit a raw nerve despite the thickening skin I was developing for this assignment.

"You can go ahead and try some of these on now," the store clerk said. "We won't be getting any new customers at this hour."

Murray held up several of my selections, giving a low whistle with each one. As he did, it occurred to me that I was making selections of dresses in styles I'd like to see on Jannine. In fact, some of them were similar to her dresses.

"These are great," Murray said. "Have you decided who you want to be?"

"I want to be a cross-dresser," I said.

I preferred to use the word cross-dresser instead of transvestite because it somehow still salvaged my identity as a male.

Murray held up a plain-looking skirt and blouse. "If you want to pass as a woman, this will work. It shouldn't draw too much attention."

He then held up a long sequined gown with hanging sleeves. "With this, people will not be confused. They'll know you're a man parading around in a dress."

"Isn't there something he can wear that's in-between," Fryman asked, "yet will make a guy's jockey shorts tighten up a bit?"

I grabbed a dress and disappeared into one of the dressing rooms. When I emerged, three jaws dropped open: Fryman's, Murray's, and the store clerk's. They didn't speak, they didn't laugh, and they didn't cover their eyes. The store clerk circled around me twice like she was in the paddock at Santa Anita, deciding to bet on a horse.

"I think we can rule out spaghetti straps and maybe even dresses completely. With those hairy legs slacks might work unless you get a waxing unless you get a waxing," she said. "Regular sizes won't work either. May I suggest we try Petites?" After racing around through the various racks, she brought out a blouse with puffed sleeves and a ruffled collar. "This will downplay your shoulders and cover your forearms. It's a ten." She then held up a pair of dark brown slacks. "With these you'll probably have to wear a gaff."

"A what?" I asked.

"A gaff. It's sort of a cross between a jock strap and a container for your—" She paused as though getting up her courage, then said, "—equipment." She looked past me at the lone shopper still milling around.

The public address system announcer asked customers to proceed to a check out station since the store would be closing in ten minutes.

"Equipment!" bellowed Fryman. "I've heard it called many things: dick, schwantz, johnson, family jewels, even junk, but never equipment. Tool, maybe, but equipment?"

I expected her to turn red, but she remained indifferent and stoic.

"How do you know so much about our...equipment?" Murray asked.

I wanted to crawl into a hiding place. These two guys were hardened cops and nothing fazed them, even using suggestive language in front of a lady. My Mexican-

Catholic upbringing still demanded respect in the presence of women.

"I'm the one who must stay after hours when men make appointments to try on dresses. We get one or two every week, along with some regulars," she said.

I finally found the courage to speak. "And do you, I mean Macy's, sell these…" It was almost impossible for me to say the word, "gaffs?"

"I tried to get them to stock a few," she said, "but management over-ruled me, saying that a display would be impossible. Our manikins are not anatomically correct."

"Do these things come in sizes?" Fryman asked. "Regardless of what the bible says, all men are not created equal."

"Well, it depends on the man," she said.

All three of them looked at me and I had to fight the urge to cup my hands over my *equipment*. I was sure the equality issue was in the constitution and not the bible.

"They are sort of one size fits all," she said. "It's kind of an elastic tube that produces maximum compression and presses against the body under the…well, you know."

Fryman looked puzzled. "What happens if the guy finds himself in a situation of seeing a gorgeous young— never mind," he said. "I get the idea."

"You can buy them on-line at Shirley's of Hollywood or at Janet's Closet. I'm told they come in all colors and they ship the same day."

Murray took out his notebook and jotted down the websites. "Do you have any other wonderful suggestions?"

"Has your boyfriend done any make up before?" she asked Murray as Fryman blurted out a laugh.

"No I haven't. This is part of a job I have to do," I said.

I wanted desperately to tell her we were cops, this was all part of our undercover work, and Murray was not my boyfriend.

"Well, as your companion here said, do you want to pass or do you want to be Avant guard?" She remained business like through all of this painful discussion. "Passing," she said, "will be a lot harder because your aim is to deceive."

The realization, that I would have to decide if cross-dressing was a lark or a serious endeavor for me, began to set in. The illusion was always easier than the reality, especially if you were a young cop with great ambitions. Perhaps Captain Wilson and I were on different tracks and now I would have to decide my next step.

"I guess I want to pass," I said.

"Then you'll need to learn how to apply make-up without ending up looking like Bozo the clown. I suggest that you stop at a Merle Norman store where you can pick up literature on make-up. You can also try YouTube for some free lessons from the manufacturers. Then, of course, you can come back here because Macy's has a full line of cosmetics. I can even recommend someone in that department who can help."

Murray busied himself on his iPhone probably with the websites she mentioned.

As she described some of Macy's products, Fryman rifled through the selection of garments. He held up an orange blouse I'd picked out then twirled it around. "Do you have this in black?"

I wanted to crawl under the nearest dress rack and hide.

Chapter 8

Cookies

Fryman and I were dispatched to follow up on the lead, which Murray considered hot. In fact, it was the only lead we had at that time—a late night phone call. Although I was excited to be off duty, Fryman seemed blazé and uninterested. He must have had a bad night because he wasn't his usually jabbering self. He looked drawn, listless. There was no sarcastic greeting, no off color jokes, and only a vague hint of a hangover. We headed up the 405 Freeway across the Valley in silence to an address near the San Fernando Mission. It was at Sherman Way before he managed his first words.

"Ninety percent of these types of leads add up to nothing," he said. "Usually they consist of eighty percent imagination and ten percent lies. The remaining ten percent don't want to get involved. So here we are on the trail of nothing."

"Murray said the woman sounded sincere, claimed she had important information about the Carlyle case she heard about on a TV newscast."

"Bullshit. She just wants attention. That's what most of them want." Fryman sounded annoyed. "A cheap way to get their fifteen minutes of fame."

"Murray says she saw two women at the Quick Stop around three in the morning. She was on her way home from work and stopped at the drop box across the street: clothes, shoes, and a couple of blankets, she said."

Fryman interrupted with, "Bet she changes her story when we get there."

"Yeah? Why do you think she'd do that?"

"Sometimes you ask dumb questions, always with the *why*. Are you such a chatter box at home, too?"

We drove along in silence again for several exits with the only chatter coming from our central police radio.

"How is asking *why* so dumb?" I said.

"I know why you got put on this case, but why are you doing it? Why didn't you just say no when you had the chance?" He shook his head in disbelief. "Wilson was just bullshitting you about putting something in your file. I can't figure why he would say that."

"Now who's asking why?"

"Fuck it. I don't care."

"Captain Wilson ordered me to observe this case."

"So he took you off patrol, he wants to dress you up as a tranny, and he says it could be dangerous, but that we'd have your back."

"Yes."

"I'll be straight with you. I don't like anybody tailing my ass when I'm doing my job. And you know what? I think there's more to it than what you're telling me. I think Wilson's got some ulterior motive like using you as bait."

"That's not what he said."

"Oh yeah?" Fryman took his eyes off the road and

stared at me. "Carlyle was five-foot-six and had a small frame. "And you know what? Burgess was five-foot-five, small boned, and was only a year older than you. That sure sounds like mackerel to me."

I already knew about the comparisons of the two victims with me. Maybe I was dumb for agreeing. "I really didn't have a choice," I said.

"Bullshit."

A long pause.

"Yeah, I coulda said no."

Another long spell of silence.

"Then why didn't you?'

"Because I'm trying to make DIII."

"You, a detective?" He sounded incredulous.

"Yeah, me. Why?"

"Well, first of all you're a shrimp. Second, you gotta take a test and you gotta be on a list. Third, you don't have street smarts. Without them you could get yourself killed."

"I took the test and I am on the list and there has been no height requirement since 1978. I was third in my graduating class at the police academy."

"Big fuckin' deal. Wow, third," he said.

I could feel the blood starting to rush up to my head. What would he know about how hard I worked at the academy?

"I was the only Latino in the top five," I said.

"That doesn't mean crap for becoming a detective. As they say, it's not who you know it's who you blow."

Fryman was beginning to get to me as I clenched my fists to control my anger.

"I'm not gonna blow anybody."

"And fourth, you're too naive."

"Did you?"

"Jesus. It doesn't mean you have to actually blow

someone. It's an expression. It means you have to kiss ass, you have to brown nose, or you have to be a lackey."

"I'm not going to kiss ass or any other part of anyone's body."

"Then you better love being a patrol cop, kid. Look around you. Have you ever seen any short detectives? In my opinion, you don't stand a chance."

"Well, it's not up to you."

"Can you ride a horse, kid?" he asked. "Because Napoleon was short, too." With that, he bellowed out a laugh.

Another much longer silence passed between us. I wanted to tell him how I hated being called a kid. I wanted to tell him to mind his own business, to shut up, and drive. I didn't care for the opinions of a stupid, loudmouth gringo.

Suddenly, I yelled, "Oh damn, we just passed the Rinaldi Exit. We should have gotten off there."

"See what I mean? You had one simple job of watching the GPS and you fucked it up."

"You better get off at the next exit."

"You think so? Brilliant! Get you guys out of Boyle Heights and you don't know what the hell you're doing."

It was a welcome silence that followed because it let my anger cool down. I gave him one-word directions of where to turn; left here, right at the next corner. I wanted to work with Fryman and Murray but, with his attitude, there seemed little chance of either of them commending me.

We parked in front of a multiple-unit, California-style apartment building, in the loading zone. Two tall Queen Palms stood as sentries at the front entrance where a recessed alcove displayed a line of mailboxes in front of a broken iron gate. The small swimming pool in the center court was full of dead leaves and a ring of scum on the blue tiles. Two empty lounge chairs at one end had broken straps hanging from pitted frames. A few window air conditioners hummed and the tinny sound of a TV filled the courtyard. The steps to the second floor were surrounded by weedy Birds of Paradise.

"Her name is Valerie McCourt," Fryman said. "Can you remember that?"

We stood in front of apartment 204 and I wasn't sure if it was me who was to press the doorbell button just above the peep-hole. I assumed I should because he outranked me. Before either one of us decided to ring, the door swung open, and there stood a vision of loveliness from a past era with large golden hoop earrings, make-up that looked like it was applied with a putty knife, and a dress whose seams struggled to hold together. She looked like a character from the funny pages. When she smiled, all those drawbacks seemed to disappear. It was warm and sincere.

"Come in," she said, beckoning us to step over the threshold. "Come in. Sorry, the place is a mess."

We entered and she was right. There were empty microwave popcorn bags on the coffee table, along with a half-filled ashtray of cork-tipped cigarette butts.

"Thank you for calling in your information, Mrs. McCourt. I'm detective Robert Fryman."

"Not at all," she said as she turned to me. "And you must be his helper. Are you a cadet in training?"

I disliked her from the moment she uttered those words. "No, Mrs. McCourt, I'm Officer Espinoza."

From the corner of my eye, I could see Fryman choking back a smirk. I felt more than dislike for him, too.

"He's almost a veteran on the force," Fryman teased.

"Oh?" she said. "Please sit down."

Fryman pushed all the cutesy couch pillows to one side before he eased his ass down on the sofa. The only place left was for me to sit was wobbling on top of the pillows.

I mustered as deep a voice as possible and hoped it would have an edge to it. "Would you mind if we recorded our interview, Mrs. McCourt?"

"No. Not at all." I pressed a few icons on the screen of the iPhone and set it down on the coffee table next to the empty popcorn bags.

There was something too eager about her tone. She began talking very decisively, first about her job and then about her husband. When she got to the part we needed, I took a few notes.

"I had been sitting in my car, looking for my glasses," she began. "They had fallen under the seat. I had to find them because my driver's license says *corr lens* on it, which means I have to wear glasses when I drive. I can see perfectly well without them, but you know—it says I have to.

Then, just as I was going to start my car, I noticed the big black car in the parking lot of the Quick Stop. Two women, who were in the back seat, got out, and stood for a while, just talking. One of the women was standing sorta close behind the other one. I wondered why they didn't go into the store. I thought it was a little odd. It looked to me like they were arguing. Then they walked around the corner toward the back of the store."

"What time was that?" Fryman asked.

"I'm not sure, but it had to be just after midnight. That's when my shift ended. The others leave early but I stay and do a little clean up because—"

"Can you describe what they were wearing?" Fryman interrupted.

"That seemed odd too because one of them had a big sun hat on, you know with a wide brim. It was too dark to see their dresses. But can you imagine wearing a sun hat in the middle of the night? I wouldn't wear one of those in the daytime."

"Anything else?" he asked.

"Well yes, the other one was a lot shorter and she was wearing a long evening dress."

"What color?" Fryman asked.

She took off her glasses and put them on the coffee table. "It looked blue, but I'm not sure because it was dark out."

Fryman just stared at her.

"I sat there for a while and I noticed that the man in the driver's seat was smoking. I could see the end of his cigarette flash bright every once in a while, though I couldn't really see him."

"How did you know it was a man? Could it have been a woman?" Fryman asked.

"Well, I just assumed he was a man," she said.

"Did you get a chance to see the license plate?" I asked.

"I couldn't make it out, but it looked kinda different than our usual California plates."

"Different how?"

"Frankly I wasn't that interested at the time. It did seem like it had only a few letters or numbers on it. I think the first part was 5 S H. I don't know. I'm not sure about the last part."

"Did you notice the make of the car? Cadillac? Mercedes? Lincoln?"

"Oh, these new cars all look the same to me."

"How about inside the store? Could you see anyone in there?" Fryman asked.

She shook her head then began to ramble about her husband again. "Even though he's not working, he sleeps a lot." She threw a glance at the popcorn bags. "You'd think he'd clean up a little when I'm working."

Fryman tried to close down the meeting but she continued to prattle on about trivial things. Three times he said, "Well all right then, Mrs. McCourt."

It was futile trying to keep her on point. Finally, in desperation he asked the key question. "Would you be willing to testify in court if the district attorney asked you?"

"Well, I don't know. I'm not sure. Isn't this interview enough?"

"Actually you could be subpoenaed," he said.

"Well, I couldn't afford to get a lawyer or anything like that," she said then glanced toward the door leading to the bedroom. It seemed clear to me she was pulling back.

I saw a chance to get even with Fryman's digs at me in the car.

With great dramatics, I turned off the recording on my iPhone and said, "That will be all, Mrs. McCourt. Thank you very much for your very valuable information. We have to go now, we have others to interview."

"Oh—oh." she sputtered. "Would you like some coffee?"

I gave her a flat, "No."

Fryman just stared at me with wild questioning eyes.

"I baked some cookies."

"No thank you, ma'am," I said. "That was very thoughtful of you."

I staggered up from my pillow throne and gave Fryman a look. He followed me toward the door, gushing appreciative comments at Mrs. McCourt.

On our way back to the station, Fryman was incredulous and angry.

"Maybe we could have taken a few cookies with us. What the fuck's your hurry? Now we gotta kill a couple hours so we don't get back too soon."

"She was starting to stonewall so why hang around?" I said.

"I shoulda asked what kind of cookies they were," he lamented.

I wanted no part of the cookies after seeing the condition of the living room. What might the kitchen look like or the ingredients of her baking?

"Ya know, Espinoza, you were terrific in the way you took control of the situation. I'm impressed. You know, there just might be hope for you as a detective."

"I got tired of listening to her," I said. "What did she give us? Nothing! Unless she considers her unemployed husband to be a suspect. And who knows, maybe there is no husband. Did you notice how she kept looking at you?"

"I'm not so sure she gave us nothing. There was something she said that didn't ring true and could be important. Play back that middle part where she is describing the two women getting out of the car."

I fished out the iPhone and tapped various combinations but nothing came out. I became frantic, searching for the recording. I even turned off the device and turned it on again, hoping to clear whatever was blocking recall of the interview.

"I must have pressed the wrong icon when we started." I was annoyed with myself. "Sorry. I'm just not used to working with these devices."

Fryman said nothing for a long while then hit the steering wheel with the palm of his hand. "Shit." He hit the dashboard, barely missing the muzzle of our shotgun, and this time he yelled at the top of his voice, "And I'm not used to working with assholes."

Sarcasm blared from every word as he re-enacted the interview.

I managed to squeak out a weak comment. "I did write down her name and address so maybe we can go back."

He took his eyes off the road and glared at me. "Go back? And then what? Tell her were a couple of jerk-offs who don't know what they're doing. No. No, I got it." He waived his hand at the windshield. "We'll go back and tell her we'd love to have some cookies and then we can ask her all the same questions." He slammed his hand on the steering wheel again.

"Why not? That's a good idea. Then we won't have to kill some time before we go back." I tried to sound cheerful and hopeful.

"You better forget about becoming a detective," he said, shaking his head back and forth.

"Why?"

"Because in your case, even an actual blow job won't help your chances."

Chapter 9

Chinese Night

I laid all the women's clothes we purchased across the bed, dresses on one pile, slips on another, panties on another, blouses and skirts on still another. The two bras were white and had snaps on the back with some lace along the edges. I tried one on and the material hung down over my vestige nipples hidden among curly hair. Since I had ordered self-adhering breast forms from The Breastform Store, I wondered how they would stick to my hairy chest. The attachable nipples had to be ordered separately and they had not yet arrived.

I tried stuffing some socks in the brassiere just to simulate what it would look like and that convinced me I had to use the silicone ones. The socks made my fake breasts look uneven and lumpy. I wondered if an astute observer would suggest I get a mammogram.

After slipping on the five-inch-heeled shoes, I liked the feeling of being taller, even if I wobbled when I walked. The sensation of falling forward was hard to deal with, while also being conscious of the pressure on all ten toes. Getting used to walking with my knees pointing the way would engage a whole new muscle group. I took five steps and fell down.

I decided to put on a tight fitting blue dress that had long sleeves and a high ruffle collar that hid my chest hair. I was pleased that I could manage the one hook at the top of the dress at the back of my neck. After a quick check in the mirror, it looked okay except for the bulge in front at my crotch level. I wondered what I was supposed to do with my dick and balls so I took off my jockey shorts and put on a pair of pink panties. Since the gaff I ordered had not yet arrived the problem had to be dealt with in some improvised way.

I pushed my rear end out behind me but that was no help. The front of the dress still bulged. I understood why a guy dressed as a woman had to use a gaff to hide his "equipment." I thought I would try an alternative.

I pulled out my gym bag and located my jock strap which, under the panties, now outlined my crotch. Trying desperately to solve the problem, I took off the panties, turned the jock strap around backward. Not only did the back straps pull down and pinch my testicles, creating extreme pain, but my rear end looked like I had filled my pants. The straight, tight-fitting dress was definitely out until the gaffs arrived.

I had stripped down and just had the panties on when the phone rang. It was Captain Wilson.

"Did you get the clothes?"

"Yes, sir. I got a several different outfits and I think I've narrowed it down to two dresses and one skirt that will work for my first time out in public."

"How does it look? Do you think you'll pass?"

"I look like a cross between a nun and a hooker. Frankly, my problem is what to do about my Adam's apple and my balls—they both show."

"Wear a loose scarf to cover the Adam's apple and with the other you might try taping them down underneath. Otherwise, the only other option is to have them surgically removed."

"Oh no, sir. I wouldn't agree to anything like that."

"Do the best you can. Look, tomorrow is Friday night and I understand that's a big night at the Velvet Glove. A lot of the regulars will be there. I want you to get taped up, dressed up, and start to mingle. Got that?"

"Will I have any back up?"

"Victor, you won't need any. This is not a deployment. You're just going to be seen and to keep your eyes and ears open. Because of all the news coverage in the case, I'm sure there'll be some talk. We need to get more leads because our case isn't going anywhere fast."

"Yes, sir."

Somehow, this wasn't the detective work I'd had in mind. I had visions of stakeouts, apprehending suspects, questioning possible witnesses, and even shoot-outs. Mincing around in a dress didn't fit the bill. I realized Halloween was less than two weeks away—when everybody dressed up and nobody noticed. Somehow, the holiday didn't help how anxious I felt about my new persona. It was a cultural thing, too. For a Latino man, anything that hinted of femininity was taboo.

My next stop was the bathroom where I had piled up all the various creams, lotions, and cosmetics I purchased that morning. Miraculously there were no nicks after my shave. I read every bottle, jar, and tube before taking a first pass at making my face look like the Maybelline cover girl. After a good hour of work, I put on the black wig and examined the results in my door mirror.

The hair hung down over a face that looked like the make-up was applied with plastering trowels. I looked like a candidate for a horror movie. The bare chest had curls of hair down to my navel and my penis stuck out from the side of the panties. Other than that, I thought it was pretty good. Not gorgeous, mind you, but pretty good.

I went back to my computer and replayed the Merle Norman videos on make-up. It was my fourth pass at the process. I had all the items laid out: foundation, concealers, color-blend stick, eyeliner, eye shadow, lip gloss, lip stick, blush brush, and neck cream. I was never more thankful to be a man. There was little risk of me snapping my fingers and singing a chorus of "I Feel Pretty" from *West Side Story*.

I laid out the plastic fingernails on the kitchen table along with a bottle of blue nail polish and a gloss finisher. The fake thumbnail was a bit smaller than my nail, but I assumed it would fit.

The phone rang again.

If it was the captain, again, I was going to tell him the job was not for me. It just wouldn't work because I was sure I could not pass.

"Hello."

It was Jannine.

"I thought you were going to call me?" she asked.

"I got involved in something and forgot. Sorry, honey. Remember I told you we couldn't tonight—"

"I'm not spending another night eating by myself."

"But I have to—"

"Well I'm at the China Wok picking up some of the chicken you like. Is there anything else I should get? Like it or not, I'm coming over?"

I had to think fast to stall her. My face was caked with various coatings of make-up. I didn't want to start World War III by telling her not to come. Besides, hearing her voice was checkmate to my resolve.

"Oh, yes. Yes. I need milk and get me some fresh

fruit, maybe bananas or blue berries or see if they have mangos. I'm going to start a diet tomorrow."

"What? I'm at a Chinese restaurant not a super-market."

"Please."

Just then, I heard a click followed by a dial tone. I started my own Chinese fire drill, running from one point to the other. I ended up throwing clothes, bottles, cosmetics, and even some of my things into the closet. I used several towels to try to wipe off the layers of make-up and lipstick to no avail. I should have purchased the eye make-up remover. After I snapped closed the new lock on the closet, I rushed into the shower and used soap and shampoo on my face. Conditioner made my face slippery. The washcloth became so discolored I used a second one.

As I wrapped the towel around me, I heard the front door open. Jannine called out my name several times while I combed back my wet hair. She barged into the bathroom, holding a container of orange-crusted chicken in a white box with a wire handle.

She smiled and wrapped her arms around me while still holding the box of chicken.

"You showered," she said. "And shaved." She pushed away and rubbed my cheek. "What's this new saving lotion? It smells like cleansing cream."

I had to think of another lie—a descendant of the original one. "It's a sample I got in the mail. Do you like it?"

She wiggled closer to me and pulled on the towel until it fell to my ankles. She tightened her arms around me and we kissed. However, I was in pain because the corner of the box of chicken was digging into my back. Confucius would say *it payback for lies*. In my case, she should have drawn blood.

"Ouch."

"Honey, I'm sorry. Did I hurt you? You must be starving."

She put the chicken on the counter and reached down to pick up the towel then stayed down there longer than what seemed appropriate. I felt a sudden pull at my testicles, which seemed too kinky, even for Jannine. She stood up holding a small piece of white medical tape.

"What were you taping to your crotch?"

"Oh, that?" I said feigning indifference, but I was stalling for time as I tried to think my way out of this with a new lie. "That was when I was at the gym."

"And?"

"And...I had used some tape to fix a tear in my jock strap. It didn't hold very well." I picked up the chicken and swung it back a forth in front of her face. "Let's eat."

"With you looking like a scene from *The Naked Lunch*? I loved that movie."

"No. I mean yes. Should I dress?"

"It won't take very long to eat and why waste a perfectly good naked body. Yes, of course, you should dress, you jerk." She turned to leave then stopped. "For a little while at least."

Chapter 10

Tail Lights

On October nineteenth at 8:30 p.m. I walked into the Velvet Glove, wearing the only outfit I had that I assumed would look as convincing as any cross-dresser in LA. It was my entrance into a new world. The place had a long bar with a mirrored-glass backing which extended from the door to the rear of the room. To the left were clusters of tables that surrounded a small bandstand. Amber-colored lighting behind the bar accentuated the whiskey bottles on glass shelves in front of the mirrors. It took a few minutes for my eyes to get used to the minimal lighting.

Several heads turned my way as I stood there, nervous and unsure of myself, wondering if I was passing. About half of the patrons appeared to be females or perhaps men dressed as women. In the dim light, it was hard to tell. I girded myself to appear steady in high heels as I walked to a section of the bar where three stools were empty. I sat in the middle one. The bartender stood in front of me and waited. He said not a word.

I pushed my voice to as high an octave as possible without sounding stupid. What the hell, I thought, I'm a cross-dresser not someone trying to sound like a woman.

"What do you have on draft?"

"Heinekens and Budweiser provided you have a driver's license."

He took my ID and he put it under a small lamp next to the cash register. After he looked at the license, he then turned, stared at me, and then back to the license. He came back, laid it on the bar, and said, "You looked better with a mustache. What'll you have?"

"Bud."

Craziness went through my mind. I kept adjusting my fake boobs which weren't adhering to my chest and the discomfort from my taped up crotch—my gaff still hadn't arrived—had me squirming on my stool. Getting dressed as a cross-dresser was a problem for men because of our external equipment. There were risks, since sitting down on taped-up equipment could cause serious pain. My beer arrived and saved me from my own anxious mind.

I looked around the room, hoping I could identify some of the types Wilson described. In the subdued light, it was impossible to tell who was trying to pass, who was an amateur, or who was a gender fucker. I didn't see any outrageous outfits. What was worse, I couldn't tell if the real women were *real* women.

The captain was right. What conversation I could hear was about the Carlyle case. The place literally buzzed with hissing S's that sounded like tires loosing air. I heard *she this* and *she that* and *she certainly*. One of the enigmas for me was why—there was my why again—cross dressers referred to themselves as *she* or had women's names. I guess someone in a long gown and opera gloves would sound silly being called *George* or *Oscar*.

More than half of the patrons at the bar were in street clothes and chatted away while the couples at the tables were huddled in close conversation.

Half way through my first beer a young cross-dressed man lifted himself on the stool next to me. He looked at me. "Were you saving this for someone?"

"No. It's yours."

After he put his purse on the bar, the bartender greeted him with, "Hey, Stan. The usual?"

"Better make it a double."

The bartender laughed and I wondered why he didn't card Stan. The new arrival was dressed to the nines, including short gold gloves. He exaggerated the gesture of putting his purse on the bar. I must have appeared obvious, staring at Stan and his outfit. I dressed trying to minimize showing my hard handball shoulders while Stan was wearing a strapless dress that showed off his small upper frame. It was easy to miss the fact that his Adam's apple was almost nonexistent. He looked at me staring at him and asked, "What?"

"Oh. I was just looking at your dress. I'm Vic." I extended my hand into which he placed his gloved hand and smiled.

"Stan."

The question raced through my mind, *Is he or isn't he*? In women's clothes or in street clothes, it was hard to tell if a man was gay or straight. I had no clue. He didn't seem to fit any of Wilson's groupings of cross-dressers.

"Is this your first time?" he asked.

Before I could think I blurted out, "For what?"

"Here at the Glove. I haven't seen you here before."

"I just moved here from Chicago." I was getting really good at telling impromptu lies to fit the moment. Worse still, I stopped feeling guilt over telling them.

"What brings you here? I understand there are some great clubs on Chicago's north side."

More lies, which no doubt would come back to haunt me, seemed to just roll off my tongue. I wanted to change the subject and got some help from the bartender who returned with a tall glass of an amber colored mixed drink.

"Where have you been?" the bartender asked. "Haven't seen you since Freddie caught his lunch."

I wondered if his "Freddie" could be Fredrick Carlyle.

I took it as an opening. Stan gave some excuse about being upset and not sure of what to do. The bartender shrugged and left and I moved in.

"Is that the murder I've been reading about?"

Stan took a long drink, gulping down more than half, then just sat there, not saying a word. Before I could speak, he drank down the other half. "Yes, it's been all over the TV, I guess," he said.

I ordered another beer for myself and a second drink for Stan. Nothing worked better than a well-oiled machine. When it arrived, he put both hands across his fake breasts. "For Me?"

I nodded and again he swallowed a big gulp.

"Just because you're buying me a drink, don't think I'm easy because I am."

"Was that the guy's name? Freddie?" I said, trying to act inquisitive yet banal.

"Yes, poor Freddie. He was one of us, but he didn't much take advice," Stan said.

I felt lucky that I probably hit a jackpot with someone who knew the victim.

I instinctively tried to swing my leg around the bar stool to face Stan, but the dress limited my range of motion so I wiggled to the side. My brain was wired for pants and definitely not coded for breasts—I kept knocking my elbow into the right one pushing the insert to the middle of my chest. No suction.

"What kind of advice?" I asked.

"Well, he was warned not to—"

"Hey gorgeous, where have you been? Who's your friend?"

A man dressed in leather pants and jacket interrupted Stan. His black hair looked greasy and a scar on his right cheek gave an uneven symmetry to his face, causing the right eye to droop lower than the left. He came from the far end of the bar and put his arm around Stan.

'Hi, Greg. This is Vic. Vic, this is Greg. Stay away from Greg," Stan said to me, "because he's big trouble with a capital T."

"Don't flatter me, Stan," Greg said.

"Should I consider myself warned?" I asked.

They both laughed and I wondered what Stan meant.

As Greg left, he patted me on my padded ass. "Don't be a stranger. Come in again." He looked me over. "And soon."

After he left I asked Stan, "A friend of yours?"

"I'm not his type," he said.

After the third amber cocktail, Stan began to loosen up. He seemed more willing to talk.

"What type does he like?" I asked.

Stan looked at himself in the mirrored bar and I saw pain in his face.

"Freddie was his type but he didn't give Greg a tumble because Freddie didn't dig men."

"Did you know Carlyle?" I asked.

"The cops have it all wrong," he said.

"About Carlyle?"

"I know stuff about that—plenty of stuff, but I can't tell you or anyone."

My investment in amber drinks was starting to pay off. I signaled the bartender. "About the murder?"

He took another long swallow of his drink and waved the empty glass at the bartender. "As usual the cops have it all wrong," Stan repeated.

"How so, Stan?"

"Because of their snitch."

"What snitch, Stan?" I was suddenly aware that I was sounding too much like a television sit-cop show.

Wilson had told me to keep my eyes and ears open but he didn't tell me exactly how. Stan got me so keenly interested that I wanted to push harder. However, I didn't want him to become suspicious. The drunker Stan got, the less he was willing to talk about the murder. He wanted to know more about Chicago and I had to improvise new lies. I had been to Chicago once to watch the Dodgers and the Cubs at Wrigley Field. I hoped he didn't know the city well enough to challenge me.

It was just after midnight and the place was slowly emptying out which seemed strange for a Friday night. The show had been cancelled because of the Carlyle murder so the crowd didn't hang around. Stan was visibly drunk and I felt mostly to blame. I had nursed one good beer and one stale beer for the whole evening.

Stan ordered another drink but the bartender took his glass away and said, "No more, Stan. It's not worth losing the boss' license."

"Come on. Just one more, Brandon," Stan pleaded.

"No, buddy, because cops are liable to come in here, maybe even in drag, and bingo, shut us down. If they nail you for drunkenness in the street, ABC comes in and investigates and I lose my job."

"I'm not worried about the copsh because I've got a get-out-of-jail-free card. Sho let's have another drink."

The bartender smiled, looked at me, and shrugged

his shoulders. Suddenly I panicked. Was it possible that he knew me? What was he trying to do or say? I wanted to get out as soon as I could.

I refused to believe that I looked like a cop but, then again, I wasn't that sure that I looked like a woman either.

Stan was a mess. He propped his elbows on the bar and cradled his head in his hands. His blonde wig had pulled slightly to the side. My cop mode snapped in and wouldn't let me have this drunken man/woman driving the streets of LA. Not only could he kill himself but he could kill innocent victims.

"Come on, Stan. Let's go for some coffee and maybe we can talk some more."

We paid our respective tabs and he almost slipped getting off the barstool. He staggered a bit heading for the door. I did too, not from drinks but from the high heels. I realized coffee would be hopeless. He would still be a drunk, but a wide-awake and nervous drunk. Coffee wouldn't change his blood-alcohol level or the speed of his reflexes. Once outside, the fresh air didn't help the situation much. He didn't know where he had parked his car so we stood there, speculating on which way to go on Lankershim.

"Look, Stan. Why don't I take you home and then you can get your car tomorrow morning? Okay?"

"I can drive. I just can't walk."

"My car's right here. Okay?"

"Okay."

I rolled him into my passenger seat and we drove along with him giving me wrong turns and vague directions. I concluded he didn't know where he was going. As we drove I caught sight of a pair of headlights in my rearview mirror. It probably was nothing but it seemed they hung back about two hundred yards, making the same turns I did. I wondered if two beers could make a person paranoid.

"Stan, you gotta help me. Where the hell do you live?"

He had fallen asleep, his head leaning against the window. I turned left on Chandler Boulevard and slowed. Sure enough, the headlights behind me turned left as well. When I got to Wilcox, I made a quick turn right, pulled over, stopped, and turned off my headlights. The pursuing car slowed to nearly a stop in the middle of the intersection, then continued forward on Chandler. I just sat there and waited.

Finally, I reached over, unhooked Stan's purse from his golden glove's grasp, and opened it in search of his address. His driver's license gave me what I needed. Stan Gorecki 23 years old 14374 Chester Avenue, Van Nuys, Apartment number 7. Hair: Brown. Weight: 142 lbs. Height: 5 feet, nine inches. I jotted down all the information, including his birth date July 3 1989, and his license number F07447041. In the picture, he looked much younger than 23 years. The notepad in my glove compartment had only one entry; the address of the Velvet Glove. The second entry was Stan Gorecki's information. I returned his wallet to the purse, dropped it in his lap, and wondered where the hell Chester Avenue was. I had a rough idea because of the number.

I started up and drove about two blocks when I noticed the headlights turn the corner and hold back about two hundred yards again. One thing was certain. The tail car made no attempt to hide itself. It seemed that the driver didn't care if I knew of his presence. Though I didn't know where Chester Avenue was, I did know this neighborhood since it had been in my patrol area for over two years.

I pushed the gas pedal to the floorboard and the tires

squealed around the corner. When I got to Whitmore Avenue, I slid around another corner and was a few hundred feet from Riverside drive where I turned right again and gunned the gas. This time I was sure I had lost my tail. Driving straight down Riverside, I mixed in with the few cars on the road. Late, I hugged the center median as I activated the GPS on my iPhone. I entered Stan's address and found I was nine minutes from his apartment. For the following nine minutes, there were no headlights behind me.

In all the sudden twists and turns, Stan's body flopped back and forth like a rag doll and his wig had fallen between the seat and the center console. He was now half-awake. With his false eyelashes, heavy make-up, and his short hair askew, he looked like a music-hall clown.

A block away from his apartment building, I stopped and waited. One car approached and passed, as did a second one. Assuming I had lost my tail, I pulled up in front of his building in a loading zone. After I fished out his keys, the two of us made our way into the courtyard. When I unlocked the door to Apartment number 7 and we walked in, the lights suddenly turned on. There in the living room sat a man in his sixties, holding a pistol pointed directly at me.

Chapter 11

Wire

Murray, Fryman and I sat waiting in Wilson's office, making small talk, first the weather then the World Series game that had started at one o'clock. Fryman kept looking at his iPhone. The two detectives were not fans of the Giants, which set up a partial bond between us. The American League champion Tigers were coming back to San Francisco for game six and we hoped they would end the World Series there. I didn't care who won as along as it wasn't the Giants.

Captain Wilson stormed in, holding our respective reports and the murder book.

"It looks like Alan Kemper wants to get some mileage at our expense. He's using the media to ask for more action on the Carlyle case. He's trying to garner the fear vote. The SOB is trying to indict the whole LAPD in the process." He slammed the reports on his desk. "Even the chief of police is pushing me on this. So what have we got?"

Murray started cautiously. "Not much."

Fryman jumped in with, "We got a fragment from a possible witness, not to the murder, but what might be the murderer or murderers. The woman we interviewed wasn't really paying that much attention because she thought it strange but not significant. She wasn't sure she was wearing her glasses at the time."

"Says here you got a license plate number."

"A partial."

"Looks like Victor had quite a night with a patron named Stan. According to this Stan, we got it all wrong and he implied we have a snitch in the cross-dress community. Do we?" Murray asked.

"Not that I know of," Wilson said. "What have we got on Stan?"

"Tell us again, what happened, son." Murray seemed exasperated.

I felt very uneasy relating the evening to Wilson. "I met this Stan Gorecki at the bar and he kept saying we, the police that is, had it all wrong.

I tried to find out what he meant but the best I could get was that we had a snitch. I bought him too many drinks. He got drunk and I took him home. I got concerned because we were followed. I'll admit I was a little scared."

"That was us, Captain. You told him we'd watch his back, and so we were," Murray said. "I might add this Victor's a pretty good driver. He managed to ditch us, which is going some when Robert is driving."

"What's this in the report about a gun?"

"Well, sir. When I got Stan to his apartment and opened the door, there was his grandfather pointing a gun at us. He seemed relieved when I told him Stan was very drunk and I just brought him home. When I asked him why he had the gun, he said he was very concerned about his grandson getting involved with murdering *re-dressers* he called them. Said he'd come to grips with the boy's condition but wasn't taking any chances."

"Did the grandfather tell you anything relevant?" Wilson asked.

"Actually it was his step-grandfather, as Stan calls him. His real father split when Stan was a baby. He told me his mother remarried twice after that, but that she too split when Stan was ten. Welcome to LA."

"Did you get Stan's car license number?"

"No, sir, I didn't."

"Dammit." He slammed his hand down on the reports we gave him. "You were there when you got a partial license from the cookie lady. Didn't you think the two might be connected?"

I thought best not to answer since what I might say would throw logs on the fire.

Fryman suggested that Stan might be a suspect because the bartender hadn't seen Stan since the murder. His absence from the bar certainly raised suspicions. As they speculated, I broke in.

"I don't think so," I said. "I've got a good feeling about this guy."

"What?" Wilson boomed. "You've got a good feeling? If you want to be a detective, or even a cop, you can't have feelings. You gotta be about your wits at all times. Feelings get in the way. Do you read me, son?" He stopped long enough to take a breath. "For a cop, instincts are good but feelings get you killed. In our business feelings are dangerous." Wilson's whole body seemed to shake as he bellowed at me.

All of this was starting not to add up for me. With Jannine liking the idea of me being a cop but hating the hours I had to keep and me screwing up at every turn in the investigation, it seemed like a bad idea. I remembered Wilson telling me I could back out any time I wanted.

"Maybe I shouldn't be doing this undercover work?" I said. "Some of these people are weird and queers freak me out. You said I could quit any time I felt like it was too much for me."

"LAPD does not use the term queers. Get used to the word gays," Wilson said.

"Yes, sir."

"And don't try and blackmail me, son. Unfortunately, it's too late for you to back out. Everybody gets cold feet when they get into the thick of it." He smiled. "Look at Fryman over there."

"No, Captain, please," Fryman pleaded.

"Did he tell you that the first time a suspect pointed a gun at him, he wet his pants?"

"Oh fuck. How was I supposed to know the gun wasn't loaded?" Fryman mumbled.

"Speaking of guns," Wilson said. "I requested a Smith and Wesson 38 caliber Bodyguard pistol for you, so you need to schedule some time at the range to get certified on it. It should fit into your purse because the barrel is only two inches."

I wondered what happened to the "no danger" aspect of the assignment or the "we've got your back" part. "I will, sir," I said.

Wilson stood up and paced behind us. He stopped at my chair, put his hands on my shoulders, and said, "I want you to get back to that bar. Sidle up to Stan. He knows more than what he's telling us. I want you to meet some other cross-dressers and gain their confidence. I want you to become a regular there so there's no question about your presence.

"Mostly, I want you to put all feelings aside and do your job. Got that?"

The captain's phone rang and he just looked at it.

"That's gotta be Kemper. He's been calling me all

morning. You guys stay on for a minute. We need to talk some more."

He answered the phone and gave Kemper a convoluted story about license plates, witnesses, and hot leads. "We're pursuing them all," he said. He cupped his hand over the mouthpiece, turned to us, and whispered. "He wants to call a news conference tomorrow morning and he needs something concrete for the chief of police to report." He gave the phone the finger. "We'll have something for the chief by noon tomorrow."

He listened for a long while and then snapped back, "Councilman Kemper, you and the mayor govern Los Angeles for the people of the city and we will protect them. Remember our motto is to serve and protect." Wilson listened for a long time. "And the same to you, sir. Good-bye."

He slammed down the phone and when he turned back to us, we smiled and gave him thumbs up. His anger boiled up again.

"Since that son-of-a-bitch became chairman of the council's Police Oversight Committee, he thinks he runs our operations." He turned to Murray and Fryman. "Let's put a wire on Victor so you two can keep track of what's coming down in that bar."

"A wire? Where am I going to keep the transmitting unit?" I asked.

"Hell I don't know: how about inside one of your falsies," Fryman said.

"That's where I keep my badge and ID."

Fryman made an obscene gesture with both hands cupped over his chest. "Is there something bigger than a D cup?" he asked.

As bizarre as it seemed, I began to feel good again about staying on the job. At least, Fryman and Murray hadn't lost their senses of humor. I was sure that joking with me was a form of acceptance into their inner circle as well as some tension release.

"Victor, put a dress over that skinny ass of yours and hit the Velvet Glove tonight. Don't pull any more tricks, if you'll pardon the expression, the way you did with Stan. Work on him but don't let him get suspicious."

"Stan's probably got a hell of a hangover. Maybe he won't show tonight."

"Then reel in somebody else, but be there. Don't be shy."

"There's no risk of that," added Fryman. "He has no trouble asking why."

Fryman and Murray stood up to leave then stopped when they saw me still sitting. Wilson gave me a look that said get your skinny ass out of here and get to work.

"Excuse me, sir, I'm going to need more cash. If I have to loosen people up I have to buy them drinks and…"

"And what?" Wilson asked.

"And I have to stop and get some more foundation cream."

"Next thing you're going to tell me that you have nothing to wear."

"Actually, sir, I hate to be seen in the same outfit again tonight."

"Jesus," Fryman said. "He's beginning to think like a woman. Next thing, he's gonna tell us he's got PMS."

I stood up to my full five feet five and a quarter inches, gave Fryman the finger, and said, "Fuck you, Detective."

We all laughed, including the captain, and I felt good about starting to become one of the team.

"New dress or old dress," Wilson said. "Be there tonight."

Chapter 12

Eye Liner

I spread every piece of women's clothes I owned on the bed, chairs, and dresser, trying to decide what to wear. When I looked at the clock, it was almost two thirty and Jannine was due at three so I went back to my Chinese fire drill of stashing everything in the closet. I snapped closed the lock just as I heard her car pull into the driveway.

I headed to the door, unlocked it, and then stopped abruptly in my tracks. I dashed back to the bathroom scooped up a few items I had left on the sink and stashed them under some towels in the cabinet. Back in the living room, I threw myself down on the couch just as she came through the door.

She was wearing a kelly-green blouse with white lace around the neckline and sleeves. Her white stove-pipe slacks must have been satin, the way they clung to her legs. Holy shit, I thought, what was I doing looking at her clothes instead of how gorgeous she was with that disabling smile of hers? I could feel the electricity stirring in all the molecules of my body and in some parts more than others.

Maybe it had been five years from when we first met but she still excited me the way she did the first time I saw her.

"Well, aren't you going to say anything?" she said.

"Jannine, you are the most beautiful woman in the world and I am the luckiest man in the world."

I stood up and took her in my arms. We kissed for what had to be a new Guinness record.

"Whoa. Slow down," she said. "Is it me or is it getting warm in here?"

"Both I hope. How about some iced tea?" I sat down on the couch and waited.

She stood there, hands on her hips. Maybe in five years I had become complacent about our relationship because I assumed she would wait for me to move. She was better at iced tea than I was so it was a no brainer for me.

"It's in the kitchen." I said, pointing.

When she came back and sat on the couch, we clinked glasses, sipped tea, and looked into each other's eyes.

"Have you forgotten what day it is today?" she asked with a coy tone that was unusual for her.

"Of course not," I said as my mind raced through hundreds of possibilities in a matter of seconds. "I intended to stop and get a card," I said. Not her birthday and not her graduation anniversary.

"I don't think they have a specialty card for the first day you meet someone," she said.

Bingo. I suddenly remembered. "Yeah, I was thinking about that first time I saw you at the library. You had me at first smile."

I was getting good at deception because Jannine had

a sense for picking up mendacity. It must have been all the practice that I had with my current assignment.

"Well, I suppose so if you call waiting in line at the DMV the library," she said with a sardonic note.

Shit.

She smiled at me then leaned back, kicked off her shoes, and propped her feet in my lap. I proceeded to give her a foot massage which, after several years of experience, I knew was the best place to start.

"You have just one hour to stop that," she said so I ventured to her ankles and then the calves.

She scooted herself up onto my lap and we kissed tenderly as she stroked my face. I kissed her neck then reached around and unbuttoned the back of her blouse. They were the tiny white pearl buttons, which were quite easy for me because I had a blouse with similar buttons. As I rubbed her back and neck, she hunched forward. Her shoulders and the blouse slid down between us. With no brazier on those beautiful breasts, she captured me in a way that I knew would cost me my control. I reached down and kissed each nipple. I could feel her give a hint of a shudder. She moved in closer and pulled off my Dodger T-shirt. It was the shortest foreplay on record—if anyone actually kept such records.

The pace of undressing each other increased to a frenzied pitch until we were both naked and lying on the couch. I wanted that afternoon of love to last longer so I held back the more insistent she became. Even though we'd been together five years, this time, like every other time, seemed like the first. We were lost within each of our bodies. Neither of us was aware that we had kicked over the iced tea glasses. At least not until I had stepped onto the wet carpet with bare feet.

Jannine just lay there, smiling, as I brushed away the tiny drops of perspiration on her forehead. I squeezed in next to her. We kissed and relished the silence that underscored our oneness. We had emptied ourselves within each other, basking in the aftermath of an ancient ritual that validated our love, a primal force that drove a man and woman into helpless submission. The quietness increased our sense of hearing, a car passing out front, the happy chatter of kids playing outside, and the insistent tone of my iPhone announcing a message.

"I'm going to ignore that," I said.

"I guess I should shower before I get dressed. Where are we going for dinner?" she asked.

"Oh, yes. Dinner. I forgot to tell you—" I was suddenly frozen silent. I didn't want to spoil the afterglow of our afternoon of lovemaking. "I might have to work tonight," I whispered.

She pulled her head back and gave me, not a look of anger, but one of incredulity. "You know Victor, you've changed."

"Changed? How?"

"Well, we don't see much of each other lately. There's something different going on with you. I can't quite put words to it because it's something I feel."

"That's because of this weird assignment I'm on now."

"It's not just that. You look and act different. I loved your mustache and you used to have that sexy black stubble that made you look—" She paused and studied me. "I don't know. Kinda older and sexier."

"Hey, what was I this afternoon, a potted plant?"

"And your face. It's like a baby's butt."

"You're not going to start the baby business again, are you?"

"No. I'm not, but I am going to take a shower."

With that, she jumped up, sloshed through the carpet, and disappeared in to the bathroom. I wondered what she meant by different. Her statement touched something in the back of my brain like a faint spark about to light a fire. Somehow, I felt different but I couldn't explain how.

I picked up our various items of clothes, laid them out on the couch, and got newspapers to sop up the spilled tea. I listened and enjoyed her singing "The Moon and I," one of our favorite Nikki James numbers.

Suddenly, I remembered her asking about dinner. I had to tell her I was on duty that night. She would be angry, but understanding. The singing stopped and yet she didn't come out for a good ten minutes. I tried to slip on my jockey shorts but they were soaked with iced tea so instead I cleaned up some of the mess.

She stepped out, wrapped in a towel. "You have changed," she shouted with more than a touch of theater in her voice. "Or should I say, you haven't changed?"

There was an urgent tone in her voice. I watched, somewhat bewildered as she dressed. There was a determination and a pace that was unusual for her. As she searched the couch for her clothes, I picked up each item and handed it to her. She didn't take it, she grabbed it and if it was one of mine, she tossed it across the room. It was more a fastball pitch than a toss.

"You bastard," she screamed. Her tears were beyond anger. She raged. "'I'm on assignment tonight, Jannine,' you said. 'No, Jannine, I can't meet you today because I'm doing undercover work.' You meant under the covers you Son of a bitch."

After she dressed, she threw a tube of lipstick and an eye liner at me. When I caught the lipstick, I realized what I had done.

In my rush, I didn't put everything away. By now, she was yelling every obscenity known to man and some that I, as a cop, had never even heard before. It only got worse when I tried to calm her down.

"Jannine, it's not what you think. Give me a minute and I can explain."

"Oh no. You've already explained. Apparently, your new girlfriend likes you clean shaven and no facial hair. Is that it? She also likes blue eyeliner. Oh my God, when I think of the five years I spent." She paced up and down. "Dammit, where's my other shoe?"

"It's part of my job, Jannine."

"Don't pull that bullshit on me. It's a damn lie and you know it."

"If I could tell you, I know you'd understand. I just can't because my captain has—"

"I musta been crazy," she yelled. "I should have known there was a reason you wanted to leave things so indefinite about getting married. How long has this been going on? No. Never mind. Don't start lying some more." She started to head out the door and I ran to stop her. She tried to hit me but I grabbed her wrists. "Let me go," she yelled.

"Not until you hear what I've got to say."

"Oh for God's sakes. Put some clothes on. Or are you waiting for girlfriend number two to arrive. Or am I number two?" she screamed. "Get out of my way."

She ran out of the house, got into her car, and peeled rubber backing out of the driveway. I pulled the curtain back and watched her just miss an elderly lady walking her dog. She looked at Jannine's car then looked up at me and smiled. I forgot I was nude. I staggered back and re-alized I could be cited for indecent exposure under Penal Code 270.

I tried to call Captain Wilson to tell him I wanted off the assignment. I wanted to tell him that my relationship with Jannine meant more to me than being a detective. He would have to explain to Jannine the bizarre assign-ment I had.

No answer.

I thought about just leaving him a message that I quit, however, I couldn't just not go on duty at the Velvet Glove. It would be insubordination. His last words were ordering me to go. I couldn't risk getting fired from the LAPD.

I found my iPhone and dialed Jannine's number. It rang to her message machine.

"Jannine, call me. Please."

I sat on the couch with my feet in the damp carpet and realized I had to get ready.

I unlocked the closet and pulled out the dress with the high neckline, the black pumps, and the large size panty hose. I balled up the dress and, like a forward pass, I pitched it into the corner of the bedroom. I put on the panty hose and, with no other clothing, I looked like Joe Montana in a TV commercial.

My cellphone rang and I ran back into the living room looking for my pants. I knew it had to be Jannine but when I answered, it was Fryman.

"Hi, Vickie, honey. It's me. What time are you going to be at the Velvet Glove tonight?

"Fuck you."

"Don't tell me it's PMS?"

"Nine o'clock." I slammed the phone into the couch pillows,

I surveyed the mess of the living room. My clothes were scattered and my socks were drenched with the tea. Carelessness was creating major problems for me. Despite the captain's edict for secrecy, I would have to tell Jannine because I was sure she would understand. I punched in her number again, but still no answer. In the meantime, I had to get ready for my evening's assignment. Wilson's last words ricocheted in my brain.

"Be there!" he'd said.

I decided to go but this would be my last act involving the Carlyle case.

Because the job of make-up took more than a half hour, I realized I had to start immediately. I dropped to my knees and crawled around the living room looking for my blue eyeliner.

Chapter 13

Plumbing

I assumed Stan would be at the Velvet Glove, and though I didn't feel like talking to him or anyone else, I decided I had to do as Wilson had ordered. There was a boisterous Saturday night crowd that was a mixture of heterosexual couples, cross-dressers, and various men in street clothes. I opted for a barstool about halfway toward the back wall. The entertainment resumed after its partial suspension because of the Carlyle murder.

The trio band, consisting of a piano player, a drummer, and a saxophonist, set up for the evening's show. After I ordered my beer and my eyes got used to the dark, I became aware of a man in street clothes at the curved end of the bar near the rear of the room. The first time I looked his way, he was staring at me, so I quickly looked away. It made me feel both uncomfortable and ridiculous.

A hand on my shoulder startled me. It was Stan. He sat down on the stool next to me with his back to the strange man.

"Been here long?" he asked.

"This is my first beer," I said.

"And probably your last, the way you drink," the bartender said, showing up with Stan's unusual drink: an amber colored cocktail.

Stan took a sip and launched into a long explanation involving his grandfather. "I'm sorry about Walter and his gun routine. I think he sleeps with it under his pillow, which worries me that some night I'll come home and he might think I'm the serial killer."

"Do you think Carlyle was killed by a serial killer?" I tried not to sound officious but it came out that way.

"You sound just like a cop," he said and I had a moment of panic.

I thought better of pushing too hard so a change of subject seemed in order. "Don't look now," I said. "But there's a guy at the end of the bar that keeps staring at me.

Stan turned around then turned back and said, "Oh him."

"What do you mean, 'Oh him'? What's his story?"

"Victor, it's best you steer clear of him. He's beyond spooky. Never talks to anyone and I can tell you he doesn't come here for the drag shows."

Trying not to sound like a cop, I asked, "Have you talked to him?"

Stan remained silent, which I took as a yes. He took a long draft of his drink and waved his almost empty glass at the bartender. He looked away from me but not at the mystery man.

"Do you know him?" I asked.

Before Stan could answer, the trio played a loud intro of a few bars to get the attention of the crowd. A spotlight went on. A Ru Paul look-a-like stepped up to the microphone and introduced himself as Queen Mary. He quickly broke into a stanza of "There's No Business Like

Show Business," which soon broke down into a parody of popular songs. These were familiar song melodies with Queen Mary's saucy lyrics.

"*We kissed in the shower at the YMCA. Our meetings were few, but terribly gay*," sung to the tune from Man of La Mancha.

I had turned with my back to the bar to watch the show and, when I reached around to get my drink, I stole a quick glance at the mystery man. He was not watching the show but still staring at me. I turned back to watch the show, but couldn't concentrate on it. I wondered if he knew me or if I had busted him during one of the arrests I had made in the past few years. That seemed unlikely since my current dress could hardly pass as my police uniform. The performer droned on with old jokes: "I'm so tired I can hardly keep my thighs open."

The audience's laughs were more polite than spontaneous.

The first set ended when Queen Mary sang a final parody: "*We leave you for sanitary reasons.*" He made a dipping bow with the crowd laughing and lightly clapping.

I checked my iPhone, hoping for a message from Jannine. There being none, I entered her number again, but still no response. I struggled with myself about how to bring Stan back to the question I asked before the entertainment began. He would surely get suspicious if I asked him once more about talking to the mystery man. Why would he be big trouble?

Queen Mary came up and stood between Stan and me. The aroma of cheap drug store perfume accompanied him. "Stan, where have you been hiding this treasure?" he asked.

Stan introduced me as a new friend. Queen Mary shook hands with exaggerated motions that looked like his hands were disjointed at the wrists as he offered two fingers. An air kiss would have been more appropriate.

"You've got to come back on Monday night and participate in Amateur Night. I just know you'll win, hands down or should I say legs up." He laughed at his own joke.

"What do I have to do?" I asked, almost afraid of the answer.

"Not much, Victor. Just walk up and down. Sing a song or tell a few jokes. Then finish with a kind of a strip tease. You know, pull off your wig, unzip your dress and get down to your jockeys, boxers, or bloomers. It's great fun. You'll love it."

"What about the hair on my chest?"

"That's even better," he squealed. "Remember, it's all tongue in cheek, if you'll pardon the pun or should I say the bun?" he said, carrying on as though he were still on stage.

The bartender stood there, smiling. "Maybe not."

"Why not?" Queen Mary yelped.

"The boss thinks the Carlyle case has everybody spooked and he doesn't want to draw too much attention to the place. Amateur night is out for a while."

"Well, I hope he doesn't cancel *my* show." With that, he turned on his high heels and walked back to the bandstand.

"Don't mind Jess, that's his real name. He can get carried away," Stan said.

I used that as an opening. "I hope he's not the snitch you were telling me about?"

"What snitch?"

"You said the cops had it all wrong about the Carlyle case and then referred to their snitch."

"I musta been drunk or something. I don't know anything about that."

There was something unconvincing about his denial. He clearly did not want to talk about the murder or what he knew. He fell silent and began looking about the room as though searching for someone. He called the bartender over and ordered another drink. "How about you?" he asked me. "Another beer? This time let me buy you one."

"No. I'm good," I said. "I'm beginning to feel like a middle man with all this beer. I gotta go pee."

I made my way to the back of the bar, then down a long hall. There were two doors at the end. Neither was marked men or women. Instead, one door had a caricature of a cartoonish character with the tips of his genitals hanging from a kilt and above it the sign: *Outside Plumbing*. The other door had a cartoon of a woman with her legs crossed and a sign: *Inside Plumbing*.

After I entered, I chuckled to myself at the sight of me holding up my dress with one hand and pulling down my panties in front of the urinal. I wondered how I would do this if I had a gaff on. Just before I started to pee, the door swung open and in stepped the mystery man. Suddenly, I couldn't pee. He stood watching me as he reached behind his back and flipped closed the lock on the door. What the hell? Why did he lock the door? I felt foolish with one hand on my penis and the other holding up my dress with a weird man staring at me.

He took a short step toward me as I let my dress down and took my purse off my shoulder. *Don't panic*, I thought, as I unsnapped my purse and reached in to feel the handle of my Smith and Wesson 38. I tried to step back away from the urinal but my panties had fallen down to a point above my knees. In small steps like an oriental geisha girl, I moved toward the sink still poised to use my weapon if needed. At no time did I take my eyes off his hands. Any quick move on his part would draw an immediate reaction from me. I had never shot anyone but with adrenaline pulsing through me, I would not give it a second thought.

"Hey, man. What's going on?" I asked.

He said nothing, took a short step toward me, then stopped. I didn't want him moving behind me so I angled sideways toward the paper-towel holder.

"What's your name?" he asked.

"Why?" I responded.

He took another step toward me then stopped again. "Any friend of Stan's is worth knowing," he said as he moved toward the urinal.

Even though his moves were slow and deliberate, I took no chances and curled my index finger around the trigger of the pistol. If either hand moved toward his pockets, I knew I could beat his time on the draw. Instead, his right hand unzipped the front of his pants.

The tension decreased for me as I heard someone trying to open the locked door. The doorknob twisted and rattled and both of us were statues staring at each other. Two or three heavy pounds on the door did not cause me to move or speak. He turned, zipped up his pants, unlocked the door, and left. I started to breathe normally again. I hoped that the person entering would be a gender fucker. That I could handle.

The door swung open and a tall man in street clothes started in. He looked surprised when he saw me pulling up my panties.

"Oh. Sorry. I thought it was empty," he said and waited for me to leave. I returned to the urinal, still needing to pee in spite of my bashful kidney. The man stepped back outside. The adrenaline rush made my need to go even greater.

When I had finished and washed my hands, I snapped closed my purse and made my way to the bar where I looked back for the mystery man, but he was gone. The trio had started to play a set and, as usual, the sound was deafening. People were almost shouting to be heard. When I got to my stool, Stan was not there so I called over the bartender.

"Did you see where Stan went?" I asked.

"Yeah," he said. "They just left."

Chapter 14

Funeral

An October Santa Ana wind was adding to the discomfort at San Fernando Mission Cemetery where Carlyle's remains would be laid to rest. The coroner had released the body seven days after the murder because the autopsy took longer than expected. The toxicology reports would not be available for another ten days.

White roses rested on top of the coffin at the start of the gravesite ceremony. The Reverend James Sothworthy of the Calvary Lutheran Church officiated. He wore a large white stole over his black suit. Small beads of perspiration formed on his brow, and his thinning hair flipped in the wind.

The two boys fidgeted as they stood beside their mother, Mrs. Carlyle, who was draped with a heavy veil covering her face. The large awning, spread over the gravesite and the guests, flapped in the warm autumn breeze. The small groups that congregated outside of the awning appeared to be colleagues from Rocketdyne.

Mercifully, the prayers were short. After the casket was lowered and the final invocations recited, the funeral director handed everyone a long-stemmed rose. As each person approached the boys and Mrs. Carlyle, they embraced her then passed the open grave where they tossed in the flower as a last good-bye. Then they headed for a holding section several feet away from the awning.

Aaron and I were in full-dress uniforms, cooking in the blazing sun. Our presence had been explained to Mrs. Carlyle as a precautionary measure to guard against demonstrators, curiosity seekers, and detractors. Aaron hated this kind of duty because hidden behind his rough exterior was a sensitive and emotional soul. He leaned in and whispered, "How much longer is this going to go on?"

I just shrugged my shoulders. The more emotional the situation the rougher his exterior became.

"How should I know?" I didn't think Aaron knew the difference between a Catholic service and a Lutheran one. Neither did I.

"Weren't you an altar boy or something?"

His whispers were getting louder so I didn't answer.

Fryman and Murray stood in the last row behind the principle mourners. Mrs. Carlyle, flanked by her two sons, was cold and detached with her head bowed. The younger boy, Fredrick Jr., fidgeted through the entire service so I guessed he had to go to the bathroom. The older boy, Douglas, never stopped crying. They were not great sobs, but quiet whimpers. The sight of him not wanting to say goodbye to his father almost made me cry.

The attendant who accompanied the vicar held a small golden cross on a wooden base. After the last mourner stepped aside, Mrs. Carlyle stood and looked down into the dark hole in the ground.

"We commit the soul of our brother, Fredrick Carlyle, into your hands for eternal salvation, Lord Jesus Christ. May he rest in peace, and may You bestow strength to his sons and his wife to bear the burden of this loss."

Standing at the far edge of the grass, but not with the group, was Alan Kemper with two other men in dark suits. Why he didn't join with the rest of us was a mystery since he was the type never to pass up a chance at public visibility.

The funeral director invited everyone to a luncheon at the Presidente Mexican restaurant across from the cemetery on Sepulveda Boulevard.

Some of the mourners stopped at their cars and watched as the small family said their last good-byes. Mrs. Carlyle and her two sons were last to place their rose in the grave. Fredrick Jr. stepped to the side and reached out to drop the rose but stopped and pulled back his arm. He just stood and stared. Douglas wept as he threw the flower in. Mrs. Carlyle lifted little Fredrick and helped him stretch his arm out, shaking it so the flower would drop. The boys and she stood for a long moment. There was no expression of sorrow or grief. Her movements were almost mechanical, which seemed unnatural.

"Aren't they going to throw dirt on the casket?" Aaron asked.

"How should I know?"

"Because you're into the religion scene, aren't you?"

As the crowd dispersed, Fryman walked over to me, taking care not to step on any tombstones. "Did you recognize any of the people here?"

Aaron was surprised by the question. "How the hell would he know anyone here?"

So there was Fryman, blowing my cover and adding another piece of the puzzle Aaron was putting together. Fryman too looked surprised at his own stupidity. He forgot that Wilson wanted total secrecy on my assignment. He gave a lame excuse for the question and Aaron produced a satisfied face.

Fryman, and his loose mouth, regained composure. "Come with me, Espinoza. We should offer our respects to the widow."

Aaron pointed to himself with a surprised look. "I respect widows, too."

"Just hang loose," Fryman said.

Aaron headed back to our squad car as Fryman and I stood in line to speak to Mrs. Carlyle. We were the last ones. Fredrick Jr. was pulling at his mother's dress while dancing from one foot to the other. Alan Kemper and his two friends remained at the same distant spot, not making any moves to come over or leave.

"Freddy, ask Aunt Elaine to take you to find a bathroom. Doug, you go with him." As the boys trotted off to find their aunt, Mrs. Carlyle turned to us and said, "Thank you for coming."

It was a cold and apathetic dismissal as she turned her back to us and started to walk away.

Fryman touched her elbow and she stopped and turned her head toward us. "Can I have just a few minutes of your time Mrs. Carlyle? I have some questions."

"This is hardly the time or place Mr…"

"I'm Detective Robert Fryman from the homicide division and this is Officer Victor Espinoza."

"I've already spoken with your Detective Murray," she said. "I expect the police department to have some respect and sensitivity." Her voice was haughty and dismissive.

"I am very sorry Mrs. Carlyle but time is very important to us where a murder is concerned." A shudder passed through her at the sound of the word, murder.

"I'm afraid I can't right now." She dabbed a handkerchief to her eyes, though I couldn't see any tears forming. "If you would care to join us for lunch, perhaps we can set up a time for your questions."

"That's very kind of you Mrs. Carlyle, but—"

"We'd be happy to," I interrupted.

Fryman gave me another of his looks that I had come to realize meant, 'I'm running this case, not you, punk.'

"Thank you very much, officer," she said and gave me a small smile.

She extended her gloved hand to me. When we shook, it was a gentle connection that carried a message of understanding. I headed back to the squad car where Aaron was leaning on the fender, reading the sports page of the L.A. Times.

"Well, did you recognize anybody?" he asked.

"Yeah. One of your ex-girlfriends was there wearing a black veil and a tight black leather dress that was backless for quick access."

"Was Gloria here? That woman follows me everywhere. She's crazy about me."

"Actually, she's just using you to get to me," I said.

After we got in the car, he asked, "Back to the barn?"

"Sorry Aaron, we've got to go to lunch with the mourners."

"Oh, shit." After a brief scowl, he smiled and looked at me. "Do you think Gloria will be there?"

As we drove away, I noticed that Kemper's group was chasing along after Mrs. Carlyle. She appeared to quicken her pace back toward the stretch limo that had brought the family following behind the hearse. It looked to me like Kemper was catching up to the victim's wife, who, I might add, looked pretty good. The boys and their aunt were waiting in the limo.

"She didn't strike me as a grieving widow," I said.

Just as she entered the car, one of Kemper's men snapped pictures of her and the departing limo.

"Aaron, stop for a minute."

He jammed on the brakes. I took out my iPhone and snapped several pictures of Kemper and his antics. When they departed, I reviewed each of them to make sure I had at least one good one. When I looked up, Aaron was staring at me and frowning.

"So, you did recognize somebody."

My lies were getting glib and rapid fire. "I just wanted to get a picture of the councilman. He's running for mayor, you know. It's always nice to know people in high places because it's not who you blow, it's who you know."

Aaron looked incredulous, "What?"

"Never mind," I said. "Let's go I don't want to be late for lunch."

As we drove along my iPhone's ring tone was that of Captain Wilson's. I ignored it.

"Aren't you going to answer?" Aaron asked.

"Nah. I'm too hungry."

Another lie.

"Mind telling me what the hell is going on, Victor? I get a new partner, and then you ask to pay your respects to a hot-looking widow, a smart-ass detective wants to know if you recognize anyone, you want pictures of a city council man, and now we have to go to lunch. What am I missing?"

"Some world class Mexican food, amigo."

Chapter 15

Insurance

Captain Wilson's message was a demand for yet another meeting at 3 p.m. on Friday. I was getting used to his escalating concern about the Carlyle case. I wasn't getting used to his frequent meetings. It seemed like all we did was sit and talk. It was always the same BS. "We gotta be on the same page," or "This is a team effort," or the one I disliked the most was, "Let's do the math." Even though math was my favorite subject in school, I didn't see a connection with this murder case.

He must have sent Fryman and Murray similar messages because as I headed into the precinct, I noticed both men sat at their respective desks outside Wilson's office. Presumably, my presence at the meeting would not raise any questions because of my patrol assignments in the case. Wilson arrived and we all marched in, single file.

Wilson got right to it. "Have you been able to connect anything from the James Burgess murder besides the obvious method of murder?"

Murray scooted his chair closer to the desk and

opened a large file. He also opened the Burgess Murder book and leafed to a summary page. "The Burgess murder is not a cold case because it is still open. The victim was thirty-five years old, married, no children, was an account executive for Price Waterhouse, and had no previous record of arrests or convictions. There is no forensic evidence or even circumstantial evidence to point to a suspect. The similarities to Carlyle are few but significant."

"List them for me," Wilson ordered.

"As far as we know Burgess was not gay. He periodically was involved in cross-dressing and frequented the Velvet Glove. And here is the kicker: at the time of the murder he was wearing red lipstick yet had a tube of blue lipstick in his purse. He was killed with a huge gash to the midsection and was found dead behind a Vons supermarket near a dumpster. The market was closed at the estimated time of the murder and the three restocking employees inside said they saw or heard nothing. A bread delivery driver discovered the body at 6 a.m. That's when they open the rear gates for the delivery trucks. The body was outside the gates, about twelve yards east."

"What about suspects?"

"Everyone we questioned as a possible had an alibi. There was one person that one of the bartenders at the Velvet Glove said was a frequent customer there and who was last seen talking with the victim the night of the murder. The bartender didn't know his name nor has he been in there since. The guy was in street clothes."

"What about the other bartenders or the waitresses?" Wilson asked.

"All the others were not forthcoming. The place hates cops, which is still the product of a couple of raids we staged there a few years ago. That kind of publicity is bad for business."

"Did his wife give us anything?"

"She gave us nothing. Said she didn't know about the cross dressing. In the three years they were married, there was nothing that made her suspicious. They lived together for almost two years before they married. She said they were very much in love."

"You're right. There's not much there. So, let's do the math. What about Mrs. Carlyle? Have you had a chance to question her?"

Fryman spoke up. "I tried at the cemetery but she refused to discuss anything. The only thing we have is her trip to the morgue to ID the body. At that time, she said very little before she left. We offered to drive her both ways, but she said no. She said she would be able to meet with us on Thursday afternoon."

Wilson leafed through the report on his desk then looked up at Murray and me. "Does that surprise you, Robert?"

"May I say something?" I asked.

"Go right ahead, son," Wilson said and again I hated his implication that we were somehow blood relations let alone father and son.

"The fact that we have so little to go on, no physical evidence, and if we are certain that the same man killed both Burgess and Carlyle, then is it possible that the killer knows what he's doing and is very good at it."

Fryman scoffed, "No shit." He then turned to Wilson. "Do you think our young Detective Espinoza has hit on something?"

At first, I missed the edge of sarcasm in his voice. "Maybe this is the work of a professional," I said. "Like maybe a hit man."

Murray and Wilson agreed but with very little enthusiasm since it was obvious to them that the targets were selected at random in some bizarre ritual. I couldn't see that, but these three together represented more than fifty years of homicide work, so who was I to question?

"We need to talk to Mrs. Carlyle," Wilson said.

"Send Espinoza," Fryman said. "She seems to like him."

"Okay, Cliff, I want you and Victor to pay a visit to Mrs. Carlyle and don't leave there until you have covered every possible aspect of the man's background. We have to get moving on this because I'm getting a lot of new pressure for a fall guy. The election is only six months away. The mayor wants a second term and he's got two challengers right on his tail, especially that bloodhound Kemper."

"All due respect, Captain," Fryman said.

"I know. I know. It should be you and Cliff following up with her. Let's let those two placate her. She just might mention something that rings a bell with what Victor has picked up in the bar. I mean picked up as in information."

Nobody thought it was funny and I wasn't sure what placate meant but it didn't sound dirty.

"We don't want to overwhelm her with three guys asking questions," Wilson continued. "Oh and Victor, don't wear your uniform and certainly not a dress. Just go 'soft cloths.'"

"Do you actually have men's clothes?" Fryman asked.

"Cut it out," Wilson warned.

When we left his office, I could feel Fryman's eyes boring holes into the back of my skull. When he got to his desk, there was much slamming of drawers and kicking of the trash can. Murray was on the phone, making an appointment with Mrs. Carlyle.

"She's agreed that we can come any time," Murray said. "Let's go now."

As he drove, we went over some of the questions we might ask. Clifton Murray was a very serious detective. He was analytical to a point of annoyance and methodical to a point of exasperation.

He had received many citations for his work with the department. The most important ones were the LAPD Medal of Valor and the LAPD Medal of Heroism. I couldn't imagine the bravery it took to be in a shoot-out with a gang-infested fortress. As difficult as it was, I spoke little during the drive.

"When we get there you better let me do most of the talking," he said.

"Do you want me to record the meeting with my iPhone?"

"No. I'll take care of that, too."

Fryman must have told him of my fuck up.

"What will you want me to do?"

"We will want to put her at ease, so at first we, I mean I, will not ask any direct questions about their marital relationship. She will no doubt be very emotional and will probably cry. I can handle that. If she gets hysterical, we probably will have to end the interview and reschedule, perhaps in a public place like a restaurant."

"I don't think she will break down," I said. "I've got a strange feeling about her."

"Victor, we don't operate on a feeling level. As Sargent Friday says, we get just the facts."

I knew I should have known who Sargent Friday was, but I didn't. "Is he in the Van Nuys Division?" I asked half joking.

The way Murray looked at me I knew it was the wrong question to ask so I tried another one. "Rampart?"

"Ah—Sargent Friday is not a real person."

At that moment, I didn't feel like a real person either. I even entertained the thought of waiting in the car while

Murray conducted the interview. I was about to bring up the idea when we pulled up to the Carlyle home.

"I want you to just keep quiet."

"Doesn't it seem strange that she didn't cry at the funeral and she didn't cry when she came down to identify the body? She was real cool," I said. "If I saw Jannine's mutilated dead body, I would go to pieces. Man, I would freak out and bawl my head off."

"Look, Victor, if you want to be a detective, you'll have to learn something. Like baseball, there's no crying in police work. Cops don't bawl their heads off."

"Why not? If your wife was murdered, don't tell me you wouldn't cry."

"Yeah, maybe, but in private where no one could see me." He glanced back at the house. "Who knows? She's probably in her bedroom right now; alone, maybe even crying."

"She acts suspicious to me," I said.

Murray didn't appear impressed at my analysis. He just opened his door. "Let's go."

The Carlyle home was not exactly like a tract house since it was located south of Ventura Boulevard, overlooking the San Fernando Valley at 4107 Ridge Road. The two-story Mediterranean style had a circular drive that led to a three-car garage at one end and a beamed double-door entrance at the other.

Murray let out a long whistle as we walked through a front section ringed with tree roses. "This guy must have been a big wig at Rocketdyne. Look at this house."

We had to push the doorbell twice and, after a long while, the door opened a crack. The eyeball and cheek of the older son, Douglas, stared out at us.

"Good morning, Douglas. Is your mom at home?" I asked.

I could feel Murray nudge me aside.

"Yes," Douglas whispered.

"I'll take it from here, Victor." Murray turned back to the eye. "Could you ask her to come to the door?"

The door opened another few inches. The boy turned and yelled, "Mom, it's the cops again."

I wondered how this kid could know we were cops. A few moments later, the door swung open and Mrs. Carlyle stood there, looking pale and haggard. She motioned us into a foyer that had a broad circular staircase to the second story and an arched opening to a living room of pastel furniture and large artwork on white walls.

"Please sit down," she said, gesturing toward the living room. "Can I get you something to drink? Tea or soda or there might be some beer left."

"Nothing, thank you," Murray said.

Douglas sat on one edge of the couch and watched us get comfortable. "Where are your guns?"

"Douglas, go up and stay with your brother in his room," she said.

"Aw, Mom, do I have to?"

She gave him a look that carried with it a history of strict discipline.

After the boy left, Murray jumped right in. "On the night of the fourteenth can you tell me what time your husband left the house?"

I wondered what happened to the warm-up he planned in the car, or was that just for my benefit?

"He said he was going to a Halloween party at a colleague's house with a bunch of Rocketdyne people. It must have been about 9 p.m."

"Did you think it strange that two weeks before Halloween he would be going dressed in women's clothes?"

She glanced over at the staircase, I assumed to confirm that neither of the boys was within ear shot. Her hands twisted in a sort of a wringing motion. "No. I had no concern about it at all." The answer was mechanical and her face remained unemotional.

Murray leaned forward slightly and spoke softly. "Mrs. Carlyle, it's extremely important that you be very candid with us. If we are to track down his killer or killers, we need factual information in order get legitimate leads."

"Yes, of course."

"Were there other occasions when he dressed up in women's clothes?" Murray asked.

She looked away then back at the staircase again. She was clearly anxious when she asked, "Did you say yes to the tea?"

We had said no, so this was a ploy to change the subject.

"No thank you, Mrs. Carlyle," Murray said.

"How about you, Detective Espinoza?"

"I'm fine, thank you." However, I did like the sound of the title she gave me.

"Are you familiar with the term, transvestite?" Murray asked.

After another long pause, she blurted out, "Yes, I am and Fredrick was not what you said."

"Did the boys know about his dress-ups?" Murray was pushing hard.

"No. And they must never know," she said as she stiffened with defiance.

"Did he have any friends with…similar interests?" Murray asked.

"I resent your implication, Detective Murray."

"We're trying to track down a murderer, Mrs. Carlyle. You've got to be straight with us."

At the risk of getting thumped down by Murray, I had the temerity to jump in with a question. "How long have you known about his problem?"

Murray's head reared back and he stared directly at me.

"Problem?" she asked.

"About his cross dressing," I added.

When she began to cry, I handed her my handkerchief.

Murray started to ask another question and I raised my hand to silence him. I wanted to let her cry. After several sniffles, she looked up at me but it seemed strange that there were no tears or even a hint of clouded eyes.

"Yes, I did know. We talked about it. He told me he wasn't seeking sex with men and I believed him. He was a wonderful husband and father."

She began crying again, with what I felt were false sniffles and we said nothing.

"He would go along for several months and everything would be fine," she said. "Then, almost as if he were possessed, he would put on elaborate clothes he kept in a locked cabinet in the garage and go out. I never knew where but I trusted him." She heaved a deep sigh. "I loved him."

For a brief flash, I thought of Jannine and wanted to call her. I wanted her back. I wanted to tell her I loved her.

Then Murray ventured in with, "Did Mr. Carlyle use drugs?"

She looked surprised at the question and then glanced at the staircase again. "Yes, but a long time ago. We both smoked some marijuana when we were single and for a short time after we got married. But when I got pregnant with Douglas we both stopped. We made a conscious decision to stop."

"Any other drugs?"

"Once, at a party, we both tried some meth, but never

again. It scared me because it felt like my whole body was tingling and the pleasure was so intense. I knew I couldn't do that again. I'm sure Fredrick—"

"How about Mr. Carlyle? Could he have continued to use meth or some other drug?" Murray interrupted her in mid-sentence, which seemed to annoy her.

"I don't think so because I pay all the bills and manage all the family's money and investment accounts. I would have noticed any unusual expenses."

"What were the sources of your family income?"

"Fredrick was a head project engineer and made a good salary. But most of our income came from royalties on patents that he held in electronic sensors. He invented those after he left the University at Stanford."

"Time is important to us, Mrs. Carlyle. We have to have something to work with. What about email accounts? Was he on Twitter or Facebook, other social media under a different name? Did he have on-line friends?"

"I have his iPhone and he had an iPad and, of course, he had a personal Google account, a laptop, and a desktop upstairs in his office. He also had a Rocketdyne account. I don't know any of the passwords or anything."

"Could we send someone to pick up those items for analysis?"

"I don't know. Perhaps I should be contacting our attorney to help me with these questions."

"Time is very important Mrs. Carlyle," Murray repeated.

"If it could help, yes, I suppose so."

I decided to jump in again with a question. "Mrs. Carlyle, did Fredrick have life insurance?"

She seemed to hesitate and dabbed at her cheeks with my handkerchief. "Why, yes he did."

"For how much?"

"I believe it is for four million dollars."

Murray could hardly contain himself. "When was that policy taken out?" he asked.

"Are you suggesting that I killed my husband for his insurance? Money was not a problem for us."

"No, of course not. That just seems to be an enormous amount for an individual policy."

"He wanted to make sure the boys would be able to attend a private university if he should—" She paused and looked at the staircase again. Her word "die," was barely audible.

"We have to check everything, every lead, Mrs. Carlyle. Are you and or the boys beneficiaries?" I asked not caring about the looks I was getting from Murray.

Her eyes grew wide and her face began to morph into anger. Suddenly, she stood up and said, "Do you have any other questions, Detective Murray or Officer Espinoza? How long is this going to take?"

"Yes, I do," he said.

"You will have to ask them when I can have our attorney present." There was a coldness in her manner that suggested more defensiveness than evasion.

"Could you arrange that? We are available full time on this case so you can pick the time and place," Murray said. "Please make it as soon as possible."

"I'll try," she said with little conviction as she stepped toward the door.

"Just one more thing, Mrs. Carlyle. Did Mr. Carlyle have any close friends, other than work colleagues, who could tell us about his relationships at Rocketdyne?"

"No. Not that I can think of. He had a friend from college that he occasionally played golf with but he was a very quiet and distant man." She started to walk to the front door again and we followed.

"Thank you, Mrs. Carlyle, you've been very helpful," I said as I opened the door.

She hesitated. "I never did understand one of his friendships. It was a puzzlement to me how he could become friends with a young man more than half his age. I only met him a couple times when he came by."

"Do you have a name?" Murray asked.

She thought for a long time and then said, "I think he referred to him as Stan somebody. Yes I'm sure his name was Stan but I don't have a last name."

"You've been very helpful, Mrs. Carlyle," Murray said.

"I would also like to help in another way. How would I go about adding an additional $50,000 to the reward offered by the city council?"

"We can certainly arrange that, Mrs. Carlyle."

Murray gushed with enthusiasm, however I wondered if she was sincere or just setting up a smoke screen.

"I'll have my attorney contact you and set up the meeting you want and he'll handle the reward paperwork." She turned and left us at the open door.

As we left, I looked back and Douglas Jr. was sitting on the top step, staring down at us.

Chapter 16

Bartender

Not counting shaving, and doing my nails, I spent over forty-five minutes just preparing my face. I watched the Merle Norman YouTube lessons on make-up so many times I could lip-sync the cosmetologist's words about foundations, highlights, and shadings. I took special care that day because I wanted to show Brandon, the bartender at the Velvet Glove, that I was a serious cross-dresser who wanted to pass, not titillate. There was just so much that make-up and clothing could disguise of a native level of testosterone. I had to keep in mind that this was a project and not a way of life.

The Velvet Glove opened at four in the afternoon, not because customers were rushing in to drink and socialize, but because the place needed preparation for the evening's activities.

On this particular Wednesday, I arrived at five in the afternoon in the hope of getting Brandon to talk about the various regulars. I wore a long-sleeved blouse, a knee-length blue skirt, and a pair of comfortable shoes that didn't make me look taller. I was the only customer in the place. Brandon had ear buds in as he inspected glasses in the bright overhead light. When I entered, he turned to me and pulled out one ear bud.

"What the hell?" he yelled.

"Hi. I'm Vic," I said, stretching my hand out for a handshake like some kind of overeager salesperson.

He wiped his hand on his apron then took mine. It was a firm grip on both ends, which caused him to look down at our clasped hands. Shit, I thought, I should have given him just two fingers.

"I'm Brandon. We're open but we usually don't get customers until around seven. What can I get you?"

"I was just on my way to meet someone for dinner and thought I would stop and have a cold beer."

Throw another lie on the falsehood barby for me. I wondered when the day of reckoning would come when I'd have to account for them. When he delivered the beer, he stood with one foot propped up on the stainless-steel sink where he was washing glasses.

"I know you," Brandon said, "you've been in here a couple times in the evening. You asked me about Stan the other night."

At five in the afternoon, the Velvet Glove had a completely different ambience. Besides the light streaming in from the soffit windows high above the bar, the odor of stale beer hung in the air.

"Victor. Victor…" He thought for a minute. "Victor Espinoza. Right?"

I nodded and realized he was a good bartender who could not only remember faces but names as well. It took only a few seconds to read my driver's license, yet he had total recall.

He could be a storehouse of information for me if I could orchestrate it without drawing suspicion.

"Sure. I remember. You're a friend of Stan's. Got him drunk a few nights ago."

"It seemed like that happened so quickly," I said.

"Quickly? You had two beers all evening and Stan had at least seven drinks."

"You've got a good memory."

"It's part of my job. I have to know what's going on in case ABC starts checking up again."

What did he mean by again? Had there been a problem or some violation of regulations?

"ABC?" I hoped that acting dumb would be a way to get him talking.

"Alcohol and Beverage Control," he said.

"Did you know much about the guy that was murdered?" I asked. "Did he ever come in here?"

"You mean Carly? Or should I say Freddie Carlyle?"

"Was that his name?" I asked, but I realized my silly inquisitive look didn't cut it with Bandon because he just stared at me.

"I read about it in the papers," I said.

"And you talked about him the first night you came in here," Brandon added.

There was a directness in his voice that concerned me. Or was it my implied lie that caught up with me?

"What was he like?" I asked, hoping he would accept the change of direction of our conversation.

"He wasn't Nellie like Stan. About your height and build I'd say." He seemed to drift off into what he was thinking or just disinterested. "Funny," he continued. "When I was in the marines, we used to beat the crap out of guys like you who acted effeminate and now, here I am working in a bar that caters to them." After a long pause, "Funny world," he said and walked away.

Brandon was a big man with heavy shoulders and large hands. A scar below his right cheek and thick eyebrows announced a mafia look that I assumed was invaluable for a bartender. When he finished adjusting whiskey bottles at the back of the counter, he returned and put one foot on the sink. He held up my empty glass and wobbled it.

"Yes," I said, "I'll have another."

"What time is your dinner?" he asked with a tone that said, "I don't believe you."

"Late. Know anything about this guy named Greg?" I assumed a change of direction and of people would throw Brandon off.

"Why?" he asked.

"He made a move on me the other night and I was wondering if you have him figured out?"

"Strange you should ask. There were a couple of cops in here yesterday asking a lot of questions. They specifically asked about Greg."

The test was on for me. I knew I had to act like someone holding four aces. Brandon just stared at me as I took a long sip of beer.

"Wow, what did you tell them?" Our conversation was beginning to take on a cat-n-mouse format and I didn't know how to cover for it.

"We don't like cops snooping around in here. Anytime a cop comes in asking questions it means trouble. It could even mean some bad publicity. Worse, it could mean my job."

"So do you think the cops were after Greg?"

"No, he's harmless. I had him figured out the first day he walked in here." He leaned in close to me. His face was only a few inches from mine. He squinted his eyes and said, "It's you I haven't figured out yet."

His comment set off alarms in my brain. What did he mean?

"Me? There's nothing to figure. Color me run-of-the-

mill cross-dresser." He stared at me. "Vanilla transvestite," I added.

"You don't sound run-of-the-mill, you don't act run-
of-the-mill, and you don't dress run-of-the-mill."

I could feel a lump beginning to form in my throat. I
wasn't scared, just concerned. He cocked his head to one
side. "You don't look like you belong in a dress or in this
place."

"Well, I'm not from LA. I recently came here from
Chicago. A friend of mine told me about this place. He
told me the Velvet Glove was a good place to pick up
someone for heavy action." I amazed myself for talking
about something I knew nothing about.

Brandon moved his head slowly back and forth, and
then took a step backward. "No. I figure you for one of
three things. Either you're a writer doing research for a
book you're working on, or you're a graduate student at
CSUN, working on a thesis in psychology or—" A short
pause. "You're a cop."

The front door swung open and we both looked up to
see an older man come to the bar. Brandon greeted him
with, "What can I get you?"

The man produced a small piece of paper then, with
a heavy accent, asked about directions to a senior community center. Brandon used hand directions to guide
him. "Up one block on Lankershim, turn left, then
straight ahead."

The man nodded, smiled, and left.

Brandon poured himself a half a glass of beer and returned to face me. "I haven't completely figured you out
yet, but I will."

"Well, you've at least narrowed it down to three," I
said, trying to act disinterested. "Who knows? There
could be more."

"So which is it?" he said. "Or is this one of those

multiple choice questions where the last one is 'none of the above'?"

I picked up my glass, holding out my pinky finger. "I'll never tell."

"Of the three," he said. "I think you're a cop."

I forced a laugh. "Do I look like a cop?"

The edges of his mouth turned up with a hint of a smile. "Are you?" he asked.

"Would a cop drink beer in the afternoon, and in a dress?" I instantly regretted my stupid question.

A broad smile broke out and he said, "Does a bear shit in the woods?"

I laughed as authentically as I could, got up from the bar stool, and took a step back.

I put my one hand on my hip like a Versace model standing on a runway and pushed my hip sideways as far as I could. "Look at me," I said. "Do you think the police department would hire a shrimp like me? I'm barely five foot five."

I remembered Fryman calling me a shrimp and hoped it would work here. A phony smile came over him.

"So what is your story?"

I made a quick inventory of the research I had done on cross-dressers and created another lie about my persona. "I'm a guy with a fetish. I like the feel of women's clothes on my body. I like to feel pretty, but I'm not gay."

"Oh sure, you're not gay, but you like to hook up with Stan."

"He's just a friend."

"Since when do friends who meet at the Glove not hook up?" he asked.

"So what if we do?" I said, because I needed to throw him off the cop trail.

"Yeah. Well, hook up or not, I'm still going with my third choice. In fact, I'm pretty sure you're a cop."

I laughed again. "My friends are going to love that when I tell them."

"Just in case I'm right, I gotta tell you. We've got nothing to hide here. Even though were not a straight bar, we run a straight operation." He turned and clicked off the overhead lights. "We've got nothing to hide," he repeated in a loud voice.

The Velvet Glove was ready for the evening's business, but I was worried that I had compromised my cover. I took the last sip of beer and stood to adjust all my falsies. Before I left, I stopped at the front door, turned, and looked back at Brandon. He smiled and saluted me with an exaggerated motion and I wondered what I had said to make him suspicious.

After I left, a flood of ideas raced through me about Brandon. If he really thought that I was a cop, why would he give me the time of day? Why wouldn't he clam up and tell me to get out and not come back? What would he report to the boss he was trying to protect? I wondered if I should report back to Murray and Fryman the details of the visit. After all, this little trip was not cleared with either of the detectives. It was my own idea. I was following orders to get information that might produce viable leads.

Chapter 17

The Phone Call

After roll call, I told Fryman and Murray about my conversation with the bartender at the Glove. They both railed about my acting alone and working the case without first clearing with them or Captain Wilson. I wanted to remind them that I was assigned to the case to try to get information concerning the Carlyle murder.

"How many times we gotta tell you to not make a move without telling us?" Murray was angry. "Wilson's going to be pissed."

"Does he have to know?" Fryman asked.

This was a different Fryman in my corner, defending my actions.

"This isn't your case, Officer Espinoza," Murray said. "Your assignment was to be undercover at the Velvet Glove that coincided with our strategy planning."

"Sorry, I thought I was doing something I was told to do. Get information."

"Look, kid," Fryman said, "if you want to be a detective, you gotta play by the rules. There's no room for hot dogs on this case or any LAPD case. We need to know your every move, every action, and even every thought you have about your duty activities."

Murray joined in with, "And you need to remember, you're to stay in the background and remain anonymous."

I had the feeling they were talking down to me and acting like I was stupid. This was not my first assignment. My high school undercover operation for Narcotics had given me some latitude of working alone and making decisions.

Now I was getting pissed. "What about Wilson sending me to interview Mrs. Carlyle and having me attend the funeral?"

"You getting that involved was never my idea. That was on Wilson," Murray said.

"Besides," Fryman chimed in, "you haven't given us anything to work with. No solid evidence or information."

"Yeah, you may be fooling Wilson with your goody-two-shoes personality, but not me," Murray said. The three of us sat there in silence, the air thick with tension. Fryman gave a long sigh and said, "So what's the bartender's name? Let's run a make on him."

"Brandon," I said.

Both Fryman and Murray looked at me like I had a Klingon head.

"Not including our office, there must be a half a million guys named Brandon in this country. With no last name, the information you got is worthless," Murray said. He turned to Fryman. "See if you can get a last name on that bartender. ABC might have a listing cross-referenced with the name of the bar and the staff working there."

I did not dare tell them that Brandon suspected that I

was a cop. That kind of information they didn't want because it would make the hunt for a murderer harder to work. Worse still, it could get me thrown off the assignment and thwart my chances for advancement, maybe even get me an internal affairs investigation.

Fryman got on the phone to ABC and gave them the data on the Velvet Glove and a bartender named Brandon. Computers at ABC compressed the wait to three minutes flat. "Thank you," Fryman said then turned to Murray. "Brandon Crawford." He looked at me. "This time you may be off the hook, Victor."

Murray fired up his computer and did a search through police files and the county database but nothing showed up so he switched to the composite data repository. It was the finger print file that was required of all bartenders that provided a full profile. He started to read the screen aloud.

"This guy's a squeaky clean ex-marine, an MP to boot. I'll be damned, one of us," Murray said.

"Just because there's no yellow sheet on him doesn't necessarily mean he's clean," Fryman said.

I interrupted with a thought I had. "Is there a date on that fingerprint record?"

"Why?" Fryman asked.

"Now you too with the why?" Murray snapped.

"Maybe he was working at the Glove when the Burgess murder came in. This guy seems to remember a lot of detail about the Glove's regulars," I said. "Should I go back and try talking to him again?"

"No. He'll get suspicious and think you're a cop," Fryman said.

"I could tell him I'm a freelance writer doing research on murders in the San Fernando Valley. People seem to want to give it up for writers."

"You're too short to be a writer," Fryman said.

Being in my corner was very short lived because he was throwing me under the bus again for the sake of a joke.

I turned to Murray. "Were you guys in the Velvet Glove recently, asking questions?"

Both of them said no.

"Then who was," I asked, "because Brandon said there were two cops in there looking for information."

"Maybe Wilson wanted to deflect interest in you by sending in cops as a routine response to the Carlyle murder. It would be more suspicious if nobody came in."

I began to realize that withholding information was just another form of lying. I was about to tell them that Brandon suspected me of being a cop when the telephone rang at Fryman's desk.

"Fryman, how can I help you?" He listened for a few seconds then looked up with wide eyes. He spoke in a slightly louder voice. "Who?" After a short pause he said, "No, there is no *Detective* Espinoza here. Let me check the directory and see if he is with another division."

He cupped his hand over the mouthpiece and began making inquisitive searches with his eyes. He motioned Murray to get on an extension.

"No sir. I don't see an Espinoza in the ranks of LAPD detectives. You might try the Sheriff's Department. Do you want their number?...Okay, you're welcome." After he hung up, he looked at me. "What the hell's going on?"

"Who was it?" I asked.

"You tell me, *Detective* Espinoza."

"Hold on," I said and raced out of the room. JoAnn was sitting at her desk sorting papers. "Can you check on the number of that last call that came to Fryman?"

"Only if it's a listed number and not blocked," she said. She clicked through then stopped. "Here it is. We're in luck. 818-286-3753. You want me to do a cross check?"

"Yes."

She entered the numbers into the computer and, almost instantly, the screen flashed the source: The Velvet Glove on Lankershim Boulevard in North Hollywood.

"Does that help?" she asked.

"No."

So much for a straight operation I thought. Brandon did not have me pegged, for certain.

Maybe Murray was right. He was not as squeaky clean as we thought.

"Okay, Espinoza, give it to me straight," Murray asked. "What went down at the Glove when you were there?" He paused. "Were you in soft sloth or in drag?

Right or wrong, I made the decision to not start telling the truth. "Well," I began, "I went there in soft cloth, hoping to meet Stan…"

Chapter 18

Coffee Time

My phone call with Stan was brief and not very productive. I had hoped to get some specific information about his connection to Carlyle, which I could bring to Fryman and Murray. He sounded detached and indifferent. His one-word answers were getting to me.

"You can't talk right now, right?" I asked.

"Yes. That's right."

"Is your grandfather there?"

"Yes." So it went with me asking questions and him giving me one word answers that were evasive. In frustration, I made a suggestion. "How about we meet for coffee? It's 10:30 now. Let's say at Jays Diner at Tujunga and Riverside at eleven?" There was a long pause, during which I could hear Jeopardy playing very loud on the television.

"Stan, are you there?"

"Why?" he asked.

I realized I had to put on the brakes because there

was a faint note of suspicion that crept into his voice. It didn't seem logical that his grandfather could hear the conversation and pay attention to a game show that was blasting at a hundred decibels.

"Oh, I don't know. I just need someone to talk to and I thought you might listen and give me some support."

"I don't know. I'm kinda tired right now."

I wasn't sure if that was for my benefit or his grandfather's. "I was figuring you as a friend," I said, trying not to sound overly pathetic, although I did have more than a vested interest in Stan.

"Well…okay," he said with a loud sound of acceptance.

"Street clothes, Stan."

"Sure. Sure. See you there."

We hung up and I wondered what he might be telling his grandfather. The old man could be a source of some information, which Fryman and Murray could add into the puzzle.

We had woefully few pieces that fit together. Stan had to have a reason for saying the cops had it all wrong. He and Carlyle knew each other and were considered friends. I had to win him over while, at the same time, I was sure he was not complicit in any way to the murders of Burgess and Carlyle.

I had just enough time to try another call to Jannine. I knew she liked to sleep in on her day off, but my earlier call went directly to the answering machine. Either she was still not taking my calls, or her phone was turned off because the machine came on again. This time I decided to leave a long message.

"Jannine, please don't delete this until you hear me out. I deserve that much. I have a meeting later today with Captain Wilson. I'm going to tell him that I plan to tell you the nature of my undercover work. I will even ask him to call you and confirm it. If you're hearing this, please pick up. If not will you—"

"Hello." It was a hard, impatient response.

"Jannine, thank you."

"How do I know this won't be another trick of yours? You get one of your buddies at work to pose as this Captain Wilson?"

"Okay, what if you call him instead?"

"What kind of B.S. is he going to tell me? That you had to have a woman in your house in the line of duty? Give me a break, Victor."

"Jannine, the only woman who has ever been in this house is you. Or at least in the last five years. Well, maybe four years."

"You're just making this worse with your lies."

"Try me."

"Okay, I will. What's Wilson's number?"

"Well, I have to call first and set it up with him."

"Just as I thought."

With that said, she hung up and I slouched down in my chair, utterly defeated. I thought about calling her back but, instead, tossed the phone on the table. If I had let her call in cold, she would have been routed to a duty officer. Nobody ever got through to Wilson without pre-screening. I wanted to tell her I missed her. I missed hearing her voice. I missed the quiet time we spent together. I missed her touch. I even missed that hokey peach-smelling shampoo she used.

At that moment, I felt like calling Wilson again and asking to be taken off the assignment. My life as a patrol cop was so easy and predictable compared to this junior detective charade. Somehow boring was easier than lying, conniving, and evading.

In all my reverie, I forgot to call Fryman or Murray to let them know I was meeting with Stan. Somehow, this didn't seem to be the same as me working the Velvet Glove. My connecting with Stan was mostly to get more information about him and about his leaving the bar with Mr. Mystery Man. This didn't seem important enough for the two detectives to have my back. As expected, Stan was late. When he did arrive, he looked like he just climbed out of bed. His hair above his ears stuck out and the puffiness of his eyes made him look like an owl. At 11 a.m. the diner was nearly empty since the lunch bunch had not yet begun.

"Hey," I said, hoping to sound friendly and non-threatening.

"So what did you wanna talk about?"

He took me by surprise because I didn't expect such an abrupt opening. The waitress arrived and I ordered coffee. Stan wanted Diet Coke with lots of ice. Hot pipes from last night, I thought.

"You look like shit," I said.

"That's exactly how I feel."

"Big night, last night?"

"Sort of, but not for me. So what's happening?"

He seemed a little impatient. I wasn't sure of how to proceed so I started by giving him my tale of woe. I told him how my girlfriend didn't trust me and how she thought I was cheating on her. He listened about how our relationship during the last five years had grown. It was a verbal mine-field for me to avoid all mention of my job as a policeman. He listened and looked surprised.

After looking back and forth, he leaned in toward me. "Are you serious about this girlfriend bit?" he asked.

"Yeah, why?"

"I thought you were gay," he said then laughed.

I laughed with him. "And I thought you were gay."

"I am," he said.

That was a real conversation stopper.

I was at a loss as to what I could add and keep the communication going.

How could I tell him that I'd been certain he was gay?

"So here you are a transvestite *and* a bisexual. Wow!" Stan said.

"Keep your voice down, will you? No, I'm not and, yes, I do like to dress up. It's sort of my thing."

We both laughed and it seemed right for me to push a little harder.

"So you never know," I said, hoping it didn't sound stupid.

"You know, Vic, I wasn't sure about you right from the start," Stan began, "There was something I just couldn't put my finger on, even though they say it takes one to know one. I just wasn't sure."

"Yeah. You never know. Take that Carlyle guy I read about in the newspaper. I guess he wasn't gay either."

"No, he wasn't, but that's what got him killed."

"How so?" I asked.

"Well, Freddie was sorta loud and pranced about the Glove. He asked me to introduce him to—"

Suddenly, Stan clammed up, looked out the window and avoided eye contact. I knew I was on to something. I'd hit a nerve.

I could see the pain rising in Stan's eyes as he painted a different picture than Mrs. Carlyle had. She saw her husband as a loner that kept to himself and Stan saw him prancing about and gregarious. Which was the real Carlyle?

"Introduce him to who?" Stan stared at me as though seeing me for the first time. "Who was he, Stan? From what I read in the newspapers, the police don't know anything about him."

His jaw tightened with determination. "And they're not gonna find out from me."

"Why not? If this guy is that dangerous, shouldn't he be locked up?"

"If they're so eager, they could easily find out from their snitch."

"What snitch?"

He seemed to grow pensive again and I wasn't holding back. I felt right on the verge of getting a name.

"Do you know his name?" I asked. "We can let the police handle it."

"We?"

I had to think fast with my slip. "Yeah. You and me. We gotta look out for each other. We have to have each other's backs."

The pained expression on Stan's face told me he wanted to trust me, to unload the burden he was carrying. "Forget the police," he said. "If they ever found out about a guy named Tony at Jimmy's, I'd get nailed for sure."

"Jimmy's?"

"A rough bar on Ventura Boulevard. It's the drug exchange palace in the Valley. A lot of middle dealers work out of there."

"Where?"

"You sound like a cop with all these questions."

I held my breath and wished I had that damn wire on now. "Are you kidding? Look at me. Do I look like a cop?" I forced a laugh. Stan seemed to get even more distraught; he looked paler than when he entered. "What's the matter, Stan?" I asked. "Are you all right?"

"I can't talk about it."

"How come?"

"I'm really fucked up right now. If this kind of information got to the police and I became a suspect, I'd be the next victim. For sure. I don't want to die, Vic."

"Jesus, Stan, let me help you."

"You're safer not knowing anything. You'd be another case of the man who knew too much. No, I think too much of you to put you in danger."

"Hey, I'm trying to be your friend here."

"Don't."

He was holding both hands on his diet coke, which kept them from shaking.

"I can't just stop being your friend. Damn it, Stan, I care about what happens to you." This time I wasn't lying, I was sincere about wanting to protect him. "Share with me what's eating you up."

I could see puddles forming in his eyes, his mouth opened slightly but nothing came out. Fear was choking him. "If you really mean that, then I can't tell you anything," he said.

"Why?"

"Because you'd be a target, too, like the others."

"If I promise not to go to the police, will you tell me?"

"Victor, why do you want to know? I feel like it's more than just curiosity. What's going on?"

"I wanna know what we're dealing with here," I said. At that moment, I could feel myself being cornered by my emotions. *'Keep feelings out of it'* echoed in my brain but I couldn't. "I know how fucked up your life has been and I want to help."

Stan just stared at me, puddles of tears forming in his eyes as his hands twisted around his Diet Coke. After a long moment, he pushed himself away from the table, stood up, and left. He didn't look back or wave. He just walked out the door. I felt totally defeated.

I was in shock. If I reported our conversation to Fryman or Murray and they initiated an investigation, Stan could be in mortal danger. If I kept quiet, I could lose my job or, at best, have no chance for any future in police work. I started not to like myself for not having any guts or loyalty to my job, my boss, or my friend. Something was happening to me that I couldn't control and it was demanding of me what I could not deliver.

I didn't like myself very much because I had to choose. Tell Wilson and betray my friend, or keep silent and betray my unofficial oath as a policeman. Stan had no dilemma. He was staying loyal to me. I was beginning to see myself as I really was and it was painful. I was no longer seeing him as a gay man, or a queer. He was a real person and in in pain. I sat there in shock as a window of self-awareness began to open.

I wondered how Jannine saw me—selfish and self-centered on what I wanted and everyone else be damned? Why, I wondered, would she continue to stay with me since all I'd ever given her were empty words?

After I took my last sip of cold coffee, I threw five dollars on the table and walked out the door. My trail of information was just about as cold as the stale coffee. I heard my iPhone ring and felt it vibrate in my pocket. It was one of those moments when I didn't feel like talking to anyone. I just wanted a few minutes to think about what to do next. I made the decision to ignore the call. Like all the others, it turned out to be the wrong decision.

Chapter 19

Size 12

I left Jay's Diner and walked along Tujunga Avenue, passed my parked car, as I continued toward some unknown destination. Strange thoughts raced through my brain. Jannine was right when she observed that something was happening to me. Obsession was crowding out my humanity. Blind ambition was snuffing out the needs of the woman I loved, compulsion was damaging a friend who needed me, and personal selfishness was destroying my sense of values.

I heard my iPhone ring again and once more I chose to ignore it.

What's the use, I thought. I felt totally defeated.

After walking nearly a mile, I calmed down enough to look at the messages. The first one was from Jannine.

OK U win. 5 2nite. I need to pick up some of my belongings.

I raced back to my car and pushed the speed limits on way to my house because I realized the place was a mess.

My moment of realization fizzled.

When I had lived in an apartment, my house cleaning and maintenance tended to cluster around doing it all one day a week. On that day, generally my day off, I washed a week's worth of dishes—which meant some of the glasses were welded to the table—did one or two weeks laundry—losing at least one sock in the dryer—cleaned the toilet, dusted, and finished with washing my car. That was pre-Jannine.

Today I was manic, running through the house and cleaning what was obvious along with getting ready for Jannine's arrival.

Normally, I wouldn't fuss with anything just for Jannine because sometimes she would pitch in and do it with me, but this time I wanted everything to be perfect. I even put an embroidered cloth—one that she bought—on the dining area table along with five candles, one for each year we had been together. I put my iPhone in its deck and pulled up the new Nikki James album I had just downloaded from iTunes. We both loved her concert at the Nokia Theater last September.

I checked the kitchen clock: 4:15, then I rechecked my text message from Jannine.

OK U win. 5 2nite I need to pick up some of my belongings.

I also checked the text from Fryman.

Urgnt Call me ASAP.

"Sorry, not tonight Detective Robert Fryman, *honey*. I've got a splitting headache." I talked to the phone as though expecting an answer from the message machine. As I lit the candles, the doorbell rang. "Shit, she's early."

I breathed a sigh when I opened the door. It was the delivery man from the Royal Wok with Jannine's favorite Glazed Shrimp. I paid him and tipped him two dollars, which he looked at in his hand and then at me. He looked as if I had just slapped him with a wet Mackerel. We ended the standoff of how much to tip with him still looking at the money and me closing the door. I rushed to the kitchen and pulled out the two fortune cookies. I used a sharp paring knife to cut a small hole into the end of one cookie shell. It was just large enough for me to slide a key into the traditional oriental dessert that contained a vague prediction of hope.

After I placed the shrimp, fried rice, and egg rolls in the oven set at low heat, I studied myself in the dining room mirror. I hadn't shaved that morning and hoped there would be some evidence of black stubble. There was just a hint. With a splash of after shave and rub of deodorant I was ready. From then on, it seemed an eternity before the doorbell rang.

It finally did.

When I opened the door, Jannine stood with one hand on her hip and the other up against the doorjamb. "Why am I here?" she asked, her voice testier than I'd ever heard it. When I reached out to give her a kiss, she pushed past me and marched into the house. "So?" she blurted out.

This was going to be much harder than I had hoped. *Why must women always start out on the offensive?*

"I thought we'd have dinner and we could talk."

"I don't have time for dinner. I have plans. Look, Victor, I know it takes two and I feel like I must have set you up for looking elsewhere to get whatever else you need or want. I just wish you would have told me, like maybe four years ago."

"I couldn't, at least not until tonight. Please, sit down and let's eat."

"I told you I can't."

"I've got Glazed Shrimp and fried rice…"

"If you think for a minute that I'm going to give in

that easily with Glazed Shrimp, you're right. I am. Not because I'm in a forgiving mood. I'm hungry."

She pulled off her blue-knit sweater, tossed it on the couch, and headed to the dining table. I tried to hold off with any triggering comments while I opened a bottle of Pinot Grigio, her favorite wine. Through dinner, we volleyed back and forth with caustic comments that were more playful than hurtful. Finally, dessert time came. She bit down on the twisted fortune cookie so hard I was sure she broke a tooth.

"What the hell?" she said.

She spit out the cookie crumbs and held up a Shlage key.

"What's this for?"

"I hope it's the key to your heart." I tried my sexiest smile as I pushed out my stubbled chin.

"Cut it out, Victor. I'm not in the mood for playing games. Even though the shrimp was good, I'm still here under what you cops call duress."

"Why don't we go into the bedroom?" I said.

"That's it. I'm leaving."

She tossed the key at me and, with that, picked up her sweater and headed for the front door. I grabbed her hand and stopped her. Gently, but firmly, I led her into the bedroom and guided her to the locked closet.

"Open it."

"Are you going to keep me prisoner in your closet? That's way too kinky even for you, Officer Espinoza. This sounds way too romantic for someone who uses sex as pastime."

I stood my ground by not letting her leave and not responding to her jabs. I held the key in the air like a religious icon. After she stared at it, she shrugged her shoulders and grabbed it.

She unlocked the closet, opened the door, and I

turned on the overhead light. She said not a word and just ruffled the dresses, blouses, and skirts on hangers. She looked on the shelf above where a dummy head held my wig and a few silky scarfs. After taking a step back, she looked at the shoes on the floor, then at me, then at the shoes again.

"Whose are these?"

There was a little bit of a boast in my voice when I said, "Mine."

"Yours? What are you talking about?"

"Yes. Mine."

"You wear dresses, now?"

"Uh-huh."

She began to laugh out loud. "You've been carrying around this little secret for five years. Oh my God, Victor. It's okay. In a way I'm relieved to see this."

"You are?"

"I don't care about your kinky activities. I love you no matter what. Oh, Victor." She rushed at me, threw her arms around me, and kissed my lips, my cheeks, and my lips again. "And you didn't shave. Oh, I'm so happy."

"Hold on. It's not what you think. There's a lot more to this."

"There is?" Her eyes widened in amazement and I too was beginning to enjoy the release. She stepped back a few steps, frowned. "My God. You're gay and that's why you haven't wanted to get married. Hell, Victor, I don't care if you dig men. I'm sure we can work something out. I wouldn't agree if you wanted to have a girlfriend on the side, but a buddy or a boyfriend? Hell, that's okay."

"Jannine, I'm not gay. I don't dig men. It's part of my assignment."

"You have to dress as a woman? Why?"

"Yes I do, but I can't tell you why. Captain Wilson has sworn me to complete secrecy."

"Why don't they just use a female cop?"

"That's the part I can't tell you."

Jannine's expression melted from joyous to skeptical in a slow dissolve.

"Here we go again with *that* routine. Let's just not go there, Victor. This line of talk is getting me upset again."

She pulled out one of the long gowns, held it up to herself, pressed it to the front of her, and twirled around the room. Out came a second one and then a third. She held the two up, one in each hand, as though she was choosing.

"Too bad you don't wear a twelve. We could share clothes. Hell, wouldn't you know the style is headed in the direction of mini-skirts now." After searching through the rest of the wardrobe, she plopped down on the bed.

I couldn't read her. Usually I knew what she was thinking.

Suddenly, she looked concerned. "Does Bubba know about you being a…what…bisexual?"

"Will you cut that out? And no, he doesn't and it's very important this be kept a total secret. Do you understand what I'm saying? No one must know."

"So you want to stay in the closet and keep your clothes in there, too."

I smiled and decided to change my approach with her. I lay down next to her, took her in my arms, and kissed her. "Will you accept me for who I am?" I asked.

She looked toward the closet. "Well, I don't know."

I kissed her again and held her closer. The peach aroma of her shampoo caught me when I kissed her neck. I could feel her fingers running through the hair on the back of my head. We clung to each other like a pair of mollusks as we rolled on the bed. Our hands explored every sensual part of our bodies. She began to undo the buttons of my shirt. I rolled over from my back so she could hurry. We were like foreplay on steroids. She stopped and pushed slightly away from me. There was a devilish glint in her eyes, which always gave me the feeling I was standing high on a precipice.

"Put on a dress for me," she cooed.

"At a time like this, you gotta be kidding. Besides, what am I going to do with this?"

I moved her hand down and pressed it against me. She held it there and then kissed me again.

"Please," she repeated.

At that point, I'd put on a gorilla costume if she wanted as long as we would resume what I had in mind. I quickly stripped off to my shorts and picked out a gold lame gown with which I had no trouble zipping up under the arms. She giggled through the whole process. For me the moment was gone, as if someone had thrown a bucket of ice water down my back. Now it was me getting resentful with the line of talk. Talk I didn't want or need at that moment.

"This is so weird. I love it," she said.

As I started to get back into bed, the front doorbell rang. Reality washed over me.

"Don't answer it," she said, and the doorbell rang again.

"Jannine," I pleaded.

"Come on. Let's do damage control," she said. Then with a vampish deep throated voice, she whispered, "I'll make it worth your while."

"All the lights are on in the house and both our cars are in the driveway," I said.

"Damn, we're not going to go through this again. The last time I asked you to not answer the phone and look what it got me. Let whoever it is, leave."

The doorbell began to ring with successive chimes. Someone was just standing there pressing the button repeatedly letting us know they knew we were in the house. I had completely forgotten about my gown and headed for the front door. When I opened it, Fryman was standing there, smirking.

"Jesus, when you get into a role, you really live it. That isn't exactly a house dress."

Jannine came into the doorway of the living room. "What's this?" she asked.

Fryman and I exchanged glances and I knew it was too late. He had blown my cover.

"It's a salesman," I shouted back from the door. Strange how I used silly lies even when I didn't need to.

"What's he selling?" she asked.

Fryman made a Michael Jackson obscene gesture by grabbing his crotch and thrusting his pelvis. He used crassness to relieve or perhaps hide tension even when there was no need for it.

"I'll explain this dress later," I whispered though it appeared he wasn't interested or cared.

"There is no later," he said. "We gotta go now. Get some other clothes on because you're not riding in my car with that outfit."

"Why? Because it makes me look fat?"

"We just got a call. Seems there's another dead body over near the University, a man dressed in woman's clothes."

Chapter 20

Dirty Politics

Detective Fryman and I sat in the squad room, trying to look busy while we watched Captain Wilson and Councilman Kemper behind the glass window of the captain's office. Each of the men appeared to be shouting and waving their arms in nonthreatening but emphatic gestures.

When Detective Murray arrived, he joined us in trying to make sense of what was going on. Murray had an armload of paperwork that, no doubt, had details of the latest murder.

"What's going on?" he asked.

"They've been in there over a half hour," Fryman said. "And it looks like it'll go on all day."

Murray dropped everything on the desk, walked over to the coffee bar, and poured himself a cup of what looked like black lava flowing from a volcano—steaming and thick.

Wilson looked up and waved us in. We picked up two chairs and joined him and Kemper in uncomfortable silence. The arc of four chairs in front of Wilson's desk looked like we were setting up for a twelve-step meeting.

"Gentlemen," Wilson began, "you all know Councilman Kemper. He is here for an informal meeting, and I stress informal, on yesterday's murder of a cross-dresser. As you know, Councilman, Detective Murray is the lead detective on the Carlyle case. I believe he is prepared to give us an up-to-date report on this new murder."

Kemper twisted in his chair and used the opening to jump in. "We've got a serial killer on our hands and there seems to be little progress on finding him. The citizens of our great city deserve some action. There is fear in the San Fernando Valley and throughout—"

"Save the political speeches, Alan," Wilson interrupted, visibly annoyed. "Cliff, give us that update now because the councilman plans to hold a news conference this afternoon and he is certain someone will ask about the latest murder."

Murray appeared annoyed as he opened the folder. "This is case number H 1276 out of Devonshire. Lead detectives are Wyatt Johnson and Bruno Ustaski. At 1750 hours a 911 call came in from—"

"Dammit, let's skip the cop lingo," Kemper interrupted. "Just give me a capsule picture."

Murray looked up at Wilson who nodded.

"The young man murdered was Brett Holland, 23 years old, a student at CSUN, and a resident of Encino. He lived with his parents who confirm that he was going to a Frat House Halloween party dressed as a chamber maid. He had a mustache and a Van Gough-style beard and there seemed to be no evidence that he was a serious cross-dresser. Instead of high heels, he had on military style boots on at the time of the murder."

"I understand he was stabbed and there was make-up involved similar to the other two cases, isn't that right,

Detective?" Kemper puffed out his chest like a wrestler winning a match.

If he knew so much, why ask? I thought.

"He was stabbed but the wound was such that he could have survived had he been transported to a hospital in time. Seems nobody in the neighborhood called 911 soon enough so the kid bled out." Murray was visibly shaken in reading the report which, for him, was not the cold indifference that a hardened detective ought to have. After a moment he continued. "Yes, there was make-up involved, but he was made up in the exaggerated way that clowns portray themselves to be funny and not in a way to seriously look like a woman. And there was only the one color of lipstick and not two. There are more dissimilarities. Burgess and Carlyle were not robbed of jewelry and money. Holland's ring, watch, and the cash from his wallet were taken. Also, there is no connection to the Velvet Glove bar. The first two murders took place in hidden areas behind buildings. Holland was stabbed once and robbed right on Zelzah Avenue, not far from the university."

"I don't buy it and I don't think the public is going to buy that there is no connection between these three murders." Kemper pounded on the arm of his chair. "The committee meets tomorrow and I'm certain they will want answers about the progress. Are you telling me the only solid witness in the Carlyle case is the woman with bad eyesight and across the street from the murder scene who was coming home from work?"

"Other than her, we have a possible lead in a young man named Stanley Gorecki, but not much more," Murray added.

Kemper frowned and looked shaken, then recovered enough to continue his tirade. "The people of Los Angles deserve answers to these gruesome murders," he shouted.

"Only if they're guys dressed as women," Fryman commented.

"Do you think this is funny, Detective Fryman?" Kemper growled.

"Thank God the entire council is not running for re-election," Wilson interjected, which seemed to work because Kemper sniffed and quieted down. "What about the suspect in the current murder?" Wilson added.

Murray opened one of the manila folders again and flipped through a series of papers. He placed a booking picture on Wilson's desk as Kemper craned his neck to see. "The suspect, a Michael Shoemacher, 30 years old with a rap sheet that includes two felonies and three misdemeanors. He's done time in county jail as well as prison at Susanville in Northern California. He's a veteran of Desert Storm and is registered at the Mission Hills Veteran's Hospital. They have a saliva sample which is being tested for a DNA match with what they got from under the victim's fingernails. Johnson writes that they had a 911 call from a witness who saw the stabbing from her front window. She was getting ready to turn on lights and set out a candy bowl for trick-or-treaters. She said she panicked and turned off all the lights in the house and hid in her bathroom behind a locked door. She eventually found the courage to make the 911 call."

There was a long period of silence.

"Shoemacher lawyered up even before he was Mirandized," Murray said.

"So it's possible that he could have killed Burgess and Carlyle, too," Kemper said. "Gentlemen, you must understand the pressure we are under, not only from the general public but from the cross-dresser community as well. Their local convention is being held this weekend in Burbank and I have been asked to speak to the group because of my position on the City Council. Needless to say they are more than passionate about the Carlyle murder and probably now this."

"And it won't hurt your campaign either." Wilson's sardonic aside was ignored.

Fryman straightened up and threw both hands into the air like a referee at a football game. "Cross-dressers have a convention?"

"I'm told this is a local chapter. The national convention is held in April sometime. We certainly want this cleared up by then." Kemper was adamant.

As a lowly patrol officer dressed in dirty jeans and a faded dodger tee shirt, I felt out of place with the four well-dressed men in their volley of digs, insults, contradictions, and asides thrown between equals. I expected Kemper, at any moment, to ask what I was doing at the meeting.

Instead, he stood with great dramatic flair. His temper appeared to have cooled. "I have two committee meetings this afternoon and since I am the chairman of the Police Oversight committee I need to be prepared for questions. Thank you very much, gentlemen. You've given me nothing." He turned on his heel and headed for the door, where he stopped and turned. "There is no doubt in my mind that our community is being terrorized by a serial killer who has struck several times in a very short period of time. And presumably one of the best police departments in the country has come up with nothing. Unbelievable, gentlemen."

As he left, he gave me more than a double take as though I was an intruder on inside information. It was not his looking at me that bothered me, but the way he did it. I detected a slight hint of a frown as if he were recognizing something.

Wilson sat down and sighed. "Politics is a dirty business."

"I'm not so sure he isn't reveling in these recent murders," Murray said. "Nobody can be that blind to facts unless there was an election advantage."

"Or he's got some strange motive for his zeal," Wilson said. "Maybe we should be checking this guy out."

"Who the hell is running against this turkey?" Fryman asked.

"What do we know about Kemper and why he's got such a hard on for these murders," Murray asked.

"Fact remains we still have very little to go on in the Carlyle case." Wilson said then he shouted, "Espinoza." I jumped with surprise and a little fright. "I want you to check out this local convention he plans to speak at."

"Do you want me to go?"

"Only if you think you can carry it off. Do you think there's any risk in Kemper recognizing you? I mean in your cross-dress outfit."

"No chance," Fryman blurted. "I've seen this number in her—er, his—outfits and I tell you I felt a little tightening in my shorts."

"You know what," I said. "Fuck you, Detective Fryman."

"Now, now," he cooed like a mourning dove. "This is no time to speak of love."

Wilson laughed then turned very serious. "Do you think you can get that guy Stan to go with you? It might help to have a cover as well as get more information from him."

"Will he need backup on this?" Murray asked.

"Have we ruled out Stan as a suspect?" Wilson was sincere in his question.

I had, but I wasn't sure that Fryman and Murray shared my opinion.

"We have nothing concrete on him," Murray answered.

"I don't need any backup, provided he agrees to go." I wasn't that eager to go myself but I wanted Wilson to see me as a team player.

"I don't want you out there in the cold," Wilson said. "You guys back him up. Take a couple of uniforms with you."

I began to understand why I hated this assignment. Perhaps being a detective was not such a good idea, after all. Everybody seemed to be in it for their own gain. Even me, I thought, because ambition required stepping on friends and foes alike. I wondered what it was that made them think Stan was a murderer. What made me think he wasn't? Was I making the mistake of letting my feelings color my ability to reason and, thereby, distorting my police work?

I had to talk to Stan ASAP.

Chapter 21

Gutter Ball

I stopped at the Virginia newsstand on Victory Boulevard and bought the *LA Times,* knowing that the paper would put news of the Brett Holland murder on the front page and bury today's death toll of the Afghanistan war on a back page. I guessed that they weighed the value of one murder against that of fifteen soldiers. I was right. The lead story covered the few details detectives gave the reporters.

The newspaper was going to be my pump primer to get Stan to talk about the murders. I drove to his apartment.

His grandfather answered the door and waved me in as he negotiated his wheel chair back into the living room. "He's in the shower. I'll tell him you're here." With that, the old guy, with good upper body strength, whipped the chair around and disappeared through the dining area.

As I sat and waited, I marveled at how skillfully the paper had produced three columns of information that contained a scant few facts. The old man hollered from the kitchen, "You want something to drink?"

"Water is fine."

When he returned, the two of us faced each other with awkwardness where each waited for the other to open conversation. It felt strange for a motor mouth like me to wait for an opening to talk. When I finally did speak, it was stupid.

"How long have you been disabled?"

"I'm not." Just to prove it he got up walked a circle around the wheel chair and then dropped back into it. "It's just that my back gets very weak if I walk too much. I don't want to fall." He opened his bible and pulled on one of the purple ribbon markers.

"Deuteronomy gives us good advice and cautions for living," he began. "Chapter 22 verse 5. You best give it a read, sonny boy."

I tried to guess his age but it seemed futile. He could have been anywhere between fifty and eighty.

Some detective I'd make if I couldn't handle simple observations.

Stan appeared, wearing a bright yellow sweater and worn jeans that were much too tight for comfort. My comfort. I wondered if I would be embarrassed to be seen in public with him.

"So where are you boys going?" the old man asked.

Though I was getting used to the reference, I still hated being referred to as a boy.

"Bowling," I snapped.

"Bowling?" Stan said. He looked wide-eyed with amazement with his hands thrust out from his body.

"Yes, bowling."

"I've never bowled in my life."

"You'll learn. Let's go." I tucked the newspaper under my arm and headed for the door.

"Deuteronomy!" the old man yelled after us. "Read it, you sinners!"

I was speechless as Stan trailed after me, both of us trying to be the first one out the door.

As we drove to the Diver Lanes on Magnolia near Cahuenga, Stan read the lead story about the murder. I wanted my questions to flow effortlessly into the subject. "Do you think there's any connection to the Carlyle murder?"

He glanced back to the picture on the front page of Brett Holland. Stan said nothing as he appeared to be studying the face.

"Does he look familiar?" I asked.

He shook his head. "I don't recognize him. For sure, he never came into the Glove." Stan went back to rereading the story. "Says here, he was a student at CSUN. You saw that most of the guys in the bar were all a lot older than college age. You and me are probably the youngest." He turned and stared at me. "What is your birthday?"

"The first week of September."

He bought the vague answer. I tried again to steer the subject without sounding like *Law and Order*. "How old was Carlyle?"

Though I knew his age, I wanted to set up a smoke screen.

"I don't know for sure. Maybe late twenties or early thirties," he said, and then he looked directly at me. "Why?"

"No reason," I said. "Just curious, I suppose." I knew then that I had to tread lightly on the earlier murders. "I just remember you telling me you knew who killed Carlyle."

Stan clammed up and neither of us talked much all through checking in at the bowling alley, putting on shoes, and finding comfortable bowling balls. I gave him gentle instructions at each phase. We sat at our assigned alley and ordered a beer. Of course, I was carded and Stan, too, which was a good beginning to our bonding. I hoped the waitress would not make a comment about my age.

After some quick instruction and two of his gutter balls, I tried again to bring up Carlyle and the convention. The convention seemed the easier of the two.

"Are you going to the CD convention in Burbank this week-end?" I asked after nailing a strike. I wanted it to sound casual and something I considered normal for my abnormal fetish.

"No. I went to the last one," he said. "It was really so boring I left early. I'm actually afraid to go this year."

"Afraid?"

"I'm afraid of who might be there."

"Who?" I wanted to keep him talking even though I was picking up on the fear he was giving off. I knew he meant Burgess and Carlyle's killer, but I didn't want to let on. "You're up."

He got up, stood holding his ball like a pro, and then staggered to the line, and managed a split. He was delighted. "This is fun," he shouted.

Not so loud, I thought, somebody might look at us and see those tight pants. I glance at the score on the screen as he sat down.

"Why don't we both go to the convention?" I suggested.

He said nothing as I missed an easy spare: nine pins.

"I know I'd be safe with you," he began. "You're probably the only real friend I have. Oh, I know a lot of people who come to the bar, but they're not friends. I've been afraid to talk to anybody."

"Stan, you've done nothing wrong. Why not go to the police? From what I hear they will take care of you and possibly put you in what they call a witness protection program. I saw that once on CSI."

"I can't leave my grandfather because he depends completely on me. He has nobody else. I asked him if we could move and he said 'Where would we go?' Then he said, 'My doctors are here.'"

"Who is this guy that's giving you so much fear? Give me a name."

Stan slumped down into the vinyl bench seat and pressed his chin to his chest. He squirmed in discomfort as he rubbed his hands on his knees. I felt like a Benedict Arnold posing as his friend and trying to pump him for vital police information. I wanted him to tell me everything so that I in turn could spill it all to Wilson, Fryman, and Murray. Some friend.

I stood up and showed him how to deliver the ball to put some spin on it and how to not aim at the pins but to line up with the alley's inlaid wood surface. He stood next to me and followed my motions in setting up for the delivery. At that moment, I didn't care if anyone was watching because I was really into teaching him how to bowl.

"Go for it, man," I said, and he made a perfect pitch and knocked down nine pins.

The 7 pin was the only one standing. After my giving him specific instructions, he made a tournament gutter shot, but he seemed happy. I ordered two more beers.

"You know this problem of this killer is not going to go away," I said. "What if he's the same guy who killed the Holland man?"

"He's not." There was no missing the definiteness of his statement. Now, it seemed, *he* was trying to change the subject. "Should I be taking shorter steps when I throw the ball?"

Shorter steps in tight pants would be way too much.

"No. If anything, a longer stride would be better. And you don't throw the ball, you deliver it." His blank expression told me he had no idea of what I was talking about. "How can you be sure he's not?" I said.

Stan nodded his head and pressed his lips together with the determination of a two-year-old.

I pushed harder. "Who is he?"

"Don't make me tell you, Victor. I know you mean well but I just can't."

"I thought we were friends."

"We are. We are. I trust you and I feel safe with you. And I like that our friendship is not based on sex or anything like that. The sex would just ruin everything. But if anything got out about him, he said he'd kill me. So you see if I tell you, then you would be in danger, too."

"If you know so much, why hasn't he killed you already?"

Stan looked away without immediately answering. "Because of the police snitch."

The answer confused me since Captain Wilson said LAPD did not have a snitch working in the cross-dressing community. This was the third time Stan had mentioned one so I decided to try for more.

"How did you get mixed up with him in the first place?"

"If I told you, I'm not sure you'd understand."

"Try me."

The counter man came down to our alley and asked if we were through because there were people waiting for an alley to open. We had not progressed beyond the sixth frame of our first game nor had I progressed beyond point zero in getting information. There was progress, however, on the strange relationship that was developing between Stan and me. He was trusting in our bonding and I was beginning to have empathy for him and his dilemma. It was then that I remembered Captain Wilson's words that there was no room for feelings in police work.

"I'm not sure, but I think it's your turn," Stan said.

I got annoyed at the interruption so I jumped up and pitched a dead straight ball that clunked the lead pin and produced a 7-10 split, which was nearly impossible to make even for me.

"You were going to tell me how you got involved," I said.

"I made a bad choice. It was a one-night stand that he turned into a nightmare. He was strung out on meth and started to tell me stuff that scared me. I went along with his demands that night because I was scared of him. He was like in a trance when he described the murder and then he told me killing someone was not a big deal. Since then he has threatened me if I told anyone about what he said."

When he picked up his ball, I saw his eyes cloud over and one tear formed. He turned his head away from me then put the ball back onto the rack and sat down.

"I don't want to bowl anymore," he said. "Don't make me tell you, Vic."

I heard the pain in his voice. I was determined not to let his pleading deter me or activate any feelings of friendship I might have.

"Who is he, Stan?"

He unlaced his bowling shoes and headed to the counter. He was right. I didn't fully understand how he got involved sexually with a killer. I was beginning to feel his pain.

Chapter 22

FBI Profiler

After Wednesday morning roll call, Fryman, Murray, and I were asked to listen to a report by an FBI profiler Wilson called in to advise us on the Carlyle murder. For me the idea of working with the FBI was exciting and new, but Murray sniffed his disapproval about federal encroachment into a local case.

We filed into the captain's office again and did what we did best: wait.

"Why do we need a profiler?" I asked. "And what the hell is a profiler, anyway?"

Fryman turned to me and put on a mock smile. "There you go again with the Why."

I raised my hands, palms up, and gave him a look that telegraphed "Yes. Why?"

"I'll tell you why," he said. "An FBI profiler is like an overpaid consultant. He comes in, borrows your watch, writes a long report, then tells you what time it is."

"He's supposed to provide us with a psychological fingerprint of the murderer which is supposed to help us identify the suspect, if we had one," Murray chimed in. Just then, Wilson entered, followed not by a he, but by the most beautiful woman with long blonde hair drooped over one eye, wearing a lime-colored blouse that featured cleavage, and a black skirt molded to her body.

She tucked the hair behind her ear and exposed the other hazel eye. The FBI got my immediate attention.

"Gentlemen," Wilson began, "this is special agent Alexi Federovich, from Quantico, Virginia. She is support services of the FBI research division and is here going over the evidence and murder books of the Carlyle and Burgess cases. Introduce yourselves."

When Fryman shook her hand, he cupped it in both of his, and then held it there. She pulled hers out with a tug. Murray took her hand, and when he leaned over, I thought he was going to kiss it. When she came to me, she took my hand and said, "You must be Victor Espinoza."

There it was again, people recognizing me not as a celebrity cop but because of my stature. I wondered what else Wilson told her about me.

"Yes, I am, Miss Feder—"

"Please, call me Alexi," she interrupted.

I liked Alexi not because she was beautiful, though that helped, but because I was a tiny bit taller than her. We settled down in our chairs and sat like schoolboys in love with their teacher. She opened her tablet, pressed a few icons, and then set it on Wilson's desk. At first, she stood in front of us then leaned against Wilson's desk in such a way that her molded skirt showed off her shapely legs and perfectly proportioned butt. It was hard to concentrate on what she was saying because I wondered how I would look in that skirt.

"I have studied hundreds of serial killers, sexual predators, and sadistic murderers. I've interviewed dozens of convicted killers on death row in all parts of the country."

With all that experience, I wondered how old she was and how long she had been a special agent. I guessed her to be the same age as Jannine.

"My job is to give you a profile of the probable personality, traits, characteristics, compulsions, and motivations of the killer."

"You can do that from what little evidence we have in this case?" Murray asked.

"Yes, that's true, Detective Murray. We don't have hard evidence or suspects in this case so we have to rely on the FBI Crime Classification Manual or CCM."

"So, we get a boiler plate," Fryman commented.

"No. Not really. Your killer falls into what we call the 'organized category' with preconceived sexual fantasies. High risk activity is part of him."

"Or her," Fryman said. "Or them."

""Probably not a her," she said. "The idiosyncratic nature of the blue lipstick and the style of cross dressing points to a lone male killer. There is no doubt that the murderer of Burgess is the same man who murdered Carlyle."

"I've known a few idiosyncratic females," Fryman said. "In fact, I dated one a few times."

Alexi's condescending smile caused Fryman to slouch in his chair.

"We really don't have time to go through a litany of your dates," Wilson said. "Please go on, Alexi."

"Let's speculate for a moment," she said. "Your killer is a hermit who works alone, he has preconceived sexual fantasies, he comes from a single parent or no parent childhood, and he has latent homosexual tendencies. It is highly probable that he was abused as a child, by a dominant female. I would estimate his age to be between thirty and fifty."

"In other words, a psycho," Fryman interjected.

"Maybe even a sociopath," she added.

Before she could go on, the office door popped open and JoAnn, the phone operator, stuck her head in.

"We're in a meeting," Captain Wilson said.

"I'm sorry to interrupt, Captain, but it's councilman Kemper. He's called three times and now he wants to stay on hold until you answer."

"Speaking of psychos," Murray said.

"That's okay," Alexi said. "I can come back later. I have more research to do and I'd like to look for any other cold cases that fit the MO."

"Unfortunately, this isn't going to be a quick call," Wilson said. "Let's reconvene in about 30 minutes."

So far, she hadn't told us anything we didn't already know. We all stood up and started for the door.

Alexi turned to me and touched my arm. "Victor, I wonder if we could meet for a few minutes. I have some questions."

Fryman laughed. "Watch out for his latent heterosexual tendencies."

Her waxy smile trumped his attempted joke. She and I found an empty desk in the corner of the squad room. It was quiet and semi-private.

"May I ask you some personal questions?" she said, after a few niceties.

"Sure."

"I understand your undercover work has you meeting and interacting with the patrons of a gay and lesbian night club and you are dressed in women's clothes."

"Captain Wilson wants that kept secret," I said.

"Yes, I know."

"I'm supposed to keep my eyes and ears open to get leads and any other information involving the case."

"And you interact with other cross-dressed men. Am I right?"

"Yes."

"When you say interact does that include having sex with any of the patrons?"

"What? No. Look, Alexi, I'm straight."

Her eyes narrowed into a panther-like stare. "What would you do if you found yourself in a situation where you had no choice?"

"That ain't gonna happen."

"Do you have a particular revulsion toward cross-dressers and gay men?"

"Are you trying to get me off the case?" I asked. "Or are you profiling me?" I was getting angry. "What does this have to do with my assignment?"

"That's not an answer to my question."

"No, I don't. Like I said, for me this is part of my job. But I draw the line against getting it on with anybody with more hair on their chest than me." I was getting defensive. Suddenly she wasn't as beautiful as I'd first thought.

With one eye hidden by hair and the other staring at me in expectation she said, "My graduate degree is in Behavioral Science and of course I'm interested in the socio-sexual dynamics of intra-male relationships, especially in law enforcement settings."

"Huh?"

"What I mean is—" She stopped in mid statement and stood up, and closed her tablet. "Perhaps we can talk again soon about how you got this assignment or was that through some influence in the department."

"I was asked by Captain Wilson."

"You said yes because your curiosity was aroused and you became aware of an alternate side of your identity, dormant within you." She reopened her notebook and began making entries.

"I said yes, not because of all that you were talking about, but because I want to build up my experience so I can be considered for a promotion to detective."

"Oh," she said, "professional ambition would certainly be part of your motives, I'm sure. Most men would deny any interest in alternative sexual exploration not because it would be repugnant to them, but because they would not want their masks stripped away. Your costumes, for instance, become your psychological hiding places."

"Well, I do hide them in my closet, if that's what you mean."

"Aha, just as I thought. The symbolism of the closet is telling." She was almost hyperventilating, yet I had no idea of what she was talking about. "Tell me about your prepubescent sexual experiences," she said.

"You mean, like have I watched any porno as a child or when I jacked—er—masturbated?"

She appeared exasperated. I felt a wall go up that blocked any communication between us even if there wasn't any to begin with.

As she started to leave, I caught her arm, gently of course. "Aren't you going to tell me what time it is?"

Her beautiful cleavage swelled and her eyes widened in disbelief.

"Huh?" she said.

The pupils of those hazel eyes narrowed as they bore into to me. She sat back down and looked over at Fryman sitting at his desk.

"Is that it?" I asked.

"Not yet," she said and pointed at Fryman. "Do you find a kinship with him that expands beyond the emotional and extends into the physical?"

"Sometimes I don't like him, not because he's an asshole, but he's okay."

"Hmm. You've given me valuable information," she said and slammed closed her notebook with such force that her breasts wobbled. "Would you ask Detective Fryman to come over? I will need to interview him and Detective Murray as well."

"Good luck with that," I said, thinking I could be a profiler and work for the FBI. That could be my promotion to detective. Hell, I was already an expert in psycho-sexual behaviors even though I only had an AA degree.

Wilson finished his call and waved us back in.

I dialed Jannine and she answered on the third ring. "Don't tell me you have to work tonight," she said.

"No, but are you interested in some psycho-sexual activity tonight?

"Okay, but what are you going to wear?"

Chapter 23

The Invitation

Despite Captain Wilson's edict not to tell anyone about my undercover involvement in the Carlyle case, I continued to dribble out information to Jannine on a need-to-know basis. She was amazing in how she pieced together the fragments I gave her to produce a fair idea of the plan. She could be a detective. Of course, she understood that everything I told her was top secret as far as LAPD was concerned. It would probably cause repercussions if the leak were traced to me.

Jannine knew about the guy named Greg at the Velvet Glove bar, about the poor soul Stan, about the eye witness, and the mystery man. I didn't tell her about Kemper because she had seen him and Captain Wilson on a television news program. She confessed to knowing about Detective Fryman's conversation with me at my house. I also told her that Captain Wilson was requiring me to attend the Regional Cross Dresser's Convention in Burbank. What I didn't tell her was that Stan knew who the killer was and that he wouldn't tell me for my own protection. In any case, the more I told her, the better my chances were of getting back into bed with her.

Her apartment was on busy Riverside Drive and her bedroom faced the street so car noise was always an issue. It had a way of intruding on the mood. As we lounged in bed after dinner, I decided to bring up the convention again. I forced enthusiasm into my voice when I asked, "Go with me to the Cross Dresser's Convention in Burbank. I think you'll find it interesting."

A frown followed her blank look.

"Lots of wives and girlfriends go to this kind of event," I said.

"Why?"

"How should I know? Maybe they just want to keep an eye on their husbands."

"Well, I do know," she said. "They have workshops, seminars, and special programs on make-up and shopping. I Googled cross dressers and got a whole bunch of information."

"When did you do that?"

"On evenings when you are on your so-called assignment. Did you know that more than half the guys are straight and married? They just have this fetish."

"So do I take that as a yes, you'll go?"

She seemed to ignore me as though she was in a different world. "The convention in Chicago had an attendance of over a thousand," she said. "Imagine that. Well, that got me hooked so I did some more research, and about one percent of the country's population is transvestites of some kind? Who knew?"

"So you'll go."

"Tell me something," she began very tentatively. "When you put on women's clothes does that affect you in any way?"

"Affect me how?"

"Does it cause you to get an—" She stopped abruptly which was not like Jannine since she was always the soul of directness. I rolled toward her and waited. Suddenly she blurted out, "—an erection."

It made me laugh. "Are you serious?"

"Yes, I am. Because what I read was that men wearing women's clothes and underwear causes them to be erotically stimulated."

"If I tell you it does, will you go?"

"No. It's way too strange for me."

"Me too, but I have to go."

"If you were a real cross dresser, I'd go. But, you're just a shill in a shawl."

"You know, in high heels I'm almost as tall as you are?" We fell silent for a long while and then I said, "You know what stimulates me erotically?"

"What?"

"Not my psycho-sexual profile—you."

She rolled toward me and traced her forefinger along my nose, lips, and chin. She smiled, leaned in, and whispered in my ear, "I love you."

"Regardless of how tall I am even I high heels?"

"In spite of the fact that you're a motor mouth, I love you because you don't try to be a controlling macho-man. You're sensitive, sexy, and sometimes a little stupid."

She kissed me again and all the electric cells in my body woke up. I propped myself on one elbow, cradled my head in my hand, and just took in her beauty. It was a beauty that overrode her smelly peach shampoo. I wondered if this classified as prepubescent sexual activity. I completely forgot about wanting to be a macho man and controlling, but her comment "sometimes a little stupid" hung in the back of my head.

"Since we're playing true confessions, I have to tell you I can't picture my life without you," I said, choking back an emotion tugging at my throat. "Jesus, is this me talking this way?"

She scooted in closer to me.

"What do you mean a little stupid?" I asked

"You just want to have sex."

"Funny you should say that because—Oh, yes, I do, but when we do have sex it feels like the two of us become sort of like one." I was on the verge of more confessions and I couldn't understand why. I felt so comfortable having frank discussions with Jannine about my feelings, my fears, and my joys. If she had pushed any closer to me, she would have been behind me. "I love you," I said. "I truly do."

"Is this a bad time to talk about marriage and family?"

Her question was tentative and hesitant. She had me in a vulnerable pin down since I was losing control over my mind. Even the thought of babies usually had me on the brink of hives, but this time it got me excited and happy.

"I say let's plan our wedding right after this current assignment of mine is over."

"Oh, I see," she said, "the assignment comes first—as usual."

"No, it doesn't. You are the most important person in my life, but I'm not so sure about babies right away?"

"I don't see how marriage is going to interfere with your job."

There was a tiny hint of confrontation in her voice; a minefield I had to avoid.

"Are you serious about the babies part?" she continued.

I felt a lump in my throat that almost immobilized me and kept me from speaking. We were silent for a long time.

"Victor, you can put on women's clothes, you can talk and act like a woman, but you can't feel like a woman," she said finally in a serious voice. "You just can't know the drive that a woman has to give birth. I can't explain it because it's kinda primal."

"Babies by all means, but one at a time," I said, "and spaced apart."

"Well, the best means to achieve that goal is you know what. Let's start right now. Tomorrow I stop taking the pill."

"Oh, no. No, no, no, no. Your parents, and mine too, would kill me if you got pregnant before we announced the wedding. Besides, it wouldn't look good for a cop to be walking up to the altar with a shotgun pointed at his back."

"Who cares? I'm stopping the pill tomorrow. And if you don't want me to get pregnant, then that means you know what—no sex."

I pushed back the covers and those two beautiful breasts beckoned. I kissed each, and then inched my way down to her navel. I looked up expecting to see two glazed eyes staring at the ceiling but, instead, she just smiled.

"Remember, no sex," she said.

"There's always Clinton style of no sex," I said and continued kissing and exploring.

Moments later her sighs and heavy breathing were drowning out the street noises. Soon her hands reached down and gripped my shoulders as her fingernails dug into my skin. I no longer had thoughts of conventions, murders, dresses, and make-up. I was swallowed into the zone of her wonderful body's aroma. We passed from consciousness to forfeiting control to ancient biological forces that drove the mystery of life.

In movies, the lingering glow after lovemaking involved smoking a cigarette but neither of us smoked so we had our own special afterglow. Two bodies, arms and legs entwined like serpents, softly breathing, eyes half closed, returned to the real world at a pace only love understands. Though I had not reached an orgasm, a contented satisfaction fulfilled me.

The fictitious, real world came inching back when I yelled, "So, what do you think?"

"About what?"

"Will you go to the convention with me?"

It was the wrong thing to say because within seconds, we untangled and she headed to the bathroom. I heard the shower start.

Through the door she yelled, "I think you're looking forward to it."

"You could meet some of the wives and talk about their problems," I said.

We were shouting at each other through a closed door, competing with the street noises.

"Are you planning to cross-dress after we're married?"

"Only if it turns you on."

She emerged from the bathroom with just a towel draped around her. Delayed gratification only lasts for so long with me.

She stopped next to the bed and whispered, "Now where did we leave off?"

Chapter 24

Convention

Cross dressers held local conventions and a once-a-year national get-together in some major city. Wilson was convinced that attendance at the TRI-ESS convention in Burbank was mandatory since there was the possibility that the killer could be there to canvas possible new targets. I didn't understand his reasoning. Why would a killer, who stabbed his victims in out-of-the-way locations during the dead of night, attend a crowded public convention? I wondered if he had some inside information that he was keeping from us.

The plans included both Fryman and Murray and at least one black-and-white with two uniformed patrolmen as additional back-up. The officers would remain outside, since gaining access for uniformed policeman would create a stand-off with the organizers of the convention. The sight of a badge would put a damper on the proceedings.

The captain arranged for cooperation between police

jurisdictions since the Marriott was covered by the City of Burbank Police Department and out of the city of LA. It was Fryman and Murray that would present the greatest hurdle since they could not gain entry to the full program in street clothes.

Even if they dressed as women, they would still look like cops.

"No way," said Fryman. "I'm not putting on a wig and a dress to be at some drag show program. Sorry."

He stood his ground and Murray was with him. I couldn't picture either one of them trying to show a creative effort at being convincing women. I thought they were just barely convincing as men.

"After the first time you dress up, it's not so bad," I said. "Who knows? You might like it. For sure, you would look better than you do now."

Fryman gave me the finger. "Fuck you."

It felt good to have him at the butt end of a taunt. It also made me feel like I was approaching a sense of equality with them. Wilson just sat back and smiled.

"Maybe we can get the hotel to let us pose as waiters during the dinner and as a clean-up crew in the vendor presentation section," Murray suggested.

"No, that will prompt too many questions as to why LAPD would want to be in the ballroom at a cross-dresser's convention," said Wilson. "That won't work. Victor, you'll wear a wire and you two will stay in the parking lot near the entrance."

"There's not much chance the killer is going to attempt anything in a crowded area where he could risk being taken down by some of the guests and staff," I said.

"I agree. After all, these are guests in five-inch heels," Fryman said. "They can hardly take down their panties."

"I don't see this as any different than me at the

Glove. Why do we need back-up?" I said, hoping to aggravate Fryman.

Wilson made the final decision, which included me wearing a wire and two black-and-whites in the parking lot with Fryman and Murray. A few more cops on the scene and we could have our own convention.

After the meeting, I phoned Stan to let him know what time I would pick him up. Then I was struck with a horror. I heard myself discussing with him what color and style of dresses we would wear. He planned on wearing his off-the-shoulder cut in royal blue and I would wear the long gold dress with a feather boa around my neck to hide my Adam's apple. The full-length dress covered the only comfortable high-heeled shoes I owned. It also hid the Smith and Wesson in the holster strapped to my thigh.

ⱻↄⱻↄ

When we walked into the main ballroom for the opening presentation, you'd have thought we were on the runway at a Paris fashion show. We took seats to the right of the main stage at a table for eight that had two places remaining. Stan's dress was so tight he could barely sit. I wondered how many of the women in attendance actually had vaginas and how many had surgically fashioned ones.

Earlier we had walked through the vendor areas and picked up brochures and free gifts, ranging from perfume samples to beard covering make-up. The main ballroom was nearly full. Pastel colored swags hung from the chandeliers to the sidewalls, giving the feeling of a wedding reception.

I leaned in to Stan and whispered, "Do you recognize anybody here?"

Just then, the lights dimmed and a tall, thin man

walked up to the microphone at center stage. He was dressed in a women's business suit that had shoulder pads. The pads, along with his own broad shoulders, made his body look like an Isosceles triangle, upside down. He pounded the podium with a small mallet and blared over the P.A. system, "Take your seats everyone, please."

"It's hard to tell in this light," Stan said, "but I do see that Greg is here at that end table."

The speaker addressed the crowd and drew a slight twitter with, "Good evening, ladies, and ladies." He laughed at his own quasi-joke.

Waiters scattered through the room, filling water glasses and pouring wine. It was no surprise that the fare was chicken, string beans, and mashed potatoes. The following day's agenda was announced and a few business items were read. Near the end of the meal, the host introduced the featured speaker.

"It is a great honor for me to introduce a man who has served two terms as City Councilman for Los Angeles. He is head of the oversight committee to the LAPD Police Commission. Best of all he is a true friend of TRI-ESS. Please give a warm welcome to Mr. Alan Kemper."

The applause—amid some scattered grumbles—was less than enthusiastic. He stepped to the microphone, teeth gleaming, and raised a fist into the air. The scattered applause died down and his fist was still in the air. The councilman droned on about the progress made through the cooperation of the community, the police, and the city council in bringing down the crime rate. He credited the council for passing several new ordinances recommended by representatives of the LGBT community.

Someone in the audience shouted out, "What about the serial murders?"

It triggered some angry catcalls and applause. After a

few minutes of shouting, the host pounded the gavel, took the microphone, and announced, "Councilman Kemper has agreed to take questions at the completion of his talk."

After some muted exchanges, the crowd quieted down.

I turned to Stan. "This is bullshit. Let's go get a drink at the bar."

When we stood to leave and, because our table was so close to the podium, Kemper stopped speaking and watched us make our way to the exit. I assumed he thought we were making some kind of a statement because he pointed at us. "It's this kind of defiance that impedes our progress toward reasoned solutions to our problems." To me it sounded like more political bull since he was running for reelection in less than six months. Besides, there was nothing to be gained by listening to his diatribe. I'd heard much of it from Wilson.

The bar in the lobby had only a few customers quietly drinking and watching a Chicago Bull's basketball game on a large flat screen. Stan and I joined two other cross dressers who also skipped the speech. We joked about introducing each other by women's names.

Two men, sitting nearby, started talking very loudly to the bartender, mainly for our benefit. "Since when did you start letting faggots in here?"

The cross dresser next to him shot back with, "It takes one to know one, dearie."

In a flash, the guy was off his stool and in the face of our friend. "Who you callin' queer, you faggot piece of shit?"

"You, asshole," came the rebuttal.

Pushing and shoving began. Bar stools were knocked over and a cocktail glass was thrown to the back of the bar. The guy's friend stepped into the fight and it became a two on one melee. I was certain that Fryman and Murray could hear the fighting and shouting coming from my wire. Their mission was to protect me and not enter into anything that was not the jurisdiction of the LAPD Robbery Homicide Division involving the Carlyle case.

The bartender yelled, "Knock it off, NOW," but the command fell on deaf ears.

When the two bigots got our cross-dressed man down on the floor, their fists pounding and kicking him, I could no longer stand by. I kicked off my high heels and jumped into the fray.

I pulled off the taller of the two, pummeled him in the stomach with my right while my left missed a swing at his jaw. The other man stopped and seemed to watch the action. The tall guy swung at me and grazed my shoulder giving me just enough time to upper cut him twice until he fell backward. He started to get up and I drop kicked him up against a stool. The others at the bar moved backward to give us more room. He started up again. I pushed him backward which knocked his head on the steel legs of the barstool. He was out cold.

The second guy lunged toward me, however, I sidestepped and he passed to my left side. I opened my hand and chopped him in the back of the neck, an action that was the direct product of the excellent training I received at the academy. When he looked back at me, I landed a roundhouse curve to his left cheek that staggered him. He fell to the floor. My feather boa had fallen into his face, which caused him to sputter and spit, so I took advantage of the garment malfunction, and finished him off with a knee to the groin. He rolled backward, next to his friend, writhing in pain. Unbeknownst to me the bartender called the police during the fight and looked amazed that they had shown up in less than two minutes.

Two uniformed cops burst through the lobby door

and into the bar to come upon a scene that had two men sprawled on the floor and one cross dresser with a bloody nose and a torn dress leaning against the bar. The crowd all started to speak at once to the cops as they looked around in confusion. I readjusted my wig, which had tilted to one side and covered one of my eyes. After straightening it, I noticed that one of the cops was Aaron, my partner. I stepped behind Stan in somewhat of a panic. "We gotta go," I whispered to Stan.

I began to back up pulling Stan with me, but Aaron called out, "Hold it minute, ladies," and we froze.

"Were you a witness to this?" Aaron said.

I mustered a high-pitched voice and answered, "Witnesses? No, we weren't witnesses."

For once I wasn't technically lying—a participant, yes, but a witness, no.

There was a long and uncomfortable pause as the two cops studied us.

Aaron gave me a strange look. "Okay, you can go." He then looked around. "Who can tell me what happened here?"

In the silence that enveloped the room, we heard the sound of a siren wailing louder as it came closer to the building. The bartender said he saw nothing. The two guys on the floor whimpered and remained silent. Just before we left, two uniformed Burbank Policemen walked through the door. The well-groomed officers, with perfectly pressed shirts, walked to the bar and helped the two bigots stand up and lean against each other.

"Did someone here call the police?" one asked.

"I—I did," the bartender sputtered and looked at the two L.A. Policemen and then the two Burbank Policemen. He was definitely confused.

"False alarm," Aaron said.

No one was willing to give testimony least of all the two bigots. The Burbank cops took out notepads and began questioning anyone who would talk. Aaron and his new partner turned to leave, when suddenly he stopped and looked back at me just as we were backing out the door, heading for the ballroom.

We got back to our seats as Kemper was winding up his speech about each citizen taking responsibility for the community's well-being. "We must shun the notion that conflict can be resolved through violence," he droned.

"That cop looked at you kinda funny," Stan whispered to me. "Have you been arrested before for street fighting or something? Oh my God, you were great."

I glanced down at my false breasts where the wire was hidden. "I've had my run-ins with policemen and detectives in the past. They're really a bunch of pussies."

"Where did you learn to fight like that?" Stan asked.

"I watch a lot of James Bond movies. Have you seen *Skyfall*?"

I knew Stan to be a movie buff so my distraction worked and he started in on reliving his favorite movies. There were no more questions about me. I began to feel guilty about using someone whom I'd started to regard as a good friend. Stan's innocence was neither naïve nor gullible because it was genuine. I was getting blind to his feminine persona.

Kemper had finished his talk and the boisterous crowd finished their questions. When I looked up, I saw Kemper off to one side of the platform studying Stan and me. I was sure he recognized me from the meeting in Wilson's office. He came down the steps and walked directly to us. I turned and started toward the door and Stan followed.

"Just a minute," Kemper called out. "Would you mind answering a few questions?"

I stopped, held my breath, and turned toward him as he caught up.

"Thank you," he said. "I'm curious. Why did you walk out in the middle of my talk? Was it something I said that offended you? Stan, I thought that was rude of you, considering."

"No," I said. "We all had some business to take care of." I intentionally pitched my voice, spoke in an exaggerated southern drawl, and hoped he wouldn't connect me to the meeting in Wilson's office. Stan looked at me with a quizzical expression. "We have to go now. You all keep up the good work, honey," I said. We turned and quick-stepped straight to the exit. "We're going to sit in the lobby now," I said to Stan but actually, it was meant for Fryman and Murray. Stan gave me a confused look.

"Is that an order?" he said.

As we settled into a lobby couch, Greg pushed out through the double doors, saw us, waved, and headed our way. Stan and I exchanged a knowing glance.

"Get ready for Greg, aka Pauline," Stan said.

Greg was one of those people who talked with their hands, touching every available spot on your body while at the same time gushing insincerities. *This*, I thought *will really confuse Fryman and Murray.*

Stan and I hardly spoke a word until I finally interrupted Greg with, "We were just leaving, Greg." I stood up and extended my hand for a handshake. Then for the wire's benefit, I said, "Greg, I didn't get your last name."

"Please, it's Pauline. Pauline Beckett, but you can call me anytime." Greg sashayed back to the main ballroom.

"Well," I said, "I guess we could stay here and kill some time or we could go over to Jimmy's and have a drink on the way home."

I was anxious to get back on the trail of finding out

what Stan knew. He opened his mouth as if to speak but nothing came out. Even his heavy make-up couldn't hide the fear that came over his face. His eyes widened and his mouth dropped open when I intentionally said the magic word: Jimmy's.

It was no easy trick talking to Stan, Fryman, and Murray at the same time. I was certain they would think that Jimmy was a real person and not a bar.

Chapter 25

Jimmy's

The Carlyle murder had hit a stone wall. Wilson was getting pressure for progress from the chief of police, who, in turn, was getting pressure from the mayor and the city council. The *L.A. Times* was filling its headlines and the OpEd page with critical reporting and city hall had received a record numbers of calls and emails from citizens about the case. The LGBT Center in Los Angeles was pressing for the Burgess and Carlyle murders to be classified as hate crimes so the resources of the FBI could come to the aid of LAPD.

Fryman and Murray were getting pressure from Wilson. I was the only one not in the pressure loop since my role was to get information and pass it on. The fact that I had not produced much in the way of leads we could follow was beginning to worry me. Unless there was a breakthrough in the case, I would probably be going back to patrolman duties with Aaron and the Carlyle murder would soon become a cold case. Without some solid information that pointed toward success, my efforts would probably be entered as a foot-note in the files. Footnotes carried no weight on an application for a detective position or any promotion.

Fryman, Murray, and I reviewed the tapes of the two-day convention in Burbank and came to the conclusion that it was a waste of time. They replayed the section of tape during the fight and asked pointed questions of what was going on. The wire did not pick up a clear signal of the exchange at the bar and I gave a vague explanation of why I was there during the disturbance. Aaron did not file a report because the two victims did not want further embarrassment. Nobody pressed charges and the Burbank Police just shrugged their shoulders and left.

I had made a decision to go after some of the leads that Stan had given me in strict confidence. What could be wrong in checking out the bar on Ventura Boulevard to see if there might be a few new avenues to pursue? Besides, I would be a hero around the office if I could bring in some new information we could sink our bulldog teeth into. There had to be a reason why Stan did not want anyone snooping around at Jimmy's bar. My safety would be assured if I entered as a lady, commanding respect. My confidence level about my ability to pass was at its peak. I had cut down my face preparation from an hour and ten minutes to a mere thirty. Dressing, buttons, and scarves around my neck were a snap now.

This particular day, however, I spent over an hour with make-up and another half hour dressing. I had to pass, not as a lady dressed to the nines but as a business woman stopping for a drink after work. This would be my first appearance alone in a place that didn't cater to cross-dressers. My debut, so to speak, would be the real test of the new Victor Espinoza in public.

I entered Jimmy's in full dress, including a large purse and a shawl. The place was indeed rough and dirty

and I felt seriously out of place. The odor of stale cigarettes, beer, and alcohol lingered, despite the city's no-
indoor-smoking laws. There was even a faint odor of
urine.

Several tables along one wall, a shuffle board along a
back wall, and an L-shaped bar along the opposite wall
made up Jimmy's. Six grizzly patrons slumped against
the bar, with nobody at the tables, looked as if they were
refugees from Fourth and Main Street's skid row downtown. The bartender didn't look up nor did the waitress
sitting on the end barstool.

I sat at a table and waited, but nobody came to wait
on me. One scruffy customer twisted around and looked
me over, then returned to his almost empty glass of beer.
The bartender rinsed glasses and the barmaid took long
drags on a cigarette, exhaling the smoke into the air
above her. After a while, I got up and stood at the bar.
Still there was no attempt to wait on me.

"Can I get a light beer, please?" I called out.

The bartender stacked glasses and, without looking
up, said, "We don't serve queers here."

Apparently, my outfit was not very convincing since
I couldn't pass even in a poorly lit saloon. I was determined so I sat on a barstool and the ripped vinyl top
caught a section of my dress.

I blurted out an, "Oh. Shit."

The bartender looked up and yelled, "Get out."

There was so much venom in his words, I wondered
about my safety. With no Fryman and Murray waiting in
a car outside, I felt a slight twinge of fear in my stomach.
As I sat deciding what I should do, two young men entered, walked directly to the end of the bar, and stood behind the seated waitress. Whispers were exchanged between them. She got up and opened a drawer behind the
bar, took out a package, and handed it to the taller man,

who left. The shorter man waited then answered a cell phone call. He nodded to the waitress, pulled out an envelope tucked inside his shirt, handed it to her, and he too left a short while later.

I waited for my beer.

I mustered up as much nerve as any good policeman should. "I have a message for Tony."

It was like dropping a bomb on Hiroshima because the tension in the air encompassed everyone, even the indifferent bartender.

The bar maid and the bartender stared at me. Two of the men seated nearby lifted their heads and looked in my direction. She snuffed out her cigarette and disappeared into the back room. The only sound in the room was a low level of rap music playing from an iPod base behind the bar. What sounded like an argument from the back was drowned out when the bartender turned up the volume. Several customers near the front door got up and left. I opened my purse and touched my .38 for some self-reassurance. I held my hand there for several seconds then finally drew out a compact, opened it, and looked at myself in the mirror.

I wondered if I looked as scared as I felt in my throat. I closed the compact and squeezed it until I could feel my racing heartbeat in the palm of my hand. What did I expect? Stan told me this was a rough bar. Worse still, he told me to stay away from this place. What the hell did I expect to find out?

The barmaid returned and nodded at the bartender. She walked up behind me and stood there.

"What do you want?" she asked.

"A lite beer," I said.

The remaining two customers left. It was just the waitress, the bartender, and me in the din of loud rap music.

She brought me the beer and demanded payment. I lifted the bottle to take a sip and set it right back down immediately because my hand was shaking. I took out a ten-dollar bill and handed it to her.

She stood there holding the money. "There is no Tony here."

There was no move to get me change so I assumed there would be none. "Can I leave a message?" I asked.

"We don't take messages," the bartender blared from the end of the bar.

I took a sip of my beer and stared directly at him. He didn't flinch. I took another long sip of my drink and stood up in an exaggerated ladylike way. I did my best to give my response a sense of bravado.

"Tell him I'll be back tomorrow at six o'clock."

It was an academy award performance that was more like a pissing match.

"Get the fuck out of here and don't come back," the bartender growled like a pit bull.

"Tell him I'm a friend of Stan's."

The bartender walked out from behind the bar and stood directly in front of me. "Do I have to grab you by your bloomers and throw you out?"

By this time, I was on the verge of wetting my bloomers so I made the decision to leave. I walked sideways to the door, stepped outside, took a few steps away, and then leaned against the building. I was still shaking and, after a few minutes, I began to breathe normally again. I started walking slowly North on Ventura and felt a strange uneasiness. I stopped, turned around, and saw the bartender watching me from outside the bar. I knew I had come to the right place but I was coming away with nothing. I wasn't even sure of what I expected. Why was he so belligerent? Who did the waitress talk to in the back room?

After I turned the corner to the side street where I'd parked my car, I took out my iPhone and dialed Stan's number. After the fourth ring, he answered. "Hey," he said.

"Stan. How are you?"

"What's wrong? Why are you asking how I am?"

"Can't I ask?"

"Well…yes. Where are you? Are you drunk? Are you using?"

"No. I'm sober. You know me. My max is two drinks and I've only had two sips of a beer that cost me ten bucks."

"Where?"

"I went to that bar you were telling me about on Ventura Boulevard, Jimmy's"

There was a long silence at the other end of the line. It became uncomfortable. I heard him breathing and, in the background, I could hear his grandfather asking who was calling.

"Stan?" I asked.

"Why did you do that?"

"I just thought it might be interesting to try some new place."

"What is it you're after? Why did you go there?" He was shouting into the phone. "Did you say anything? Why would you do this?"

I detected fear in his voice. No, not fear—panic. "I just wanted to check it out. I was curious."

"For what? Oh my God. I'm fucked."

"What are you talking about? Nothing happened. They just don't like gays coming in there."

"Were you dressed?"

I knew he meant did I wear women's clothes. "I was, but—"

"We're both fucked," he yelled so loud I thought the

tiny speaker in my iPhone would rupture. "Did you mention anything about the murders or say anything about the Glove?"

"No. Of course not. What are you getting so upset about?"

"Was Tony there?"

I said nothing. How could I explain that I knew he was even though I didn't actually see him?

"No, he wasn't. I tried to leave a message but they claimed there was nobody there named Tony. That was it. I left."

Stan hung up and I realized my mistake. He was genuinely upset and I knew I was on to something significant. I headed for his apartment.

Chapter 26

Confession

When I got to Stan's apartment, I rang the door-bell several times with no answer. I started pounding on the door until it opened and stopped about two inches because of the chain lock. I could see his grandfather in his wheel chair.

I caught a glimpse of the barrel of his gun pointed directly at me.

"Who are you?"

I had on different women's clothes and he didn't recognize me at first, so at least I wasn't a total failure at passing.

"It's me, Mr. Gorecki, Victor Espinoza. I'm a friend of Stan's."

The door closed again and I could hear him talking to his grandson. It didn't sound like an argument, yet it was high-pitched conversation. I heard the chain being removed and when the door opened it was Stan, looking as if he had been crying. He said nothing and disappeared into his bedroom with me following.

Behind me, I heard the old man shouting, "Behold, the devil is about to cast you into the fire. Apocalypse two."

I closed the door to the bedroom.

"What is it with you, Victor? I don't get it."

There were two suitcases lying open on his bed. One was partially packed. He grabbed a stack of shirts and tossed them into the empty case. Women's garments were tossed onto a chair in the corner of the room.

"Where are you going? And why?" I asked.

"I'm not telling you anything. I've already told you too much."

"Maybe I can help."

"Victor, you haven't been straight with me. I've told you everything. I trusted you. And you?" He paused and looked out the window. "What do I know about you? The only thing I know is that you have a girlfriend that you're not that crazy about. That's it. You better be straight with me because we both may be dead soon."

He sat on the edge of the bed, cradled his head in his hands, and began to cry. A strange feeling came over me because I too came close to crying. At that moment, I didn't see him as a suspect in a murder or even a person of interest with important information. I saw him as a friend who was in trouble because of my stupidity.

I sat down next to him, put my arm around his shoulders, and just let him weep the torrents of tears that fell into his lap. We sat this way for several minutes until he finally stood and began packing again.

"Stan, if you feel you are in danger, I'm certain the police can help."

He gave me a sardonic laugh. "Are you crazy?" He slammed shut the full suitcase. "You know, what I don't understand is why you are so interested in stirring things up? Why do you keeping pumping me about the two murders?"

"I've been trying to figure how I can help you."

"I can't figure it. Who are you?"

I remained silent hoping this line of questions would end.

"Well, you better start trying to figure out how you can help yourself," he said, " because they could figure you know too much and decide to silence you—for good."

"Who are *they*?"

Was he referring to more than one killer and what would their motive be? Despite the trouble I would suffer by going against Wilson's order of secrecy, I felt I needed to tell Stan the set-up. Despite Fryman and Murray considering him a suspect, I was sure they were wrong.

"Okay, I'm going to be straight with you. I'm an LAPD patrol officer on a special undercover assignment."

"Yeah, sure. And I'm Queen Elizabeth the third."

"I'm not kidding." I pulled out my left falsie pressed it apart and showed him my badge and my ID card.

"Now will you believe me that I can help you?"

"Jesus, Victor, this gets worse all the time. Either those are phony or we are both doomed. I don't get it. Why would they need you as an undercover operation when they have a snitch already working with them?"

"You've said that before. Who is it?"

"I don't know the name but I do know that information gets out before it's official or anybody else knows anything about it."

He finished packing the second suitcase just as the front doorbell rang. After creeping silently to the bedroom door, he signaled his grandfather to not answer. The bell rang again.

The three of us held our positions like statues in a museum. Mr. Gorecki held the gun pointed at the door. Stan made his way to the front window and stood behind the drape, peeking through a small slit at the side. The bell rang again. There was no sound coming from outside of the door, no rattling of the doorknob, and no pounding on the door. More than three minutes passed with no sounds of knocking or ringing of the doorbell.

Stan held his position for several more minutes as he peered out the window until finally he stepped back and announced, "They're gone."

"Who was it?" I asked.

"I don't know. I've never seen them before."

"Did you see the car they were driving?"

"No. They disappeared up the street."

"You gotta let us help. We can keep you and your grandfather safe while we pursue the killer or killers. You have to tell me the truth of what you know about Burgess and Carlyle."

"The truth? Who the hell knows anything anymore? Are you really a cop? Do you really have a girlfriend? Are you really my friend or are you still faking it? The truth is bullshit. I have to take care of myself and him." He glanced over at the old man still pointing the gun at the door.

"Don't tell him anything." Mr. Gorecki mumbled. He waved the gun around the room and then pointed at me. "You better get out of here and leave us alone."

"Pa, I'm going to pack up your stuff. For now, we'll just take a few changes of clothes and your medications."

"Where are we going?" he asked.

"I figure we can stay at Melanie's for a couple of weeks or until I can get a job up there," Stan's voice sounded tentative yet urgent.

"No way," his grandfather said. "She won't even

open the door. By now you should know your sister doesn't want anything to do with us."

"We don't have a choice."

"Leave my stuff alone. I'm not going anywhere," he said.

"You can't stay here. It's too dangerous," Stan said.

"As long as I have my baby here, I'll be okay." He waved the gun around the room and it was clear that he had no training in handling weapons in a safe way. I wondered if he ever shot a gun.

"How will you get to the doctor's office?" Stan asked.

"I'll call LADOT. Remember, I did that once? It took forever but I got there."

"Grandpa, besides taking forever, sometimes they don't show."

"So where do I have to go? Doctors are my whole life."

Grandfather and grandson watched me punch in numbers on my iPhone. I didn't care if they heard my end of the conversation. It was time for me to take direct action. I was going to protect Stan whether he wanted it or not.

"Give me Captain Wilson, please." There was a short pause, during which they looked at me wide-eyed. "Tell him it's Victor. Officer Victor Espinoza." I stressed my full name so that they would know I wasn't lying about being a police officer.

Captain Wilson sounded annoyed when he answered, "Wilson."

"Captain, this is Victor. We have to talk."

"What have you got?"

"Plenty, sir, but I can't talk right now."

"Where are you?"

"I'm on Chester Avenue in Van Nuys, in the 140 hundred block."

"What the hell are you doing there?"

"I'm at Stan Gorecki's apartment." There was a long silence at the other end of the line. I could hear Wilson breathing. "Sir?"

"Meet me at the Red Line's South bound Universal City subway stop in thirty minutes." He hung up.

Another strange piece of the puzzle, I thought. Why at a subway station? Why couldn't I just come into the station?

Chapter 27

Fired

I expected Captain Wilson to be pacing up and down the platform when I arrived at the station. His six-foot-four-inch frame would be hard to miss in a crowd. A southbound train had just left so there were only two other people on the platform. A couple behind me on the escalator were wrapped up in each other's arms, the rest of the world tuned out of theirs. It made me think of Jannine and our dinner date later in the evening. I looked at my iPhone and realized I was about twenty minutes early.

I proceeded to read the wall tiles written in Spanish of the early days of the region. Crude drawings depicted the historic scenes.

Certain I had missed the captain or he was late, I decided to check my email but couldn't get connected so I rode the escalators back to street level. I connected, read all my new emails, and answered a few, then Googled *Jimmy's on Ventura*. Finding nothing, I changed the search to just *Jimmy's* and came up with a coffee house and a club in West Hollywood. It was then that I realized a sleaze bar like Jimmy's would hardly have a website.

I headed back down into the station. The northbound train came to a stop and people hemorrhaged through the doors but still no Wilson. The up escalator spilled over while the down escalator had a few scant statues gliding along.

Captain Wilson, the incredible hulk, stepped from the escalator and searched up and down the platform. He looked directly at me and didn't recognize me. It gave me a momentary rush, knowing that I passed. As I walked up to him, he stepped past me, craning his neck, searching for a different Victor.

"Captain, it's me," I said.

He looked startled then composed himself immediately. "This better be good."

"I just left Stan Gorecki who has given me some names and places. I have been trying to get him to talk but each time he gets suspicious of me. He put me onto a lead at a place called Jimmy's on Ventura Boulevard. He said the police, meaning us, were looking in the wrong place for the killer. So I went there dressed in this outfit—"

"Were Fryman and Murray with you?" Wilson, who was watching the arriving passengers on the escalator, snapped his head toward me and interrupted.

"No, sir. I just went to check the place out."

"Jimmy's eh?" After a short pause, he began to bloom into a bright red. "Dammit, we have had that place under surveillance for over a year. It just happens to be the central clearing house for drug traffic in the East Valley. Even the hint of cop in there could negate all the work we've done."

"I don't think they thought I was a cop." I said. "They thought I was a…faggot."

"Who the hell do you think you are? You are not running this investigation. Detective Murray is the lead man and you take it upon yourself to decide what you should be doing. Our job is to protect you, to have your back. You job is to obey orders." Fire was coming from every pore and his face was the color of the Red Line.

"I didn't think it was going to be a big deal, just checking out the bar."

"You're supposed to be an LAPD cop. You're not being paid to think. What exactly did you *check out*?" This hulk of a man was raging angry though I couldn't understand why.

"Well, Stan told me about a guy named Tony, said Tony knows about everything going on in the Valley, so I asked if Tony was there."

"Holy shit!" Wilson took out his cell phone and attempted to make a call but there was no reception in that deep tunnel of a station. He trotted, almost at a run speed, for the up escalator and I followed. On the way up, he kept checking for communication bars.

"I tried to convince Stan that if he was in danger, we would guarantee to take care of him, but he said nobody, even the police, could protect him."

Wilson stopped at the top of the escalator and turned to me. "You told Stan, a suspect in the Carlyle murder that we, the police, would protect him?"

"Yes, sir. I thought, why not get him on our side first?"

"I don't believe this." The captain started to pace back and forth as people rushed past us. At that moment I had the feeling that I was safe in a public place, a bulwark against Wilson's wrath should he consider launching me onto the third rail.

"Let me understand this, Espinoza." I sensed I was in trouble since he always called me Victor or son and now

I was Espinoza. "You venture out without clearing with the detectives and then you take over my job and make commitments of the department to a man who is considered a prime suspect in two murders. Is that right? And just how did you get this information, which so far is worthless?"

"I had to tell him I was a police officer working undercover."

"You what?" he bellowed.

"It was the only way I could see to get what we needed, sir."

His phone rang. When he took the call, he stepped away far enough so I could not hear his conversation. Somehow, I just hadn't explained myself very well which I was sure was the reason for his anger. I wondered what he would have done if he was in my shoes—my regular shoes, not the high heels. I felt awkward, watching him wave his arms while talking, then dialing again, and finally shouting into the phone. He walked over to me and without flinching said, "Espinoza, for your own safety and for the good of the department and the people we serve, I'm terminating your involvement in the case. *You are fired.* If we need you for anything additional, I'll get in touch with you."

Just then, a southbound train roared into the station below and a wave of people pushed their way onto the escalator. I wasn't able to hear his final remarks. He took a few steps away from me then turned back. "I'm ordering you to keep any and all information concerning this case in total confidentiality. No discussion of any kind with anyone. Do I make myself clear?"

"Yes, sir. But I don't understand why. What did I do?"

"The people at Jimmy's are not dummies. They can smell police in or out of disguise."

"I fooled you, didn't I?"

"And if I hear you have leaked even one syllable to anyone, I will have you fired from the force. I will personally demand an internal investigation." He turned and headed for the parking lot.

Why, I wondered, did we have to meet at a subway station? There it was, another damned *why,* but at least this one would not get me in trouble. I wanted to run after him and plead for my job, but thought better of it because he probably was in no mood to reconsider. I was completely confused because I was certain that there couldn't have been even a hint of police work with my visit. They thought I was gay and wanted me out. Then I remembered that I had mentioned Stan's name.

I just stood there, perplexed, when a tall man in his thirties came up to me and frowned. "Was that guy bothering you?" he said and then smiled.

"Yes, sort of," I said, completely forgetting that I was dressed to pass.

"Can I be of assistance? I hate to see a pretty, young woman in distress. Perhaps we can have a drink or something to calm you down."

I looked at him and laughed out loud. "That's not a bad line. I'll use it myself someday."

As I drove home, I thought about my short-lived career as a detective. At that point, going back to patrol duties didn't really seem that bad, even though I was sure that, after a few days, I would begin to hate it again. There was one bonus, and a big one at that. I would have more time to spend with Jannine. The second bonus was that I could give all my outfits, including shoes and purses, to the Catholic charities rescue missions for the poor and homeless. But why would the homeless dress in drag? How could a long gold dress help? My platform shoes would be worthless. I took them off, threw them in the back seat and drove barefoot.

Best of all, I wouldn't miss shaving so often and applying layers of make-up each time I was on assignment. For a few seconds, I toyed with the idea of keeping the false eyelashes—trimmed down, of course. What a laugh that would be at parties.

On the drive home, I chatted, via iPhone, with Jannine about wedding plans, babies, and our future life. She asked me twice about my dresses, how the case was going, and if I was all right. This time my lies came out in sputters and I knew she was aware of my evasions. With a final, "I love you," we hung up. Yet with all these changes and the prospects for the future, I wasn't really happy. Apprehensive was s a better description of how I felt. I had a promotion in my grasp and through my stupid decision to go it alone, I'd lost it. I had this strange feeling that I wanted to get into a fight, a physical fight, with someone. Anyone. I felt a need to retrieve my soul.

When I stopped in the driveway of my house, I was suddenly alerted that something was wrong. My front door was partially open—I never came and went that way because to leave I had to turn a dead bolt from the outside. That dead bolt could only be turned from inside.

It couldn't be Jannine in the house because I was just talking to her. Someone had entered my house. I drew my service revolver from my glove compartment and stepped out of the car. Normally I would have used the remote to open the garage and enter into my kitchen area. If someone was in the house, I wanted the element of surprise to be in my favor. I held the gun with both hands straight out in front of me and eased open the front door.

Chapter 28

Chaos

The door didn't swing in all the way so I pushed at it until it reached the back wall. There was no one behind it. The small entrance hall contained a closet that I pulled open, still holding my gun straight ahead. My golf clubs and jackets were undisturbed, though my Dodger baseball caps on the shelf were on the floor.

When I stepped into the living room, I saw couch pillows on the floor, lamps and pictures turned over, but I remained focused on the possibility that someone was still in the house. I stepped over items as quietly as possible and headed for the front bedroom, which served as my combination guest room and office.

All the desk drawers were pulled out and emptied onto the floor. The open closet door showed that each storage box had been opened. Again, I moved, cat-like, toward the kitchen-dining area, which was torn apart by someone who had plenty of time and was looking for something specific.

Finally, my bedroom was an even greater victim of the mess. I was satisfied that the house was empty so I relaxed my arms, which were beginning to ache from the tension of the aiming maneuver. It was then that I noticed that the closet where my dresses were kept was not disturbed. There were several bruises in the door and in the adjacent wall. Every dresser drawer was emptied onto the floor. The mattress was pulled off the bed frame and box spring. I returned to the living room, sat down on the coffee table, and dialed Captain Wilson.

I got routed to the front desk and was told he was not in his office. I left a message to have him call me. Murray's cell phone went to his message machine too, so I called Fryman and he answered.

"What's up?" he asked.

"I'm at my house and it looks like someone has tried to rob me. The place is in total chaos."

"What about your service revolver?"

"That was in the car with me."

"Sorry, Victor. Homicide doesn't get involved with home invasion robberies. Call the front desk and they will send out a couple of your buddies to make a report. Do you have homeowner's insurance?"

"I do. But there is something strange about this. I haven't checked everything but it doesn't look like they took anything. Maybe they were just looking for something specific."

"You mean, like your expensive dresses?"

"Actually they're not mine. Technically, they belong to the department. So in reality, they're your dresses, unfortunately not your size."

"Fuck you. I'll check with Wilson. In the meantime, don't touch anything before they take a report. I doubt they will get involved or even order any dusting. These kinds of bust-ins don't amount to anything."

He hung up and I walked back to my bedroom, changed into street clothes, and then picked up the framed picture of Jannine from the floor. The glass was broken but her smile was intact in spite of the distorting crack. I sat on the box spring, stared at the mess, and wondered if this didn't have some connection to the Carlyle case. I did remember that I kept a small amount of cash in my nightstand. That drawer was not spilled out so everything was still there: the small bible my parents gave me, a bottle of TUMS, and the old leather case that had eighty dollars in it. It was all there.

The home invasion robbery had a strange effect. I felt a personal affront and an injury to my private world. It was hard for me to shake the feeling that this was connected to my strange assignment.

My iPhone rang. It was Wilson.

"Hello, sir."

"I don't like this. I don't like it at all. Sit tight. Bob and I will be there in a few minutes. Are you all right?"

"I am, sir."

"Good. Don't touch anything. I'll call in a crew to document everything. Also, don't make any calls from your land line. In fact, keep all of this on the down low."

He hung up. I decided not to go through the secrecy charade again so I dialed Jannine. She would be just about to leave work.

"Victor, you never call me at this hour. What's wrong?"

"I've been vandalized. The house is a total mess. I'll have to stay at your place tonight."

"I'm on my way over."

I walked out into the backyard and looked around, not knowing what I was looking for. There was no evidence of any disruption. I thought about having a nice boring nine-to-five job where your life was predictable and no adrenaline would pump into your veins. This detective business was a high wire act. At that moment, I wondered what I would feel if ever I had to shoot someone. I was an excellent shot, according to my charts at the pistol range, but shooting at a paper picture was different than shooting at a human being. I walked to the kitchen and wanted to get a drink of water, but then remembered Wilson's order.

Seems I was finally learning to follow orders, even though a bit late. I sat back down on the box spring, but couldn't shake the feeling that Stan's panic had produced in me. Perhaps Fryman was right, that this was just a random shot, maybe even kids in the neighborhood pulling a prank.

I heard a car pull up out front so I met Murray, Fryman, and Wilson at the front door. We walked through the house like a quartet of appraisers and finished in the kitchen.

Fryman couldn't help himself. "Wow. It looks like the robbers were casing the joint. They must have thought a woman living alone was an easy touch."

"Cut the shit, Bob. Vic's house is in chaos." When Wilson spoke, Fryman backed off.

Murray looked out into the laundry room. "Looks like they broke a window to get in," he said. "Lucky you weren't here."

"Lucky? Are you kidding? I could've caught the SOB."

"You could've shot him," Fryman said, "and no body would've accused you of using excessive force. Then you could enjoy the fun of an internal affairs investigation."

"You got somebody you can call who can board up that back door window?" Murray said. "I don't think you'll get a glass man out here today."

"I've got some plywood in the garage. I can do it myself."

"You know how to use a hammer?" Fryman asked.

"Bob, you and Cliff check with the neighbors and see if anyone saw anything or heard anything. Damage to the walls and the closet door aren't exactly stealth."

The investigative crew pulled up out front and came marching in with suitcases and boxes to set up shop. One of the men set his case down on the kitchen counter and then called us over. My homeowner's insurance papers, which had all my personnel information, did not connect my employment with LAPD. However, it was spread out on the counter. On top of it was a note I had made of Stan's address and phone number. The technician pointed to a tube of lipstick and asked, "Is this your paper weight?

"This was no ordinary robbery," Wilson said. "But at least they didn't get your gun or your badge."

"Or your dresses and make-up," Fryman added.

My two-car garage was untouched and to my relief all my power tools and workbench were undisturbed. Though it appeared to be a mess to an outsider, it was an organized mess that only I knew the whereabouts of every item. Half the garage was clear and accessible for my car.

Leaning against one wall, several scraps of plywood of different sizes and lengths would work as a board-up for the broken window.

After I opened the garage door for additional light, Fryman came in and whistled. "This looks like a few notches better than high school woodshop. Is this all yours?"

"Yeah. I use it to make shoe-shine boxes." It felt good to give back some verbal hustle to Fryman. It also helped me to feel like an equal.

"Listen, Victor, I owe you an apology. Sometimes I can be such a dick. I'm sorry for all the nice things I ever said about you. For a girl, you're quite a man."

Jannine's car came screeching into the driveway. The engine had barely stopped before she jumped out, ran up to me, and threw her arms around me. She gave me a kiss, not of passion but one of relief. We hugged so long that I completely forgot about Fryman. When we looked at him, his eyes appeared to bug out under his arched eyebrows.

"Oh, sorry. Jannine, this is Detective Fryman of the Robbery Homicide Division."

He nodded an acknowledgement. "And you are?"

"Jannine Lindbloom."

"She's my fiancée," I added. "We're going to be married."

"We are?" she said. There was a softness in her expression that I had never seen before. "Okay, when."

"You better start thinking of a maid of honor because I'm asking Stan to be my best man."

"Maybe he could do double duty and be maid of honor too," Fryman said.

"You never give up, do you?" I snapped.

"You guys fight it out. I'm going outside to make some calls," Jannine said and headed for the kitchen door.

"Don't touch anything," Fryman called after her.

She waved as she left the garage.

"She's a knockout. To rate someone like her—you are one little guy with a secret weapon. Or is she just a sucker for a uniform?"

I tossed him my steel tape measure and told him to measure the size of the window. When he returned with the dimensions, Murray was with him. He too was impressed with my workshop.

"Any idea of who might want to ransack your house? Do any of the cross dressers at the Velvet Glove know where you live?" Murray asked.

"The only one is Stan, but I know he wouldn't do this."

"Why are you so sure?" Murray asked.

"Unless he mistakenly told someone else," Fryman added.

I turned on the table saw and laid out the measurements on a small sheet of three quarter inch plywood. The high-pitched zing of the blade cutting through the wood brought out Wilson and Jannine.

When the two detectives saw the captain, they headed out of the garage.

"Let's go. We gotta interview neighbors," Murray said.

"Jannine, there are some one inch wood screws in that second drawer. Bring six of them and the Phillips head screw driver."

"Nothing like having a great lover and a handyman in one little body," she said. "I'm right behind you."

When we entered, my house was crawling with police personnel. Two technicians had set up laptop computers and were pecking away at them.

I turned to Wilson. "What are they doing?"

"They are using the new Integrated Automated Fingerprint Identification System, also known as IAFIS. We will be able to identify a name with a fingerprint in less than thirty minutes; provided the print is in a local or national database."

A masked technician emerged from the bathroom. "I found a whole basket full of heavy duty make up."

Jannine broke in with, "Oh. That's mine. I stay here often."

A third technician reported to Wilson. "It looks like

your vandal was a guy, judging from the size of the foot print left in the spilled coffee grounds in the kitchen."

"Got anything on the prints yet?" Wilson asked the tech.

"Some of it is coming in now, sir."

"Did we pick up anything on the tube of lipstick?"

"The guy must've worn gloves or wiped down after himself because it's clean. So is the paperwork under the lipstick and around the table. Here's one hit coming in now for a Victor Espinoza and he has no prior criminal record."

"Not yet," I answered.

Captain Wilson and I left the house and stood on the back decking.

I boasted about building the deck myself but he seemed unimpressed. I decided to bring up my status because I hoped this new development would work in my favor.

"Am I back on the case working with Fryman and Murray?"

"No, son. I think there's too much risk here for you. Unless, of course, if Murray feels otherwise, then you would stay assigned, but I don't think you are really a team player because you do not share everything you know. In effective police work, we work collectively to solve a case. It can't work any other way."

Just then, the IAFIS technician came out. "I think we've got something, sir."

We returned to the computer display and he began reading the new hit. "Stanley R. Gorecki, 23 years old. He's got a rap sheet but no felonies: a couple of disturbing the peace, a resisting arrest, and an underage public drunkenness.

We found his prints on the living room coffee table and on the bedroom door molding."

"Stan has been here but I know he wouldn't do this," I said.

"Do we have a current address on him?" Wilson asked the technician.

"Yes, we do.

Here was the problem Wilson was telling me about. I knew that Stan was planning to leave and I knew his grandfather would not let on to where he was going.

"Okay. Let's bring him in. This could be the break we're looking for." Wilson said.

"Captain, I know he's not the murderer."

"The other dimension to effective police work is not to mix personal feelings with the job. We put ourselves at risk when we lose our objectivity."

After a long pause, he turned to the IAFIS technician. "Contact headquarters with the details on Stanley Gorecki and tell them to bring him in."

Chapter 29

Grapevine

Before boarding up the window, I headed out into the back yard where Jannine was on the phone talking to her mother.

She was giving her the news of the upcoming marriage.

When she saw me, her female sixth sense kicked in and she must have known something was wrong.

"I'll have to call you back," she said and hung up.

"I need to use your phone," I said.

"What happened to your phone?"

"I don't want to use it because it's—" I stopped short of telling her my fears that perhaps my number was being monitored. I didn't have any idea of who or how but it was just a feeling. "I have to call Stan."

"Wow, you move fast. Inside of ten minutes, you propose to me and set up a best man. I haven't even thought about a maid of honor." She gave me an eyebrows raised look as she handed me the phone. "I hope you know what you're doing."

"Not exactly." I dialed Stan's home number and his grandfather answered.

"Mr. Gorecki, this is Victor Espinoza. Can I talk to Stan?"

"No, you can't," he said.

After some prodding he told me that Stan had left about a half hour earlier. I didn't want to ask him any other questions because of my concerns that his phone too was tapped. I ended the call and dialed Stan's cell phone. However, it went directly to his answering machine.

"Stan, call me as soon as you get this. It's urgent."

"Urgent?" Jannine looked puzzled. "It's not like we're eloping—or is it?" The sarcasm in her voice negated the question.

"I have to warn him. They want to bring him in for questioning. I'm sure they are going to call him a person of interest, which, translated from police terminology, means he is a suspect."

Jannine's expression changed to one of resolve, bordering at the edge of anger. "I thought you were off the case? Are you trying to be Batman or 007 and go it alone?"

"Jannine, this is something I have to do. You're going to have to trust me that I know what I'm doing. This is for Stan, not the LAPD."

"What was all that baloney about going back to be a patrolman and settling down?"

She held out her hand for the return of her phone just as it rang. I answered and it was Stan.

"Where are you?" I asked.

"I'm on the 5 in the Grapevine, heading north. What do you want?"

Jannine turned her back to me with her head bowed. She began to walk away in slow determined steps.

"Stan, I can't talk now but here is what I want you to do. There is a rest area near the top of the Vine. Pull in there and wait for me. I'll be there in about an hour."

"Why? What's happening?"

"I'll tell you when I see you. There's good news and bad news. The good news is you're going to be best man at my wedding. The bad news can wait."

As I hung up, I heard him say, "No, it can't"

When she turned around to face me there were puddles of tears forming in her eyes. Those brown eyes had a darkness about them that brought a lump to my throat.

"Grow up, Victor. You are not dealing with a mild domestic quarrel here. Going against orders is not gonna get you a promotion to detective, it's going to get you fired. You can't disobey orders and expect to win any atta-boys for it." She paused. "I can't do this anymore."

I followed her out to her car and pleaded for understanding, but she dismissed me with, "It's the same old story," and drove off.

As I watched her car disappear at the end of the block, I felt a strange conflict within my gut. On the one hand, I wanted to please her because I loved her and, on the other, I wanted the freedom to do what I felt was part of my job, right or wrong.

After I returned to the garage, I saw Aaron's car pull up and park out front. Why, I wondered, would he be coming into the scene? Since he wasn't in uniform, I guessed it was his day off. He checked the boarded up window and seemed to stay at my elbow as I moved around, starting to straighten up the mess of my house. At one point, I noticed him chatting with Captain Wilson. It seemed strange since the two had never actually met.

I cornered Aaron to ask a favor. "Will you hang here and lock up my house after the crew leaves?"

"Why? Where are you going?"

"I've got to take care of something."

He looked concerned but did agree. As I gathered a few items—toothbrush, change of underwear—he was back with Wilson again.

Without telling anyone, I pulled out my car from the driveway and started to pull away. In my rear view mirror, I saw Wilson and Aaron run to the center of the street.

As I turned the corner, I saw them get in Aaron's car and start up after me.

It was hardly a low speed pursuit since I turned up the alley behind the next block of houses and then out onto Chandler Boulevard. Aaron was a good driver but no match for me.

Once on the interstate, I dialed Jannine in hopes of heading off a big scene when I returned, but there was only her message machine.

Before I could leave a message, the call dropped probably because of the surrounding mountains. Communication was iffy in the Grapevine.

I tried again in a flat area and got through. This time she answered.

"You know, Victor, maybe all this is happening for the best." Her voice sounded defeated and devoid of anger. There was a resignation that I found worrisome. "We don't seem to have a common goal. Perhaps we should both move on with our lives."

"Jannine, I love you. I don't want to move anywhere without you."

There was such a long pause I wasn't sure if the call had dropped again.

"Jannine?"

"I'm here. This is no way for us to discuss this—over the phone. Let's talk when you get back from wherever it is you're going," she said. "I have a lot of thinking to do."

This wasn't the Jannine who was a straight talker, ready to shoot from the hip with a heavy dose of emotion behind it.

The call did drop just as I came upon a sign that read, *Rest Area. Use right lane.*

Chapter 30

Rest Stop

The rest area bustled with northbound travelers. At the entrance, a sign directed cars to the right and trucks to the left. I cruised by at low speed to check each car, looking for Stan's green sedan, then came to a stop at the far end. Two large buildings housed rest rooms and a central plaza that contained vending machines, payphones, display maps, and a drinking fountain. I searched the picnic tables and the rest rooms, but no Stan.

It couldn't be possible that he was not there yet because he was at least a half hour ahead of me. Perhaps he stopped at a store or a restaurant and was delayed so I parked and waited at a point where I could see the new drivers entering the area. After a half hour, I became concerned. I imagined a variety of scenarios, he missed the turn off, he had car trouble en route, or he changed his mind.

I got out and sat on a bench where I still had a view of the entrance. After one hour, I decided to call his number, but stopped when I noticed an occasional car pulling into the truck area. The rows of semi-trailer trucks obscured most of the parking slots. I decided to explore on foot just in case he had pulled into the wrong area.

Some of the truck drivers were circling their rigs, checking tie-downs, tires, and lights while other trucks had no visible driver who probably was in one the buildings or sleeping in his cab. It wasn't until I reached the last truck that I saw Stan's car up against the bushes and at the rear end of a double trailer. I thought it strange that Stan would pull into the truck area and park in such an obscure location.

As I drew close to the rear of his car, he was in the driver's seat and appeared to be using his iPhone. The window on his side was down and his head was bent forward but a strange feeling of foreboding came over me. As I neared, I called out, "Stan."

He did not budge. At first, I thought he must be asleep.

When I reached in to shake his shoulder he fell forward against the steering wheel; his head bounced on the rim. When I opened the car door, his left arm dropped down and his iPhone fell to the pavement. Blood oozed down to the floorboards. My heart began to pound and my chest felt like it would explode. I held his body by the shoulder, keeping him from falling out of the car. When I pushed him back against the center column, I saw where the blood was flowing from. He had been stabbed in the abdomen in what looked like several large gashes. His shirt was ripped open.

"My God, Stan," I whispered as I fought back tears. "Stan. Stan."

Saying his name choked in my throat as I began to blame myself for his death. Then suddenly Captain Wilson's words began to echo in my brain. '*In effective po-*

lice work, you can't mix personal feelings with the job.' I wondered if I was able to do that for at that moment my emotions were overwhelming me. I had grown into a strong relationship with Stan so now it was personal.

The truck driver of the rig next to Stan's car dropped down from the cab and came up next to me. He too was horrified at the sight.

"Jesus, what happened?" he asked.

Then he took two steps back from me and appeared frightened. He must have assumed that I was Stan's murderer.

"We planned to meet here," I said. "I just found him this way."

He looked at me and another step backward told me he was afraid of me and wasn't going to take any chances. When I stood and looked directly at him, perhaps it was my tears that convinced him otherwise because he began to talk.

"I was sleeping in my cab. I didn't see a car here when I drove up."

"How long ago was that?" I asked.

He looked at his watch. "Well, over an hour ago. Shouldn't we call the police?"

I didn't want to identify myself, though I didn't understand why. I was, after all, an off-duty cop. I didn't want to use my phone so I asked the truck driver, "Would you call 911?"

"Sure," he said.

I didn't want to touch anything since police procedure in Los Angeles required the first one to do any research and declare the victim dead was the medical examiner.

However, since the murder did not take place in Los Angeles, it would be under the authority of the Los Angeles County Sheriff's Department.

"They want to know if the victim is dead?" the truck driver asked.

Though Stan's head was tilted back and his eyes were open, I could not bring myself to touch his eyeball. I wanted to cradle his head in my arms and let him know that someone cared about him. I cared about him.

"Yes. He is." I could hear my voice cracking.

I dared not think too much about Stan's death because I knew my jaw and lips would quiver and I might start a major crying scene.

We were joined by two more truck drivers who stood back several feet from the car. Neither of them spoke or asked any questions. I straightened up and approached them feeling some measure of composure return to me.

"Did you guys see anything unusual here?" I asked.

"No," the one said and the other just shook his head.

"Did you hear anything?"

"Just the noise of truck engines, air brakes, and all that."

"Any voices, arguments, or hollering," I asked.

"Well, there was one thing I guess you might call strange. I have to say that it's not that unusual. About an hour ago, I noticed a black car pull out from our truck area. What was unusual was that a big sedan like that would burn rubber. That's what caused me to look up."

"Did you get a license plate number?"

"Naw. I just looked and went back to my reading."

I returned to the open car door and noticed the iPhone on the pavement, which I picked up and slipped into my pocket. Stan's two pieces of luggage were in the back seat, which ruled out robbery.

As we waited for the county sheriffs to arrive, I realized I would have to show identification and would have to explain my presence at the murder scene. Again, I remembered Wilson's words that a loss of objectivity in police work could be dangerous. I concluded that Stan pulled into the truck area because he was trying to hide from a car following him since he would not be trying to hide from me. I wondered why he didn't call me. I also wondered if the black sedan the truck driver noticed had anything to do with Stan's murder.

"I'm going to get my car to pull it around here," I said. "So please don't leave until I get back."

As I ran toward my car, several people from the car park area headed to the crime scene. It was amazing how fast information traveled. To get to the truck area I had to drive the wrong way in the one-way lane entering the rest area. I pulled up behind Stan's car just as I heard the wailing of sirens in the distance.

I pulled out my notebook and approached the three truck drivers. I recorded the time, the place, their names, and contact numbers. I also jotted down the vehicle license numbers of the trucks and trailers. One trailer carried an Iowa plate and the two others were registered in California. Additionally, I sketched the location of Stan's car in relation to the bushes and the semi-trucks. I had to keep busy doing the business of police work, otherwise, I knew I would break down completely.

I jotted down the two statements of the drivers and then asked the people arriving to stand back from the car because everyone wanted to see the body of the victim. When a few people gave me some resistance, I showed them my badge and they backed off.

Two Los Angeles County Police cars arrived and four deputies took over the scene. A few minutes later, a fire ambulance arrived and two EMTs inspected Stan and then his car. The next hour was a blur for me. I endured questions asked and questions repeated, questions about why I was planning to meet with the victim. Though I didn't want to, I referred them to Captain Wilson of

LAPD. At first, I showed them my California driver's license but then had to produce my police ID if for no other reason except to distance myself from their investigation. The sergeant in charge kept looking at me and my two IDs then said, "How long you been with LAPD?"

"Five years. Why?" I asked.

Two hours later I was in my car, heading north on the 5, searching for a place to turn around and head back south. I stopped at the summit station for a cup of coffee. I considered myself lucky that I did not have to face reporters and television news crews. I wanted to let Mr. Gorecki get the news from me before he heard it on the TV or from the LAPD.

I pulled out Stan's iPhone and located his home number. After the third ring, he answered. His first words were, "Are you Okay?"

"Mr. Gorecki, this is Stan's friend, Victor."

"But you're calling from Stan's phone. What's wrong?"

The lump in my throat revisited me and I could hardly speak. It's your job, I told myself. Get your feelings out of the way.

"I'm sorry to tell you, Mr. Gorecki, but Stan has been murdered."

There was no response from the old man, just heavy breathing. I said, "I'm so sorry, Mr. Gorecki."

He then bellowed into the telephone, "The wages of sin is death. Romans 6:23."

After he quoted the bible verse, he wanted to know the details. What few I had didn't seem to satisfy him.

"Can I come over, Mr. Gorecki?"

"Away from me Satan," he whispered. It sounded like he was crying and, after saying nothing, he hung up.

I searched Stan's phone for possible clues or leads that could be explored, possible names or places. His phone indicated that he had an unsent message to me. I located it and it said simply, GET PIX.

There were several pictures of some of his friends, some in drag, and the most recent picture was a somewhat blurred image of a cross dresser who looked familiar. He was wearing a turtleneck sweater with a large necklace of what looked like white pearls. The wide-brimmed hat looked like a straw sunbonnet that flopped down over the eyes. Only his mouth and his wide jaw with a slight cleft dominating his chin could be seen. His lips were covered with royal blue lipstick. I was certain it was someone I had seen at the Velvet Glove. As I studied the picture and started to enlarge it, the phone rang. The ID showed the caller to be from a number I recognized: LAPD East Valley Division.

Why would they be calling Stan?

Chapter 31

Red Dress

The long ride back to the Valley gave me an opportunity to think about my own situation. One overriding reality kept me from thinking about some of the minor issues. The killer or killers knew about my connection to Stan and they must be out to get me because they probably believed that Stan gave me their identity. The fact that he didn't made no difference to them. The fact that I was in danger got my adrenaline racing through my body. I could feel my skin tingling. The prospect of being a target didn't trigger fear in me, though I was conscious of the flight-or-fight reaction. One thing was certain. I could not stay at my own house while I was in the fight mode.

I had to put aside the urge to study the picture on Stan's phone, especially the gnawing feeling that the face was familiar. Even if it was somebody that I recognized why would I conclude that this was the murderer? It could simply be a picture of a friend of Stan's taken recently. Even if it were the killer, would a picture on a cell phone stand up as physical evidence in a trial? At that moment, I felt like a real detective. I was weighing evidence and its relevance.

When I pulled up to the front of my house, I was excited to see Jannine's car parked in the driveway and most of the lights on inside. Immediately I shifted to panic mode because I thought she might be in danger. I rushed to the door and made as much noise as possible before I entered since I didn't want to scare her, though the likelihood of that was remote.

When I opened the front door, and before I entered, I hollered, "Jannine."

"I'm here in the bedroom," she called back.

I felt weak with relief to hear her voice. Almost all of the mess of the house was straightened out and everything seemed to be in order. A strong woman like her had managed to wrestle back the mattress onto the box spring. She had a large cardboard box and two suitcases on the bed packed with my clothes. I charged up to her, put my arms around her waist, which she immediately pushed away.

"Give me a hand," she said.

"What are you doing?" I asked.

"Aaron should be here any minute."

"Why?"

"We're moving you out. You can't stay here. It's way too dangerous."

"How do you know?

"Wilson filled Aaron in on everything. At first he thought it was funny until he saw all your dresses and under things. You should see how silly he looks with your wig on."

"Where am I going?"

"You're gonna stay with me until this serial killer is caught. I just don't want you to be next on his list."

I pushed one of the suitcases aside and sat on the end of the bed. I grabbed her arm, pulled her onto my lap, and wrapped my arms around her waist. I kissed her neck.

She squirmed. "Not now. Aaron is due any minute."

"I can always call him and tell him to bust a couple of speeders before he gets here."

After the doorbell rang, she kissed me. "Too late."

She jumped up. I grabbed her hand and held her from bolting. Together we went to the front window and pulled aside the curtain. There was Aaron's car.

We let him in and he made a false move to punch me.

"I didn't have a clue about your double life," he said.

"It's not a double life. I was working undercover."

"Believe me, this explains a lot. I couldn't figure why you just disappeared. And here, all I had to do was look under your skirt and see how they're hanging."

"Never mind the graphic," Jannine said. "We gotta get him out of here."

"Thanks, guys, but not tonight. I've got something I have to do. There's something I need to find out."

"Leave that job to LAPD," Aaron said. "Remember you're still assigned to Wilson. Even though he sees you as a loose cannon, he thinks you're a good man."

"Currently I'm not on the case," I said. "And I'm not on the clock."

"What are you going to do?"

"I'm going to get you two out of here so I can get ready for my date."

"Aren't you taking this job a little too seriously?" Aaron said.

"Good-bye," I said with a boldness that even frightened me.

They left with most of my street clothes. My dresses were all hung up in the closet and my makeup was still in the bathroom. I promised to lock the door after they left. It was 6 p.m., way too early for the Velvet Glove action even for a Friday night.

I showered and put hot towels on my beard before I shaved. I spent the next hour with make-up and thanking my father for giving me a Y chromosome. My flame-red dress looked good because the gaff was killing me. The pain pulsed up from my testicles to my waist and then around to my back. I set my red pumps next to the front door and put on my sneakers. I looked great. I had no idea whether the killer would be at the Glove tonight but I was determined to go every night until he showed.

I fired up my computer and downloaded the picture from Stan's iPhone. The magnified image gave me a better look at the face and the hat.

At the front-left of the picture there was a small section of his knuckles and it appeared he was holding something in his hand. It could have been a knife. What struck me was that it was his left hand and, on his pinky finger, a small cameo ring caught the light at one end. The other characteristic that stood out on the enlarged photo was the blue lipstick and the small blue line under the partially visible right eye. The floppy hat covered the left eye, forehead, and ears completely. Most of the right eyeball was not visible.

With another hour to kill, I turned on the TV in search of news channels. All the major stations were broadcasting comedy shows except channels 5 and 9 and a few of the cable stations. I surfed between them until I came upon the rest stop story. Channel 9 was not releasing the name of the victim, pending notification of his relatives. I listened as I strapped my gun to the inside of my thigh. My badge, ID, and my wallet fit into my clutch purse along with money. The channel 9 news anchor looked more like a runway model than a hard-boiled reporter. She was referring to an earlier news conference called by Councilman Kemper.

"Earlier today at City Hall our reporter Cindy Crawford spoke with Councilman Alan Kemper," the model said.

"Will the council be increasing the reward money for the arrest of the killer?" Reporter Crawford asked.

"We will spend whatever our taxpayers wish to bring this killer of three innocent men to trial," he answered. "I realize that there are those who are saying the victims got what they deserved, dressing in women's clothes and parading around. But I say they shouldn't die for the poor choices they made."

The recorded clip ended and the runway model continued the report with, "The councilman's office later explained that he could not release the names of the individuals but that they were probably supporters of his opponents in the coming election." She paused and then continued. "In other news this evening…"

I switched back to another channel in hopes of catching more information. The news ended at nine o'clock; the witching hour at the Velvet Glove. I stood in front of the full-length mirror and decided I had reached perfection. I felt confident that I could pass on the bus and anywhere else even in broad daylight.

My cell phone ring showed the caller as Private Caller. I knew it could not be Jannine or Aaron and certainly not anyone at the East Valley Division. I fought the urge to answer. After the call went to my message machine, I finished getting ready to leave.

I left one light on in the kitchen and turned off all the others. When I stood in the darkened living room, I noticed a car parked across the street with the driver sitting at the wheel. It was a light-colored hatchback, either a Toyota or a Honda. I remembered the truck driver describing a large black sedan. I decided to wait and watch. A few minutes later, a young man emerged from the house across the street, joined the driver, and they drove off.

I took a deep breath and realized how jumpy and nervous I was, maybe even a little paranoid. I even considered calling Murray and letting him know what I was doing. I dismissed the idea because he would forbid me to go. I had to go it alone. Wilson was wrong. I could not separate my personal feeling about Stan from my police work. I wanted his killer. I wanted desperately to avenge Stan's death, or was I seeking an escape from my guilt?

Chapter 32

A Kiss and a Promise

For me, driving in high heels was very uncomfortable and it was a definite hazard because of the lack of control. I was certain I could get used to it if I pointed my knees toward the dashboard. I left the house wearing my sneakers and carrying my shoes, which looked like weapons sitting in the passenger seat. As I drove down Chandler Boulevard, Jannine's warning began to sink in. If the killer or killers knew that Stan had divulged the name or names, they probably figured out it was to me and that I would go to the police. I was, and hopefully I would continue to be, the police, but whoever ransacked my house could have pieced evidence together and conclude that I was a cop. None of it sounded good to me. I wondered if it was safe for me to trust my reasoning abilities as I headed for the Velvet Glove.

As I turned on to Lankershim then on to the bar, I noticed that one of the large neon letters above the door had burned out. It read *Velvet love* so I wondered if the owner had a hand in the burn out.

The place was nearly full. Almost all the tables were taken by groups of two, three, or four and most dressed in street clothes. Many were curiosity seekers, waiting for the show to begin. The trio on the stage played cool jazz as the two waitresses darted between tables, taking orders and picking up empty glasses. I found a seat at the door end of the bar.

A few of the patrons sitting on bar stools were regulars I had seen before.

When Greg spotted me, he picked up his drink and headed my way. I did not want to talk to him. However, he might be able to shed light on Stan's death so I decided to put up with him.

"Hello stranger," he said. "You look fabulous."

It was obvious that he was not really interested in talking since he was rubbing his hand across my padded ass. I did not respond with either words or motions for fear that I might, at any moment, punch him out. My short fuse was looking for any excuse to light up. I wanted to tell him if he touched me again, I'd flatten him. Instead, I called over the bartender. Greg just stood behind me.

"What'll it be?" the bartender asked.

I gave him my order.

"Oh, and give me another," Greg chimed in.

When he delivered the drinks, I asked to run up a tab. Then I added, "Isn't it awful about Stan?"

Greg shrugged. "What was he doing cruising the Grapevine?"

"When was the last time you saw him?" I asked in my least police sounding way.

"Oh jeez. That was the night before he was murdered. He left here with some guy sitting at the bar."

"What did he look like? Was he in drag?" I asked, not realizing how easy the lingo was for me.

Brandon just listened and looked at me quizzically. After a while, Greg got bored and walked away.

"Did you see him?" I asked Brandon.

"I was off that night."

I squinted in the dim light and saw a fortyish-looking man sitting alone. He was dressed in women's clothes but didn't appear to be very well made up.

I nodded toward the man. "Is he new here?" I asked Brandon.

"Naw. I've seen him here a few times. I don't think he's a serious dresser since he seems to wear the same outfit every time he comes in. He's kinda quiet and angry-looking most of the time. He's a big tipper."

"I want to buy him a drink and when you deliver it let him know I sent it." The face and the outfit made me suspicious.

"You better watch yourself. He's kinda strange."

"Speaking of strange, where were you the night Stan was murdered?"

"Always the cop, eh, Victor?"

I watched him make the drink then present it to the strange man. Then the bartender pointed back toward me. I lifted my glass in the air and held it up as in a toast. The man took the drink, held it up, and then nodded his head before he took a sip. The next step for me was to muster the courage to walk down to the end of the bar and talk to him. What would I say? What would be my reason for buying him a drink? After all, a total stranger who sends down a drink to another total stranger is not just extending a friendly gesture. There must be some motive. Mine was to try to get information about Stan during those last few hours of his life. I decided to wait and he too waited, so it was a standoff.

As I sat and pondered my next move, I remembered Wilson's words. Even Fryman and Murray's advice to me, that to be a good detective you had to have courage and determination.

Suddenly, mine was slipping away. Why, I wondered, would a man dressed as a woman buy another man dressed as a woman a drink unless there was a motive? When the man sitting next to him paid for his drink and left, I grabbed my drink and walked to the other end of the bar. The trio stopped playing and the show was about to begin.

When I got to the empty seat, I noticed a large floppy hat hanging from one knee of the strange man. He moved it to the other knee and gestured for me to sit down. It was clearly a scene from a bad made-for-TV movie. I decided to use Greg's approach.

"Hello, stranger."

He looked at me sideways for a long moment. "Do I know you?"

"Didn't I see you in here the other night?" I hoped my lie was more convincing than those I told Jannine.

"I don't think so."

It was when he looked at me straight on that I noticed the slight cleft in his chin. A sudden realization came over me that this might be the same man in Stan's iPhone picture.

I had a twinge in the pit of my stomach. It occurred to me that Stan could have taken the picture the night he left with this man, yet I wasn't even certain it was the same man since the iPhone image was quite small.

"Look," he began, "I'm just here to have a drink and see the show."

"Well, so am I," I said.

"I'm sure," he answered and looked away.

All his body language was saying "Leave me alone." I could not take my eyes off the cleft chin. Nor could I deny the strange foreboding feeling I had.

"I know I've seen you here before with a friend of mine." I extended my hand to him and he just stared at it.

"I'm Vic," I said, leaving the door open for him to assume Victor, or Victoria, or Vicky.

Finally, he responded to my handshake, however, I had completely forgotten about the role I was playing and squeezed his hand in a manly grip. He held it there and a hint of a smile came over him. Now what? I thought. When he finally let go he took his hat and put it on. It was then that I noticed a distinct stain on the front of the brim. It was an oblong shape and the color was a brownish black.

"Look. I've gotta get going," he said.

"What's your hurry? The show is about to start."

I put my hand on the upper part of his thigh and held it there. He looked down at my hand and then back up to face me. There was uncertainty in his expression. I had no idea what I looked like to him because he kept staring at me. I didn't even know what my next move should be.

"Maybe we can get together and chat," I said.

"Chat?"

"Or, whatever."

I was now clearly in over my head. I wanted and needed to know what connection he had with Stan. What time did he see him and where? I was floundering in my interrogation skills. I removed my hand from his thigh and took a long sip of my beer. Why did I even suggest the possibility of sex?

"This is a new group starting tonight. They call themselves the Sex-n-Gin Arians. I like the bald heads," I said, trying for small talk to keep him interested.

"You know the group?" he asked.

I lied. "Oh, yes. They're really cool."

I put my hand back on his thigh and gave it a slight movement. Again, he looked down at my hand.

"It will have to be tomorrow," he said, "unless you're really horny."

"Tonight, tomorrow, or whenever," I said.

He shifted on his stool sideways and faced me directly. The brim of his hat fell forward and covered one eye. The cleft chin was in full view. I was certain it was the same person in Stan's iPhone picture.

"How about meeting me tomorrow?" I said.

He nodded.

"At the Lighthouse in Studio City at six in the afternoon?" I said. "It's not very crowded then and we can talk—and after, as they say we can do—whatever."

"Lighthouse?" There was a long pause as he thought about it. "Yeah, I guess."

"Okay," I said. "By the way, what's your name?"

"Aah…" No doubt he was trying to come up with a phony name. "It's John. Yeah, John." Then as if an afterthought, he added, "We better wear street clothes to the Lighthouse."

"How can I reach you, if I have to?"

"What do you mean?" he asked.

"Well if I can't make it, can I call you?"

The long fixed stare was answer enough, but I wasn't going to be the first one to blink. I dissolved into a smile, which I thought was seductive, however it must have been comical instead.

"You don't need a number. I know you'll be there." With that, he took my hand from his thigh and pressed it against his crotch. I resisted pulling my hand away. He pressed harder.

He stood up behind the bar stool, finished his drink, and glanced at the one I bought him that was still sitting there. He leaned down, kissed me on the cheek, and left. I had no idea of how to interpret the kiss. Was it meant to be sexy? Was it a Kiss-Off? What was it? Whatever it was, it made my skin crawl. The progress I made in changing his mind from indifference to agreeing to meet me must have been a testament to my red dress.

These were definitely uncharted waters for me. I knew that Wilson, Fryman, or Murray should know what's going on. I put my fingers into the inside of his empty glass and held it in front of me being careful not to touch the sides. I wanted those fingerprints in good condition. I took out a handkerchief, draped it over the glass, picked it up, and left. I waved to the bartender on the way out at 10:40 p.m.

I was certain he was the man in Stan's iPhone picture. Was he the murderer or was he just some guy looking for a score. Queen Mary finished her song and was going into her stand-up routine.

"I'm so tired I can hardly keep my thighs open," she said and nobody laughed.

Chapter 33

Fingerprints

I probably looked like some religious high priest carrying a sacrificial chalice into the squad room. I should have worn a feather and done a few Indian hoops and hollers as I placed the glass on Fryman's desk. In that jaded office, nobody would notice since the shift was just changing.

Murray, sitting across from Robert's desk, looked puzzled. "What's that?" he asked.

I puffed out my chest and flashed a victorious grin. "This is the big break we've been looking for."

"An empty glass?"

"Finger prints," I said.

"Whose?"

"He said his name is John but I'm sure he was lying."

Murray came over and stared at the glass, which looked very clean. "Where did you get it?" he asked.

"The bar at the Velvet Glove. Can we use the new IAFIS system?" I asked.

Without answering me, Murray put in a call to central and requested that a tech be sent over to lift prints. He then called Fryman's cell phone and told the message machine to hurry and get his ass into the division. He then asked JoAnn to call Captain Wilson.

"Glass is tough," he said, "especially if it was wet or greasy or if there are a lot of overlapping prints. Who else handled it?"

"Just the bartender," I said. "Anyway, let's try."

"What makes you think the prints are those of the perp?"

"I've got a feel—" I caught myself and corrected, "I have reason to believe this guy is it."

JoAnn called over to Murray that Captain Wilson was on seven. Line seven was a direct number which was not on the rotary with the other numbers.

It was kept private so we could have safe field communication in and out of the squad room. Murray picked up and, after several "Yes, sirs," and an "I already did," he hung up.

"Wilson wants to have a brainstorm meeting at 8:30, that's in one hour, so hang loose. You'll be happy to know he wants you included."

Fryman came in and wanted to know who was using his desk as a dumping ground as he reached for the glass. Both Murray and I yelled at the same time, "Stop. Don't touch it."

"Why?"

"I think I have the killer's fingerprints on it," I said. "And stop this asking *why* all the time.

"Fingerprints on a glass? You'd been better off to get some cum inside the glass." With that, he made a masturbating motion with his cupped hand. "Or," he continued, "maybe some spit or a lock of his hair."

We ignored his crude jokes and his raving.

"Wilson wants to have a session," Murray said, "at the white boards."

We pulled up chairs and sat pondering the myriad of circles, notations, and arrows that resembled a football coach's playbook. Every person of interest or suspect was circled and connected to boxes that contained pertinent facts. Greg, Mrs. Carlyle, and Stan (circled in red). Even the cookie lady was listed, but not her husband. Murray created a new box and drew a glass inside of it with a question mark.

Wilson arrived and looked annoyed. "Why isn't the tech here?"

"It's rush hour," Murray said.

Wilson studied the white board and started a litany of don'ts. "Victor, you say you know who the killer is but—" He paused and pointed at the white board. "We don't have a name. We don't have a witness. We don't know the motive. We don't have reliable prints. We don't know who the snitch is. We don't have hard evidence." He heaved a sigh. "We don't know shit."

Just then, the tech arrived, hauling the new equipment required for fingerprint identification. "Sorry," he said, "traffic was a bitch because some asshole on the Hollywood ran out of gas. So what have we got?"

Murray took him over to Fryman's desk and pointed.

"On a glass?" The tech sounded incredulous.

"Ah ha."

"Well, okay, but I may need some light control in this room. I need low ambient light."

The tech was a symphony in motion as he set up his equipment.

Wilson stepped up to the white board and pointed to an entry. "Okay, at 12:37 a.m. a witness saw two women walk behind the Quick Stop. The surveillance camera on- ly captures a dark, blurry picture because of poor or broken lighting. The clerk inside heard nothing: no screams, no commotion, nothing." Wilson sighed and continued. "The blue lipstick means shit. Well, it means this killer wants to be caught and is psycho, according to the profiler."

"Aren't they all?" Fryman interjected.

"The only person from the bar who knew anything is dead. So like I said, we got shit."

"We've got suspects," Murray said.

"Some suspects," Wilson said. "The wife of the dead man whom she probably hated and she has an alibi. A nutty grandfather, who hates gays, spouts bible verses, and is wheel-chair bound.

A faggoty bar patron who wants to make every guy in the bar and also has an alibi." Wilson stepped back from the board and pointed at Fryman. "And how about you, Robert? Where were you at midnight on the fifteenth of October?"

"Home, waiting for your call boss."

Murray stood up and pointed to some other entries. "The question is, what do we know and how does it fit together? We know both Burgess and Carlyle were straight. We know the killer is probably gay. We know he's strong and adept with a knife. We know there might be a second party involved."

Suddenly the tech called out, "I think we got a hit from one of the prints. It's just coming in now."

We all jumped up and stood behind the tech as he manipulated the screen information of his computer. Next to the picture of a black haired man was a listing of known data. Karl Decker, 42 years old. Last known address was in Columbus Ohio. Five arrests, two in Columbus and three in Wisconsin. There were two arrests in Milwaukee, one for stalking and the other as a suspect in a killer for hire case. There was no conviction for either one. The two in Ohio were for assault and battery. No convictions there either because he copped.

"Maybe the guy's a hit man." Fryman said.

"Here comes the info on the second set of prints." The tech pulled in another window, which showed a six-foot-two-inch male. "This print match is from a military database and he is an ex-marine from Camp Pendleton."

"Wait," I said. "He's the bartender."

"He's clean," the tech said. "Honorable discharge and no arrest record."

"Can this system give a false positive," Fryman asked. "I mean can it lift a partial print and connect it to the wrong person?"

"It's got an excellent redundancy check but, yes, I guess it could. The manufacturer says it can't." The tech sounded speculative.

"Then a good defense layer could impeach the evidence," Wilson said. He turned to me. "What do you think, Victor? Does the picture look like the guy in the bar?"

An instant of confusion hit me because I thought he was referring to the picture on Stan's iPhone.

After a long minute of studying the screen, I said, "I'm not sure, sir. The chin is not very clear on that screen. He has his head tilted downward."

"We need a positive ID," Wilson mumbled,

"I made a date to meet him at a restaurant in Studio City. Couldn't we use the print to question him?"

"No. Too risky," Wilson said.

"Let me meet him at the Lighthouse as planned," I pleaded.

"No," the Captain lamented, "there's too much at stake."

"I don't think so, sir. It's in a public place. I'll wear street clothes and a wire." Wilson studied the white board for a long moment. "Maybe he was just coming on to you."

"No, sir. It was the other way around. I was pretending to come on to him. I wanted him to keep talking. All due respect, sir, do we have to wait for this psycho to kill someone else?"

Fryman apparently couldn't resist. "Pretending?"

Wilson studied me for what seemed an eternity. His eyes showed a hint of defeat. "I don't know," he said. "It's just too risky."

"We don't have any other options, sir," I said.

Wilson shook his head and turned his back to the white board. He took a slow walk around the room.

"One more thing, sir. Can we get the lab to give us a blow-up of the surveillance picture at the Quick stop?"

"Listen to the kid," Fryman said, "He's already sounding like he's a detective."

"Sure," Murray said.

Wilson looked at me then at Murray. "Okay, but remember, Victor, this is a team operation. I don't want you going off like some hot dog."

I wanted to cheer. I was back in business. There was still a chance for me. Wilson thanked the tech for the printout picture and data and pinned them up on the side of the white board. Fryman and Murray were headed for the door when Wilson called out, "Hold on. Let's grab some takeout and plan out every detail."

Wilson and Murray groaned.

"Now?" I said.

"Yes now. I don't want any slip-ups at that restaurant." Then he turned to me, "If your ass gets hung out to dry, padded or not, I'll get the heat." He appeared to hyperventilate as he continued. "Cancel everything for the rest of the evening."

After Wilson entered his office, Fryman looked at

Murray and me. "So, Detective Espinoza, do we want Chinese take-out, Indian take-out, Thai take-out, or are we stuck with Mexican tamales?"

"I'm not hungry," I said because I was trying to figure out how not to start World War III with Jannine. I dialed her number at work.

"Hello, Jannine. It's me."

"What's up? Why are you calling me at work?"

"You know that play we were supposed to be going to at the Mark Taper tonight?"

There was no response. I waited.

"Hello, Jannine. Are you there?"

Still no answer.

"Jannine?"

A dial tone gave me the answer.

Chapter 34

The Rehearsal

Take-out turned out to be Jewish. Four giant corned beef sandwiches slathered in mustard with a side of kosher pickles and Dr. Brown's Root Beer eased the resentment we had about working into the evening. Captain Wilson wolfed his sandwich down while studying the white board, never realizing he had dripped yellow mustard down the front of his white shirt. His potbelly saved the stuff from plopping into his crotch and producing a yellow stain. When he spoke, I couldn't keep from staring at the yellow trail on his shirt.

"This whole police snitch thing has me puzzled," he said. "I've checked every division and nobody can identify a contact."

"Maybe they don't want to give up a name?" Murray said. "You know, a form of protection for the guy."

"Or maybe it's all bullshit. The snitch was in Stan's imagination," Fryman said.

"What if the killer is a cop?" I said.

The three veterans were silent, akin to the code that

was understood and never spoken of when it involved one of "our own." The stillness in the office was thunderous.

Not wanting too much quiet time, I broke through with, "Or somebody that has something on a cop."

"No," Fryman said, "a cop wouldn't use a knife. Too messy. Me, I'd use a quick clean bullet." He pointed an index finger to his temple, bent his thumb, and, with a mock pistol shot, yelled, "POW."

"We'll keep your name in the hopper," Wilson said. "Let's get started."

We went over every detail in the murder book and on the white board and kept coming to the only strong suspect; the mystery man in the bar named John but whose real name was Karl. It seemed obvious to me but Wilson had reservations.

"What are the risks?" Murray wondered out loud.

"I don't think he knows I'm a cop," I said. "He had to be the one who tore my house apart. A robber would go after money, jewelry, or stuff he could pawn and he wouldn't spend the time ransacking everything. He knew exactly where to look."

"How could he get phone numbers and addresses?" Murray wondered.

"If he knows you're a cop, then he wants you dead. Just like Stan," Fryman said. "I don't see the point of Victor walking into a trap."

"He thinks he's walking into a hook-up," I said. "I'm sure he understood that I was propositioning him."

"Remember you fit the profile of Burgess and Carlyle," Murray said.

"It's not a trap," I said. "If he's the killer of Burgess, Carlyle, and Stan, then he's not going to do anything where there are possible witnesses."

The phone rang and as the junior man of the group, I

answered. It was a message from the duty officer at the
desk. "The lab tech will be sending the enhanced blow-
ups from the Quick Stop surveillance camera." He
paused. "By the way, who is this?" he asked.

"I'm answering for Captain Wilson."

"Oh. Okay. The passcode on the site is Carlyle,
pound sign. Got that?"

In all, there were ten close-ups to review. With each
one, we could expand any portion of the screen, though
the quality and the large pixels cost important detail. One
view showed an enhanced section of a mouth and chin. I
pointed to what looked like a shaded area that could be a
cleft chin. The very same kind possessed by mystery
man.

"That's our killer," Fryman said.

"The D.A. is going to want more than this picture.
Hell, that could be my sainted grandmother," Wilson
said.

"Let me try and get more tomorrow," I said.

Wilson was visibly uncomfortable, shifting in his
seat, rubbing the back of his head, and pursing his lips.
"If we do this, we've got to have at least four cops inside
as customers or employees and four outside."

"Robert and I will be in the van parked close by,
monitoring the wire," Murray said.

"Do we bring the manager in on it?" Fryman asked.

"Absolutely. He or she has to agree. We can't risk a
lawsuit if something should go wrong," Wilson said.

For the fourth time a small knot formed in the pit of
my stomach and I could feel some dampness in my
hands.

It was more than a touch of fright. It was the excitement for avenging Stan's murder. I was doing exactly
what Wilson said I shouldn't: bringing emotion into my
police work. It just seemed right that Stan's death should

not be in vain. Besides, what could go wrong, I wondered, with so much firepower backing me up?

"What was the reason for meeting at the Lighthouses?" Wilson asked.

"It's a first date," Fryman answered and Wilson winced with more discomfort.

"Maybe he's not the killer and he just wants to put the make on you," Murray said.

"No," I said. "It's the other way around. He thinks I'm putting the make on him or at least I thought I was."

"In what way?" Wilson asked.

"Well, when we sat at the bar I put my hand on his leg and held it there."

"What part of his leg? The ankle? The calf?" There was an edge in Fryman's voice to accompany his smirk.

"His thigh," I said as I felt my face getting red. I wasn't going to tell him about the crotch part.

"Inside or outside?" Fryman pushed harder; his eyes widened in glee.

"How should I know? I'm new at this. Why? Does it make a difference?"

"Let's find out," Fryman said, "put your hand on my thigh and we'll see."

All three laughed but I didn't think it was funny.

"Look. Right now, I think he knows you're a cop," Murray began. "What he doesn't know is that we have his correct name. At some point in the conversation you should call him 'Karl.'"

"What happens then?" I asked.

"Then we hope he spills some info that we can use. We nail him,"

Wilson shook his head. "That has to be a last resort. Victor, you will have to steer the conversation, keep him talking, and maybe even bring up Burgess or Carlyle as a routine subject."

The planning then reduced to Wilson and Murray refining the scenario of who does what and when. It was decided that once we recorded the key piece of information, Murray would leave the van, enter the restaurant, and be joined by two of the undercover customers and make the arrest. It all sounded simple and I didn't feel any apprehension, at least while we were planning.

"See which detectives we can tap for this operation. Each pair in the booth should be a male and a female cop so as not to raise suspicion," Wilson said. "Another thing. Check if the Lighthouse has surveillance cameras inside and outside. If they don't, let's get a team in there right now and set up some inconspicuous eyes."

As more details were considered, my iPhone gave a text message ring. When I checked, it was from Jannine. It read, *CALL ME. URGENT.*

I interrupted the conversation. "Sorry Captain. I have to take this call. It's from my fiancée."

"What?" Fryman shouted." Already you're pussy whipped? What the hell is it going to be like after you're married? Oh, you poor guy."

"How would you know? You've never been married," Murray said and I felt good having him in my corner.

I moved several desks away and made the call. She answered on the first ring.

"What's up?" I asked.

"Victor, there is something strange going on. I'm sure I was followed on my way home from the store. Now I have all the lights out and from my front window I see a black car parked across the street, two doors down, with someone sitting there smoking a cigarette." She paused. "I'm scared."

"Can you get the make of the car and a license plate number?"

"No. It's too far to make out anything. Hurry, will you?"

"Keep the doors locked and stay unseen at the front window."

"What if he—" She suddenly stopped as though she could not find the words for the fear that must have gripped her.

"If he gets out of the car and comes to your door, don't answer. Just call 911. I'm leaving now."

Chapter 35

Phone Messages

I knew that leaving the squad room without letting Wilson know why would be a problem for me, but my priorities were very clear in my mind. This time it was not a case of me making a choice between Jannine or my captain.

As I drove toward her apartment, I dialed Aaron in the hopes that he was home. It was only eleven o'clock and the boys would be getting ready for a nap. Worst case he could be doing a shift. After the fourth ring, Carrie answered.

"Carrie, this is Victor. Is Aaron home?"

"He's in the garage, working out. Why? What's wrong?"

"I need his help."

"Hold on."

After she put the phone down, I switched my phone to speaker because I did not want the delay of being stopped for a cellphone violation. Naturally, I wouldn't get a ticket. I just couldn't afford the time. Traffic on

Chandler was unusually heavy for the lunch hour and it seemed like I had to stop at every light.

"Hey." Aaron sounded out of breath, which I could understand since domestic chores were never his strong suite.

"Can you meet me at Jannine's, ASAP?"

"Thanks for saving my ass."

"Listen, Aaron. Jannine may be in trouble."

"I'm walking out the door."

His phone clicked and my light changed to green. When I approached Jannine's, I did not stop. Instead, I cruised past her apartment building, checking each parked car on the street. I saw no lights on in her place and nobody was sitting in a dark sedan. I circled around the block once more and came to a complete stop in front of her apartment. When I phoned, she answered immediately.

"He drove away just a few minutes ago. Thank God you're here."

Aaron arrived just as I was parking my car so I waited for him to find a spot down the block. He ran toward me, nearly out of breath.

"What is it?"

"It may be a false alarm. Sorry, Aaron. She got spooked because she was sure someone followed her. When she got home, she saw the car parked out front with a guy behind the wheel."

"That's no false alarm with all the shit comin' down lately. Do they know who tore your place apart?"

The curtain in Jannine's apartment moved and I saw her waving at the window. "Let's go up because, though she looks and acts tough, I know she's scared."

We climbed to the second floor front apartment and found her waiting at the open door.

"I'm up here about to wet my panties and you two

are standing on the sidewalk probably talking dirty," she said.

I made a move to kiss her but she turned sideways and all I got was a little cheek. That seemed better than fighting.

"What kinda beer you got?" Aaron asked as he pushed by us.

"Whatever was on sale," she said then headed for the kitchen just as the phone rang. "Victor, can you get that?"

I picked up her cordless phone and said, "Hello." There was no answer so I repeated the hello again. Still no answer. "Is someone on the line?" I asked.

Jannine came back into the room holding three bottles of *Pacifico*. I ended the call.

"Who was it?" she asked.

"Wrong number," I said trying to sound disinterested and matter-of-fact.

It didn't work because the color in her face matched the foam oozing out of the bottles. "I got the same call and hang-up last night, too."

She handed us each a beer and her eyes shifted suddenly to the front windows. We sipped and speculated about the importance, if any, of the events of the past two days.

Aaron tried to make light of the situation by placing the blame on Jannine's killer figure. "With that body, I can't blame any guy for trying to meet you," he said.

"This is too weird," she said.

"Okay, pack up some things. You're coming with us," Aaron said.

"Where?"

"My house. Right now. Victor is bunking in with Taylor so you can share his sister's room. Unless, of course, we put Taylor and his sister in one room and you and Victor—"

"Carrie will never go along with that and neither would I," she interrupted. "I'll be all right here. It now seems like it was all coincidence. Maybe I'm getting paranoid," she said.

"I'll stay here also," I said. "Damn, I can't because Captain Wilson—oh shit, I have to call him. He's going to be pissed."

I dialed the private number into the squad room and Fryman answered.

"Do you know what time it is? Wilson is boiling. Get your ass back here now. We have only four hours before show time."

I hung up and turned to Jannine. "I have to go."

Aaron took a long swig of beer. "You're coming to my place, Jannine. With all the shit going on, you can't stay here. Besides, the kids will love to see you."

She said nothing, but her expression screamed annoyance.

As we prepared to leave, Jannine's phone rang again.

"Don't answer it," I said.

Chapter 36

What's in a Name?

The small office space in the East Valley Division hummed with complaints of a deployment three days before Thanksgiving. Though everyone was out of uniform, they still looked like police personnel.

Fryman was like a USO Comic, entertaining the troops with his bawdy police stories. He kept referring to me as the star of the show, which did not lower my anxiety level. "Victor will sign autographs after the cuffs are on," he announced.

The whole spectacle did not look like a run-up to arresting a serial killer. Murray called the meeting to order then referred to his yellow pad. He pointed to a large chart of the restaurant's layout.

"Officer Daniel Gonzalez will be in this center booth and wear a navy blue watch cap pulled over his big ears to hide buds that will connect him to our van outside."

"I got it here," Gonzalez yelled and stood up, pulling the cap over his ears.

"Better cover the nose, too," someone yelled.

"He will be coupled with Officer Maryann Wright."

She pushed her fist into the air. Even out of uniform, she looked like a cop with her light brown hair pulled back into a tight bun at the back of her head.

"Officer Lilly Ellis has agreed to wear a decorative head scarf tied into a bow on top of her head, covering the ear buds," Murray said.

A collective "Aww…" rang out in the squad room.

"She too will have audio connection to the van. Her partner will be Officer Albert Colletti and they will be in the booth next to Victor's."

"I'm going to be a sixties hippie," Colletti said.

His buffed out body and his broad shoulders could hardly pass as an emaciated, skinny, Hirsute flower child.

Detectives Bob Johanson and Ralph Onesti, who off duty were golf buddies, would come dressed in flashy pants and sweaters with tees tucked behind each ear. I wondered why golfers would eat at the Lighthouse when the closest golf course was in Toluca Lake, five miles away.

Since my meeting with John, aka Karl, was at six, we would gradually take up positions starting at five fifteen. I was to arrive ten minutes early and would be sitting in a booth when he arrived.

Murray droned on about procedures everyone knew. "The SWAT team will not take up positions until after the target enters the restaurant. The rear entrance presents a minor problem since positioning will have to be up the hill." He pointed to another chart showing the outside areas.

We anticipated everything or so we thought. The assumption that he would be armed was correct, that he would be in street clothes was correct, and that he would recognize my car was also correct.

Murray wanted me to arrive alone in a plain car from

the general pool of vehicles assigned to the East Valley Division.

"That might arouse suspicion," I said. "Why don't I use my own car?"

"Because the pool car will be wired and have a direction finder transmitter," he said.

My nervous level meter went up two notches. Boredom drove the chatter level in the room up to a point that Murray had to pound on the podium.

"Quiet down, everyone. We're almost finished. The group wired for communication meets at Laurel and Ventura at 5 p.m. for a sound check. The rest arrive according to the schedule."

At ten minutes to four, Wilson wrapped up the meeting and we all left in silence. At 4:30 p.m. the van parked on Ventura just east of the restaurant. I parked behind it and the final test of the system began. After Fryman said he could hear me loud and clear, I climbed into the van. One whole side contained electronic equipment for checking location, direction finding, audio, and four feeds of video into separate displays. Two bolted down swivel chairs allowed for easy reach of any module.

"Ellis, are you on?" Fryman asked from inside the van.

"Check," she said.

"Does Colletti look stoned?" Fryman asked.

In the background I heard him yell, "Dude, I'm gone."

Fryman laughed and spoke to the microphone. "Gonzalez, check in."

There was no answer.

"Gonzalez, talk to me, baby."

Still no answer, just the crackle and static of dead airways hissed from the speakers.

Fryman slid open the curbside door, stepped out, and

looked up and down Ventura Blvd. No sign of Gonzalez and his partner, Maryann. He slammed his hand on the top of the van.

"Fuck"

"You're on the air," I said.

"I don't give a fuck."

He checked his watch then trotted down to the corner at Laurel. I watched his mouth spitting out what must have been more expletives. When he returned to the van, he began leafing through a personnel manual in search of Gonzalez's phone number.

The communication system began to hiss and pop. Amongst the cacophony, Gonzalez's voice began to fade in and out. Amid the obscenities came a critical evaluation of the case, which was being broadcast over a system he probably didn't know was on while they were in route to the Lighthouse.

"I wonder if the taxpayers know..." Static noises broke up part of the conversation. "...is spent on a drag queen killer."

After more spurious sounds, Maryann's voice broke in with, "Turn left at Laurel."

"Oh shit. We're late," Gonzalez said loud and clear, on a noise-free connection, which meant they were getting closer.

"I wonder if the taxpayers know how much you are costing them by being late?" Fryman broadcast. He was seething.

"Sorry. Gonzalez and Hill, checking in."

Everyone took up their positions. I left the van and drove off to wait. At precisely 5:20 p.m., I drove up from the west on Ventura Boulevard and parked behind the restaurant. According to the plan, I was to be fifteen minutes early so I could select the assigned booth. I felt calm and reassured, though a little anxious that my wire was a one-way communication. They could only hear my conversation.

There were to be three key points in my discussions with Karl. The first came when I confronted him with his real name, Karl Decker. The second was when I asked him if Stan killed Burgess and Carlyle. The third was a simple why. If an opening occurred in the conversation for any one of these three, I was to be ready for a reaction. It was here that I was feeling more like bait than a police detective. As I got out of the car and walked into the restaurant, I wondered why, if Karl had a fetish, he wanted me to wear street clothes. Why not dress up if that was to be part of the bizarre scene? How would he recognize me? There was the why again.

The first inside curve ball came when I walked inside. Our plan was to have me sitting in a booth when he arrived. Though I was fifteen minutes early, he was already there, in the end booth, facing the front door. I wondered if he was there when Gonzalez and Wright or Ellis and Colletti arrived. I walked slowly, trying not to look at the two pairs of detectives sitting in booths that were not in the locations of the plan.

I was at a loss as to what to say, how to act, or even think about asking any questions.

"Hey." I offered as I slipped into the booth with my back to the detectives. "It looks like we're both early." I felt nervous and afraid he could pick up on my body language of uncertainty.

"Relax," he said. "We're just getting to know each other."

He was beyond cool. His confidence level reflected in his total deportment. He sipped his coffee in a slow exaggerated motion, his steel blue eyes never leaving me or blinking. The waitress arrived with a glass of ice water which I drank in gulps.

"You guys need some time?" she asked as she set down two menus.

John, aka Karl, nodded slowly. His not speaking primed my urge to fill the empty air time. "Give us a minute," I said. "We haven't even looked at the menu or do you know what you're going to have—" I paused and caught myself almost saying Karl. "It's John, isn't it?"

He took another sip of his coffee and nodded. I wanted to kill some time to make sure everyone; including the SWAT team was in place and ready.

I wondered how I was going to get this guy to start talking. True, it was I who brought about this meeting with the suggestion of possible sex.

Then I remembered Murray advising me to ask open-ended questions. Try not to solicit yes or no answers. That was the plan.

"What do you think of the Valley?" I asked and immediately realized it was stupid and obvious.

"I like it." With that, he bounced the verbal ball back into my court.

I fidgeted. "Are you from here originally?"

"No."

Shit, wrong question.

Casually, I stretched around, making sure I could see Gonzalez and company in place. The waitress returned and gave us a surprised look since the menus were still where she had put them so she shrugged and left. He never turned to look at her. Instead, he kept staring at me. If he was trying to get to me, it was working.

"So what do you do?" he asked.

"Oh, I'm a programmer. I work from home. Call my own shots so to speak."

His facial expression did not change when he said, "I mean in bed."

That came out of left field. Then I realized, it was me

who put my hand on his thigh. He was better at asking open-ended questions than I was.

"A little bit of everything, I guess." I became keenly aware that a whole squad of cops was listening in on our conversation. I also became aware that it was me who had to move this along.

"So what do you like to do?" I asked.

"I'm too old for cat and mouse games," he said. "I wanna get it on, get in, and get out."

"Right on," I said. "Let's eat lunch and then go for it."

I picked up a menu and decided it was time for me to use option one. If he knew I was a cop, why was he going along with this charade? He couldn't know or else he would be walking into a trap. Butterflies returned to my gut.

"So what looks good to you?"

"You do," he said and I forced a perfunctory laugh.

"I mean for lunch," I said.

He hadn't even picked up the menu so I tried some pointed questions. "Was last night your first time at the Glove?" I asked.

"No."

That was hardly an open-ended question. I decided to go out on the limb. "Did you ever meet that guy that was murdered? I think is name was Carlyle."

Suddenly, he tensed and looked around turning his head like a bird sensing danger. "No."

Then it happened, not as planned, because I was getting flustered. "How about the other guy? Did you get it on with him?"

He suddenly tensed and turned his head toward the front door. "The other guy?" he asked.

"Yeah, I think his name was Burgess."

His right arm moved from the top of the table to the bottom. He slowly turned and looked at the back door. He scanned the restaurant and his jaw tightened because the veins in his neck appeared to swell.

He knows. I was sure of it. I was incredibly calm when I realized I had to move to the second phase of the plan.

"Don't misunderstand," I said. "I'm not jealous if you did get it on with those guys, Karl."

"My name is John," he said as he sat up from his slouch and again searched the area as someone expecting a sudden move.

"Oh, I meant John. Sorry." I felt the initiative switch to my favor. "I mean in bed. What can I expect?"

He wasn't listening. His attention was focused elsewhere. He shifted in his seat several times. He reached into his jacket pocket and drew out a revolver, pointed it at my chest. "I'll do the talking."

A cold chill ran through me and I thought about Fryman wetting his pants, except in this case, there was no question about the gun being loaded. It began to dawn on me that a man who had killed three other people would not hesitate to add another notch. He had nothing to lose. Up to this point, we still had nothing to tie him to Burgess and Carlyle. When the waitress headed our way he shifted the gun under the table.

Chapter 37

Take Down

Currents of anxiety charged through my body when Karl reminded me of the gun pointed directly at my groin. I realized that all the cops, the SWAT team, and the detectives could not come between the muzzle of the gun and my body. The flash that coursed through my consciousness was Jannine and Aaron calling me bait. I was now on the hook, about to be reeled in, just as they predicted.

When I began to speak, Karl raised his hand to silence me. Without words, there would be no incriminating evidence, but more important the van had no way of knowing what was happening. No anticipating actions. Two things were certain: he'd figured out the police were on to him and he assumed I was part of the plan. It had all seemed so easy in theory.

Facing death with courage and resignation was something I didn't realize I was capable of. We hadn't rehearsed this part where I became the hero, where a city would mourn, and where I never became a detective.

Karl and I remained frozen like a Christmas Tableau. As the waitress neared our booth, he tapped the gun against the bottom of the table to remind me of its presence. I didn't dare move a muscle, let alone move my head. I had hoped beyond hope that she was one of the cops in on the plan. I was wrong to assume anything.

Was the gun still pointed at me? I had no idea and no intention of finding out. I remained silent. She looked at Karl then at me. The menus were back on the table, unopened.

"Do you need more time?" she asked.

I wanted to shout out, "Yes, I need all the time I can get. Please, please don't leave."

Karl nodded while continuing to stare at me. She turned and looked at me and I watched her face from the corner of my eye. In a fraction of a microsecond, an almost imperceptible flicker of her upper lids told me she knew and wanted me to know she was a replacement waitress—an LAPD cop.

"Yes," I said as though answering her question but really saying yes we're in trouble here so let the van know. She turned and left and, though I could not see her, I hoped she had stopped at the Gonzalez booth.

Karl's eyes had changed from those of a cool cat to those of a Bengal tiger that sensed danger, an animal, cunning, alert, and tense. He brought the gun back above the table with a handkerchief draped over it. I felt the perspiration starting to form on my brow with a slow rivulet easing down my face in front of my left ear. I could actually hear the rapid pounding of my heartbeat.

As I waited for the next move, I thought how I fucked up by not wearing the Kevlar vest. Depending upon what kind of bullets he was using, it could have saved my life. I kept my hands together on top of the table without even a hint of motion. When I shifted my legs, I could feel my pistol in the right front pocket of my pants. Carefully I stretched out my right leg, taking care not to touch him. Provided there was an option, it would make access to the gun easier and faster. The handle was close to the opening but the latch was on. I had to piece together the fragments of the probables I had to work with.

I decided to speak. I assumed he would not risk shooting me there in the restaurant, because he knew he would never make it out the door.

I gambled and said, "Why did you kill Stan?"

He did not answer. His eyes darted to one side, watching for any movement.

"Stan wasn't your type. Why did you kill him?"

After what seemed an eternity of time he said, "We decided he knew too much."

"And what about Carlyle and Burgess?"

He just stared at me. I assumed, as I was sure he did also, that a SWAT team was waiting outside at both the front and the back entrances. The entire restaurant seemed to fall silent. Once again, he moved the gun under the table. I watched as Gonzalez and Hill passed by on their way out the back door, without a glance at us. What my mind could not process was the thought that if Karl knew he was going to die, then my life would be just another notch in his gun belt.

I never really thought about death, sacrifice, or the bullshit of duty and honor. My only thoughts at that moment were saving my neck and not urinating. I remembered the awful odor of Carlyle's dead body, the stench of dried blood, piss, and shit.

"You got a wire on?" Karl whispered.

"Yes," I said.

"Then you're my ticket out of here. Pull it off."

All systems were a go. The van knew it, the cops knew it, and the SWAT team was in place. The only one not ready for all of this, was me. Since my whole being was focused on survival and not on catching a killer. I measured my chances of using the ruse of removing the wire and, instead, reaching for my gun. The timing was wrong. He'd shoot before I could unlock it. I reasoned that if he shot me, it would be tantamount to his own death.

Slowly I reached behind the front of my shirt and tugged out the microphone attached to a long wire, laid it on the table and folded my hands.

With the butt of his gun he smashed the tip of the mike and I winced at the thought of the gun going off from the jolt.

"Karl, this doesn't make sense. I know you can make a deal—no special circumstance—that's a minimum deal. Why not go for it?"

His face showed no reaction. I couldn't tell if he was considering the offer or he was off in some other world. I decided to press further.

"No special circumstance could mean no death penalty," I said.

The slight movement of his lips gave no hint of rage or a smile. "No chance," he said.

"Why? What did these three men do to you?"

His eyes narrowed and the edges of his mouth turned down. His lips tightened. He had to know, now, that he wasn't being recorded.

"My job," he said. "Same as you do your job. They meant nothing to me. Nothing."

The slight hint of regret in his voice gave me enough hope to continue.

"Karl, I can help you with a deal, but I'm no good to you dead. What do you say?" I regretted that none of this conversation was getting to the van. I needed to keep him talking because the more he said the more I could read my chance of negotiation and life. "There's an army of cops out there with fire power you can't match."

"I don't need to," he said. "I've got you to help me get downtown."

"We can help each other, Karl. I can help you cut a deal with the D.A."

A strange smile—more like a sneer—came over his face.

"Get up," he said. "And face the front door. Stand perfectly still. Do you understand?"

"Wait, Karl. Why are we going downtown?"

"Shut up and do as I said."

I did exactly what he said but also considered my chances of reaching my gun. They were a lot better if I was standing.

"Keep your hands folded in front of your stomach."

One again, I sensed hope slipping away, yet I knew I had to stay alert, watchful, and ready to seize an opportunity. He kept his back to the rear entrance door with me in front of him. The muzzle of his gun was hurting my back. I watched Lilly stand up slowly and I prayed she would not do or say anything. She and Colletti exited through the front door. We stepped backward, like two performers from *Dancing with the Stars*. Karl suddenly waved the gun sideways, urging me to move. When some of the patrons saw the gun, they remained frozen with fear. Nobody headed for the front door. Though I could not see her, I heard a woman sobbing. A man and a woman at the far end wrapped themselves around a little girl sitting between them as they ducked down behind their booth.

When another woman screamed, Karl yelled, "Shut up."

She began to whimper.

Plastered together, we took tiny steps backward. I let

my folded hands drop slowly below my belt as we reached the rear door. None of this had been in our rehearsal so I, like Karl, was moving one step at a time toward some unknown objective, which only he knew about.

Suddenly, I felt the barrel of his gun press harder into the center of my back.

"Get those hands higher, he said.

"Karl, we can make a deal with the captain. I'm sure of it. You can save your neck."

"No deal."

There was finality in his voice that weakened my knees. In fact, I could almost not feel my ankles and toes.

"When we step outside, you're going to turn sideways and then face out. You got that?"

"Where are we going?" I asked.

"Did you hear what I said?" The impatient edge in his voice became another warning for me.

"Yes," I said.

I knew exactly my role; I was to shield him from SWAT getting a clean shot. I wondered what they used as a margin of error before shooting. Mostly I hoped they would grant him whatever he wanted.

When he opened the door, we were like a duet on a ballet stage. We stepped out, turned in unison, and faced a full battery of police weapons pointed directly at me. The thought of a trigger-happy or trigger-nervous cop crossed my mind. An LAPD negotiator on a bullhorn announced his presence from behind the open door of a police car.

"Karl Decker, this is Officer Martin Uribe. Toss your weapon on the ground in front of you so we can stand down and listen to your requests."

"I want my car brought here and guaranteed passage," he shouted from behind my ear.

"Toss down you gun and your keys then put your hands on your head." The officer's voice was a numbing monotone. It was also a stupid request, the keys, maybe, but not both.

I heard Karl whisper, "Fuck."

He wrapped his left arm around my waist and pressed me tightly against him while his right hand held the gun to my side just below my elbow. Each time I tried to move a little to one side or the other, he dug his left fist into my stomach and pushed the gun further into my body.

It became an excruciating pain.

I watched Captain Wilson join the negotiator. Fryman and Murray were right behind him. He took the bullhorn. "Mr. Decker, this is Captain Wilson. I want you to know you can make things much easier for yourself by cooperating." After a short pause he added, "What do you say?"

I watched Fryman and Murray step up next to Wilson.

"No deal. Make your team disappear. All of them."

"Okay, toss your keys out and we will stand down," Wilson said.

I realized that the captain was trying to create an edge for me. When Karl reached for his keys, I could bolt and SWAT could get a clean shot.

"They must think I'm stupid," Karl said.

We were at a complete standoff. Neither Karl nor the police were willing to budge or make the first move. I realized it all came down to me. I would have to do the set-up and hope SWAT would do their part. For the next few minutes, Wilson made several offers, each rejected by Karl.

"Move everybody out and clear the alley," Karl demanded.

I could not hear the exchanges between Wilson and the cadre of cops behind him. In what looked like slow motion, pairs of cops moved away toward their vehicles and drove off. Most of the cops were gone except the SWAT team, Wilson, and the negotiator.

"The keys, Karl. We need the keys," Wilson shouted.

A loud noise at the far end of the parking lot spooked everyone. Karl watched several police look in that direction. When I felt his left hand loosen slightly as he turned his head to the right, I used that instant to twist my way to the left and push at his hand holding the gun. We were both momentarily off balance. I heard a single shot. That single shot was followed by a volley of gunfire. On the ground, I realized I was hit. It seemed strange that I wasn't in any great pain. I felt a strong burning sensation on my right side. I reached around with my left hand and felt the wet sticky fluid of my blood, though I couldn't tell where it was coming from. I heard footsteps running. I felt an arm under my neck. When I looked up, it was Fryman.

"God dammit, get an ambulance here, now," he yelled over his shoulder. He cradled my head in his arm. His voice had an echoing sound like he was in a large empty room in an old mansion. "Easy, Vic. Just take it easy," he said.

I sensed him getting close to my face, and then I felt his forehead touch mine. The shouting sounded far away and I didn't feel any pain. I had the sensation of flying over rooftops and swooping down on baseball diamonds.

I heard Wilson's voice say, "He's dead."

The last thing I remembered thinking was I didn't want to wet myself or shit my pants.

I felt Fryman's cheek against mine and the last I heard was him yelling, "Where the fuck's that ambulance?"

Chapter 38

Vicodin

LAPD's contract for medical and hospital services landed me in Providence St. Joseph's Medical Center in Burbank. I was grateful for that. How and when I got there after the shootings I did not know. Only vague snippets came to mind before I lapsed into unconsciousness. It was a scary feeling not being able to account for a large chuck of time. When I came to, I had wires and tubes extending from every part of my body. I certainly didn't have to worry about wetting my pants because I had a tube extending from my penis to a bag hooked to the side of the bed.

"Where am I?" I asked a beautiful Pilipino nurse adjusting plastic bags hanging above my head.

She smiled, adjusted the bed covers, and checked the various connections. "You're in ICU for surgical recovery at St. Joseph's," she said. "Welcome to the living. Are you in any pain?"

I wanted to leap up and tell her, "Pain is good! Dead is bad."

"Yes, but I love it," I said instead.

"On a scale of one to ten how would you rate the pain?"

"About a fifteen," I said, "but don't give me anything for it. I want to feel it."

"We will be moving you to a private room this afternoon, once the doctor gives the order."

After pressing buttons on various screens and machines, she started to leave.

"Can I ask you a favor?" She nodded. "Would you call East Valley Police Division on Burbank Boulevard and ask Captain Wilson or Richard Fryman to come here as soon as possible. It's urgent."

"Right now only family members are allowed a few minutes visit," she said.

I spent the rest of the morning, squirming and shifting in my bed. At first, I hated having a catheter and a pee bag hanging from the bed and me. After the first couple of times, I got used to just letting it go whenever I needed to. After lunch, the medical tech came in and announced that she would be removing the catheter. I had mixed feelings about that. What was more, I had a new appreciation for women who had to undergo a cervical examination as I lay there with my hospital gown pulled up to my chest, the bright lights of the room shinning down on my equipment, and a tall, beautiful black-haired woman medical tech holding my penis as she withdrew the tube. Normally such activity would lead to an erection.

Sadly, not this time.

After the extraction, the nurse returned and told me the good news. I could now urinate into a plastic bottle.

"Did I get any inquiries from a Jannine Lindbloom?"

She gave me an understanding sigh. "This is the fourth time you've asked me and I'm sorry, but there have been no phone calls or visitors asking to see you. Your parents are in the ICU waiting room. They were in here several times while you were out."

"Thanks."

"Do you want me to call her? If you give me the number I'd be glad to."

"No, that's okay. Thanks. Just ask my parents to come in."

❧❧

They wheeled my bed, with me in it, to a private room on the fourth floor where Wilson, Fryman, and Murray were waiting for me. I lifted my head and saw Fryman holding up the LA Times with a headline reading *Serial Murderer Killed*. A smaller sub-headline read, *LAPD Closes Case*.

"You're a gutsy little guy, Victor," Fryman said.

"Now that the case is closed, the mayor, the chief of police, and a certain city councilman want to have their picture taken with you," Wilson said.

"It's not closed," I said. "The mastermind behind the killings has not been arrested."

"What are you talking about?" Murray asked. "You yourself nailed him."

"Karl was a hired killer," I said. "He did the stabbings of Burgess, Carlyle, and Stan, but for him it was only a job. He had no personal stake in any of those victims. He did it for money."

"How do you know this?" Wilson asked "And if that's the case then who is the real killer?"

The nurse came in and apologized. "I'm sorry, but the doctor has limited visits to only one person and for just a few minutes. Tomorrow he will be a lot stronger and you can stay longer."

"Just a couple more minutes, nurse." Wilson made it sound like a demand.

She turned on her heel and left.

"What makes you so sure, or are you still shooting for job security?" Murray said.

"When Karl did talk, he used the word *we*. Like when I asked him why he killed Stan he said *we*. Didn't the search find out that he was involved in a hired killer case in Wisconsin?"

"He was acquitted," Murray reminded me.

"That doesn't mean he wasn't guilty," Wilson added.

"During the stand-off at the Lighthouse, he kept saying he had a get-out-of-jail card downtown." At that moment, the pain in my side and my shoulder was kicking my ass. I wanted to buzz for the nurse and get a magic Vicodin pain pill, but I also wanted to get going on the case. "I think the guy behind the killings was Kemper."

"What?" all three said at the same time.

"You forget he was the crusader for finding the Carlyle and Burgess killer," Wilson argued.

"Yeah, I know. That's what we have to find out. Why?"

Fryman was beginning to consider Kemper. "He is running for election. Maybe he's desperate."

"Or maybe there's something more in his history," Murray added.

"Remember when Stan thought there was a snitch working for the LAPD and you found nobody in our division or any other that had such a contact?" I asked Wilson.

"Stan didn't know about Kemper so he thought it was a snitch providing the inside information," Murray said. "That's possible."

I was beginning to get excited, but the pain was also getting more intense. "Why did Karl want to get downtown when an army of cops surrounded us? Who was he going to contact?"

"Did he mention Kemper?" Murray asked.

"No."

The nurse came in and stood at the foot of the bed with her arms folded like a top sergeant. Her facial expression and body language shouted louder than any words she could use.

"Wait, before you go. When Stan and I were at the convention of—" I didn't want to say the word in front of the nurse, but she didn't budge. "—cross-dressers. Kemper was the main speaker and, after the program, he came down to talk to both Stan and me. For a minute then, I thought Stan and Kemper knew each other. Just the way he addressed Stan made me a little suspicious. Then he said something to Stan that told me they had a history."

Wilson frowned. "I think we'll do some checking. Bank statements, phone logs, personal background, and basic research might give us some clues. Who knows, you may be right?" He then turned to the nurse. "How soon will we be able to return? I have a lot more to discuss with him."

"Let's give him at least twenty four hours of rest," she said. "He now has a phone so you can call him later."

With that, the three of them left and I begged for a double dose of Vicodin. If I got hooked, I'd worry about kicking the habit later. It couldn't be any worse than hitting on a joint.

At four o'clock the call came in from Murray. "Victor, you're a genius. Turns out Kemper had a son who was molested by a cross-dressed man when the boy was thirteen years old. We also found large deposits to an account owned by a K. Decker that corresponded to withdrawals from A.J. Kemper's account." He was talking so fast I was sure he would hyperventilate at any moment.

"And—" He was almost yelling now. "—he owns a black Chrysler Town Car with license plates 5SHJ210."

"Where is he now?" I asked.

"In lock-up. When we arrested him, he gave no resistance. He lawyered up right away. It should be a slam-dunk and mostly to your credit. You should be able to see the arrest on one of the channels. They were all there."

"Are any of them coming here?"

"Ah—" There was a long hesitation. "The captain wants to keep you on the down low for now. He said he'd call you later today."

I had hoped for some exposure but it was not in the cards. I'd had enough Vicodin that I didn't care. What I did care was about Aaron and Jannine. I couldn't understand why neither of them had not come to see me. I rationalized that perhaps they didn't know because the paper had only sketchy reporting as per the chief's preference. "Keep a low profile" was always his mantra, for the good of the force.

Maybe just one more Vicodin.

Chapter 39

The Cross-Dresser's Ball

M y fourth-floor room overlooked the 134 Freeway, which gave me a lord's-eye-view of the endless stream of humans in their metal shells going about their daily lives, unaware of the dark underbelly of crime in the valley. Waiting in a hospital room, gave me pause about life in general and my own in particular.

Aaron came to visit the second day and brought me up to date about Claire and the kids but nothing about Jannine.

I, too, wanted to get moving, but mostly I wanted to get away from the pungent antiseptic hospital odors, the hard bed, the constant blood tests, the IV bags, and the reruns of Two and Half Men. I wanted out.

Aaron agreed to pick me up at 11 a.m. and now he was seven minutes late. Even minutes in a hospital room are torture.

The nurse stood outside my door with a wheel chair and my discharge papers, which she read to me twice before I signed. I was not going to be pushed through the halls and the elevator like some produce on a vegetable cart.

"I can walk," I said. "My legs are fine."

"I'm sorry, Mr. Espinoza, it is hospital regulations that we deliver you to the front entrance," she said.

"Look. It's my shoulder and my arm that got hit, not my legs."

She smiled her response, shrugged her shoulders as she flipped the two foot rests of the wheel chair up, and gestured me into my rolling caddy. "I told your friend to bring the car around to the front where we will meet him."

I lowered myself into the chair and she put a strap around my waist, no doubt insurance that I wouldn't jump up and run. She dumped a plastic bag filled with my belongings into my lap and off we went with me avoiding eye contact with anyone we passed.

Aaron folded me into the passenger seat of his Grand Cherokee and then buckled me in so that the shoulder strap did not cross over my bandaged chest. We drove along in silence for a long stretch. Finally, he announced, "You're going to stay at my place for a few days."

"Bullshit. I want to go home."

"Not until you learn to drive, cook, and dress yourself with your left hand."

"I know I can manage."

"Claire is itching to play nursemaid, so you might as well resign yourself."

"What about Jannine's place?"

"You tell me. Did you talk to her? Did she visit you at the hospital?"

"I guess I burned the last bridge, this time for good."

We dropped back into silence as he turned off the freeway at Lankershim. It seemed strange that Jannine did not even call. I assumed she didn't know what had happened. I was lost in my thoughts about her so I hadn't noticed the streets we were taking.

"Where are we going?" I asked because Aaron's house was off the Woodman exit.

"I need to make a quick stop at the station for some paperwork. This new pain-in-the-ass rule about filling out a form for overtime pay has got us all crazy."

When we pulled into the parking lot I said, "I'll wait in the car."

"No you don't, Victor. I don't trust you because you might decide to take off and hail a cab. No. You come in with me."

I was in no mood to argue with him so I agreed. When we entered the squad room, it was nearly empty. All the information about the Carlyle case was erased from the white board, the lights in Wilson's office were off, and none of the detectives were at their desks. JoAnn, who manned the phones, waved at me and I pumped my left fist in the air.

"We missed you," she said.

I felt a little sad that my short career as a detective was over. Seeing the squad room filled me with nostalgia.

JoAnn stood up and walked to a side counter where she switched on an ancient Boom Box that started to blast the drums and brass of the old tune, *The Stripper*.

With that, the side door to the locker room opened and in marched, single file, the entire gang all dressed in drag. Murray, in a ballet dancer's pink tutu, headed the group. Somehow, his black sideburns and mustache spoiled the image and the make-up on his face didn't hide the serious pain he was suffering as a great gender-fucker. He took it all very seriously.

Fryman followed, wearing a brilliant red miniskirt that accentuated his knobby knees and hairy legs. He seemed to be enjoying the chance to let loose. The false eyelashes weighed down his lids and gave him a dreamy appearance. I got a little suspicious at the way he wiggled his ass as he marched in. It struck me that he was enjoying it far too much or maybe he wasn't wearing a gaff.

Jim Franklyn, the cop who kept the log at the crime scene, was dressed in a large maternity outfit that made him look like a fat social worker from Child Protective Services. He seemed to be doing his best to sashay.

Captain Wilson followed, disguised in a nurse's uniform with an unlit La Paloma cigar. The little pill box hat kept falling to one side and each time he straightened it he bellowed a loud "Son-of-a-bitch." Pillbox or not he was undaunted.

Finally, the bartender from the Velvet Glove came in, wearing a maid's apron and a bra over his hairy chest. He was waving four bottles of champagne above his head. I would have bet money that he was the snitch before I knew about Kemper.

They were all comic caricatures of powerful men compromising their power and reveling in their conception of the weaker sex. We the stronger sex had not progressed very far in the area of understanding the female personae.

The last to enter was not a caricature but a beautifully dressed woman in a large brimmed straw hat, a full length royal blue gown, white elbow-length gloves, and oversized sun glasses. Everyone watched as this vision of loveliness circled around me, bumping to the beat of the music. After the third time around I said, "Aaron?"

She stopped and lifted her dress above her knees and showed off two large sized fishing boots.

"Aaron, it is you, isn't it?" I asked.

Just then, a champagne bottle cork popped. She pulled off the hat and sunglasses and let out a booming belly laugh. The bartender poured the bubbly into paper cups and Wilson yelled out, "Quiet everyone. I want to make a toast."

Before he could say another word, the outside door swung open. I knew it couldn't be a raid because all the cops were in the room. To my surprise, in burst Jannine, wearing a black leather biker outfit, her long blonde hair tucked under a Nazi general's hat.

"Hold everything," she shouted and then looked around the room. "Who's Wilson?"

A somewhat embarrassed Captain Wilson tentatively raised his hand as though he was being called upon to recite. "Who are you?" he asked.

"I'm the only real thing in the place, baby," she said as she used her wrists to push up on her beautiful breasts.

"What do you want?" he asked.

"Who do I have to see about cancelling a restraining order that I never filed?"

"You've come to the right place," Fryman said. "You'll have to talk to our soon to be new detective."

Jannine came up to me, put her arms around me, and kissed me as catcalls and whistles drowned out *The Stripper* music.

I gently pushed her back and said, "You're killing me," and pointed to my bandaged body.

Wilson came over to us. "See that desk over there?" He pointed to an empty desk next to his office door. "As soon as we get the budget clearance, and I don't know exactly when that will be, I'm going to put a name plate on it that says, 'Vicky Espinoza, Detective'.

"Ah, Captain, let's make that Victor Espinoza so there's no chance of confusion," I said.

The Stripper music stopped and everybody cheered and started to sing, "For she's a jolly good fellow. For she's a jolly good fellow. For she's a jolly good fellow.

That nobody can deny." There was something off key about the song that worried me.

JoAnn came up to me with a note. "This came in a little while ago," she said.

I opened the note and it was a phone message from Douglas Carlyle.

Thank you, Detective Espinoza. I love you.

About the Author

After serving in the U.S. Navy and the U. S. Maritime Service, Charles Alvarez explored the various islands of the Pacific: Hawaiian, Marshalls, Tahiti, and the Marianas. He completed a bachelor's degree from California State University, Northridge, along the way doing graduate work at the University of Houston, during which he received two grants from the National Science Foundation. He is the author of four books in the sciences, published by McGraw Hill and Science Research Associates.

Dressed to Kill is his first novel. He has completed four screen plays and is an active member of the Alameda Writers and the LA Writers. Alvarez is married to Patricia Ann Hurley and they have four children: two girls (Christina and Elizabeth) and two boys (Raymond and Thomas).

www.ingramcontent.com/pod-product-compliance
Lightning Source LLC
Chambersburg PA
CBHW062123170626
46813CB00002B/548